M. S. Power was born in Dublin and educated in Ireland and France. He has worked as a TV producer in the United States, but now lives on the Oxfordshire/Buckinghamshire border. His first novel, *Hunt For the Autumn Clowns*, was published to wide critical acclaim in 1983. *The Killing of Yesterday's Children*, the first novel in his 'Children of the North' trilogy, was published in 1985, followed by *Lonely the Man Without Heroes* in 1986, and *A Darkness in the Eye* in 1987.

LONELY THE MAN WITHOUT HEROES

'His achievement is to give expression to the bitterness and suffering that have been provoking Ireland for so long'

TLS

'Casts a sober and humane light on the war on Britain's doorstep'

New Statesman

D1346913

Also by M. S. Power in Abacus:

THE KILLING OF YESTERDAY'S CHILDREN
LONELY THE MAN WITHOUT HEROES

A DARKNESS
IN THE EYE

M. S. Power

SPHERE BOOKS LTD

Published by the Penguin Group
27 Wrights Lane, London w8 5TZ, England
Viking Penguin Inc., 40 West 23rd Street, New York, New York 10010, USA
Penguin Books Australia Ltd, Ringwood, Victoria, Australia
Penguin Books Canada Ltd, 2801 John Street, Markham, Ontario, Canada L3R 1B4
Penguin Books (NZ) Ltd, 182–190 Wairau Road, Auckland 10, New Zealand

Penguin Books Ltd, Registered Offices: Harmondsworth, Middlesex, England

First published in Great Britain in hardback by William Heinemann Ltd 1987
Published in Abacus by Sphere Books Ltd 1988

Copyright © M. S. Power 1987
All rights reserved

Printed and bound in Great Britain by
Richard Clay Ltd, Bungay, Suffolk

For
Martin and
Alison Deeley

. . . Still, as we well know, 'the fault, dear Brutus, is not in our stars but in ourselves'; and yet with what facility and sleight of mind we ascribe our foulest deeds to that great charlatan, destiny. How sad that in reaching for those stars, those bright and burning emblems of man's most noble and holy aspirations, we dim their radiance by treachery, and eclipse their brilliance by furtive acts of duplicity and shame. Oh, tragedy proclaimed! We yearn and cry for dignity in death, but death merits only scorn if the life it extinguishes has been useless, futile, and a sham. Surely it is the giving of life that is glorious, and the living of life that merits dignity. Is it not life, with all its sufferings and tribulations, that elevates us to the region of the stars, makes us worthy of our place in the presence of God? Death is a grim and inevitable defrayment, nothing more. I do not believe that any man dies bravely: he dies in peace – reward enough; or, with an awful darkness in the eye, he dies screaming for the power of Shekinah to protect him. Alas, by then it is too late for mercy, too late, even, for pity . . . . But reach for those stars, reach and strive to clasp their wondrous splendour, remembering always that they are, however, cold. The warmth for which we hunger is in man's glowing spirit, attainable, and so very close at hand.

'The Visions and Visitations of Arthur Apple'

· ONE ·

THE KILLING OF Seamus Reilly would unquestionably have made the headlines in every morning newspaper in Belfast had not, on the same evening, and at approximately the same time, a young man from Clones decided it was his turn to be featherweight champion of the world, and bring about the miracle of uniting a battered community if only for a few hours. Consequently, Seamus Reilly's untimely mishap was relegated to page 2 and allotted only a dozen or so cryptic lines: even in death, it seemed, Reilly was capable of shrouding himself in shadows, and of advancing his soul as collateral for further intrigue.

Indeed, even the London dailies, intoxicated by the euphoria surrounding the young boxer's outstanding and surprising victory, were reticent to intrude on Northern delight with a terrorist's murder. The *Telegraph* headed its single, terse paragraph with TERRORIST LEADER SHOT, explaining that police had identified the man shot dead by Security Forces the night before as Seamus Reilly, 44, the 'self-styled Godfather of the Provisional IRA', ruthless, callous and vicious.

The reporter might have been correct about his name and

age. However, the claim that the Security Forces had terminated Reilly's life was pure, if unwitting, fabrication: *that* information was a piece of trickery the likes of which would have done credit to Reilly himself, and of which he would surely have been proud.

Colonel Matthew Maddox stared out of the bedroom window of his Berkshire home, a cup of black, sugarless coffee in his hand, an open copy of the *Telegraph* on the floor, a small, moustachioed triumphant boxer smiling up at him. For some months now he had taken to having breakfast upstairs, away from his nattering wife and her recent addiction, morning television. So Seamus Reilly was finally dead. Hoist on his own petard, Maddox mused. He stood up and opened the window wide, breathing deeply: he had given the huge expanse of lawn its first mowing of the season the evening before (perched on the seat of his newly acquired rotary machine, and playing a gloriously childish game, imagining he was Fangio no less as he twirled the mower round the base of the enormous copper beech, pretending it was a particularly tricky chicane, leaning extravagantly sideways, and shouting wheeeee), and he relished the scent of the freshly cut grass under the dew.

The thought returned: Seamus Reilly was dead. Perhaps it was the weight of this knowledge that made Maddox feel suddenly giddy. He sat down, resting his slippered feet on the window-sill . . . He had probably been cheerfully wheeeeeing his way round the tree at the moment Reilly had been crying for mercy. But no. Reilly would certainly not have made any fuss about dying: it would not have been his style at all. He would have accepted death with dignity, welcomed it as an inevitability. The fact that it came violently might, even, have appealed to his cruel, warped sense of justice.

Maddox smiled wryly. The awful irony of it! Just when Reilly was trying his utmost to bring about an end to the violence that crippled the province, he had fallen victim to that violence. The Colonel sighed, a sincere sympathy for the murdered terrorist welling up inside him. At least Reilly had tried! But there were,

2

alas, no rewards for trying, unless one considered death as a reward – which, come to think of it, was not too flamboyant an hypothesis. What was it Reilly had told him? 'Colonel, I am long since dead. That old fool Mr Apple was quite right, you know. We are all dead in this blighted land. The innocent and the guilty – we all died a long, long time ago.'

– You know that what you propose to do will – , Colonel Maddox had said before Reilly interrupted him by holding up his hand. As long as you know, the Colonel concluded.

– I know.

– 'It is a far, far better thing,' Maddox began. Reilly winced at the quotation.

– Nothing so dramatic, I fear, Colonel. Nor for such noble reasons.

– Sacrifice is always noble, Maddox countered, as though longing that the opportunity for sacrifice would step his way.

Reilly was cynical.

– You're still missing the point, Colonel. It has nothing to do with sacrifice. Years and years and years ago I swore I would do everything in my power to see to it that Ireland was united. And, from time to time, violence was the only option.

– I don't –

Again Reilly had held up his hand.

– You know it's true, Colonel. You won't admit it, but you know it's a fact. You saw for yourself how things worked when you were stationed here in Belfast.

The Colonel nodded.

– Yes. Yes, indeed I did.

– Well, Reilly shrugged, things have now changed. There is just a glimmer of hope that we can achieve our ends by political means so the violence has got to stop. Unfortunately, there are some, even within our own ranks, who disagree with this policy. They see negotiation as weakness, terror as strength. Some of our most loyal followers have broken away from us and have sworn to continue the killings and bombings. Someone – finally – has to take a stand against violence. Someone from within our organization. So . . . Reilly smiled thinly and raised his eyebrows.

So – Seamus Reilly was dead.

'I see you've heard.' The senior editor of the BBC's current affairs programme 'The Right To Speak' eyed Declan Tuohy's grim face with some apprehension.

Tuohy nodded. 'Yes. I've heard.'

'I'm sorry, Declan.'

'We killed him, you know. As surely as if we held that gun to his head and pulled the trigger we killed him.'

'Come off it, Declan. We – '

'Oh yes we did. We made a deal with Reilly. He kept his side of the bargain. What did we do? What – '

'It was taken out of our hands.'

'Ah – that's to be the excuse, is it? That's how we make everything all right? Christ above! Reilly was supposed to be the conniving bastard. What we did to him was worse than anything he would ever do. He trusted us, dammit. He trusted us.'

'I know he did, Declan. But it had nothing to do with us that – '

'Oh, piss off.'

Inspector John Asher of the RUC learned of Reilly's death about an hour after it had happened. He was appalled. On the face of it, he should have been delighted, of course. But for all his innate Protestantism, his suspicion of everything Catholic, and for all his fundamental adherence to law and order and his loathing of terrorism, Asher felt an inexplicable loneliness at the death of Seamus Reilly. For the first time in his life, he knew what it was to be saddened. He knew that he could never be seen to grieve and would have to smile and rejoice and pretend he fully endorsed the myth that Belfast would be a better place now that another IRA bastard was killed.

It was some consolation that he had tried to warn Reilly: what he proposed to do was folly. Reilly had agreed that perhaps he was being foolhardy, but he had then gone ahead and done precisely what he had intended to do in the first place. Asher sighed again. That was the bloody IRA for you: let them get an idea in their heads and it became a damned obsession that nothing, not even their Holy Roman Pope, could remove. His years of wheeling and dealing with Seamus Reilly had taught him one thing: the IRA were just ordinary men doing what they saw as fit and proper for their cause, resorting to violence because otherwise nobody would pay them any heed, prepared to take life if it enhanced the chances of realizing their dream, yet equally prepared to sacrifice their own lives for the same end. And, or so it seemed, that was exactly what Reilly had done. He might, at least, have hoped for a more dignified execution. It would have been the betrayal that would have hurt him most. Asher poured himself a large whisky. He raised his glass. 'Here we go, Seamus, you devious old bugger. I'll miss you.'

Apart from those actually involved in the murder, the Commander in Chief of the Provisional IRA was probably the first man to know that Seamus Reilly was dead. For several seconds he stared at the messenger before dismissing him with a vague, preoccupied wave of his hand (a gesture he had unconsciously picked up from Reilly himself) and slumping into the leather armchair. He stayed like that for some twenty minutes: unmoving apart from an occasional twitch of the scar that ran the length of his bearded jowl. It wasn't until his youngest child yowled upstairs that he sat up. He removed his horn-rimmed spectacles and, taking a handkerchief from his breast pocket, wiped his eyes, smiling sadly to himself, thinking that anyone seeing him do this might have suspected him of crying. They would have been tears of frustration, not loss or remorse. He was angry at himself for not speaking out, for washing his hands of what had become known internally as the 'Reilly affair', for having allowed himself to get into a situation from which there was but one, inevitable, tragic escape; and afraid because now the precariousness of his own position, despite his treacherously diplomatic neutrality, was clearly evident. That, of course, was always the trouble when one chose sides, particularly when the strife was within the ranks: and for the best part of a year the internal wrangling had been going on, gathering force and becoming more aggressive and spiteful with each passing month, the two factions (the hawks and doves as they were classified by the tabloids) entrenching themselves ever deeper in their opposing beliefs, the menace of outright rebellion only just held at bay, mostly through the efforts of Seamus Reilly who had somehow become ensconced in the role of mediator, while the Commander in Chief had sat quietly in the background, smoking his pipe, watching coldly, summing up the arguments, preparing the decision that would ultimately be his, allowing Reilly to take the flak, allowing him to make himself vulnerable.

– Damn you, Reilly, the Commander now thought, getting up and walking to the window. No, not damn you. God love you. God love and protect you.

Upstairs the child screamed again, and was immediately comforted by its mother who crooned. 'Slower and slower and slower the wheel spins,' she sang, the words lulling the child, and sweeping over the Commander who found them distinctly mournful. Slower the wheel spins . . . and when it finally, irrevocably stopped? Involuntarily he shuddered, as if someone had walked on his grave. A vengeful spirit in search of retribution perhaps. He pressed his forehead against the cold glass of the window. Away to his left, only just visible in the yellow light of the moon, the mist surrounding its peak like a gently falling shower of pollen, rose the Sugar Loaf Mountain. The feeling had been growing within him for longer than he cared to remember, but now he knew and recognized that the real and true calamity of Seamus Reilly's death was the almost certain evaporation of any hope of peace within the IRA. The chance, slim though it might have been, had been there. But he had abandoned it; abandoned, too, far worse, his friend Seamus Reilly. If only . . . ah, if only.

6

He turned from the window, stretched and yawned, and made his way to bed. If only. . . .

A neighbour mentioned to Rose Duffy that Seamus Reilly had been killed.

'Oh, dear. Poor man,' Rose said, hawing on the glass she was polishing.

'He's probably better off, though,' she added, smiling brightly. 'Still, I think I'll set his little place at the table just the same – in case he feels like coming back. He's a terrible man for that – popping in when you least expect him. Always better to be nice and prepared for the unexpected. That's what I say,' she concluded, holding the glass at arm's length away from her, and admiring the glitter with bright, crazy eyes.

· TWO ·

COINCIDENTALLY, AND NOT without a certain irony, four separate meetings were scheduled to take place in the first week of May 1984. All, in their various ways, were to lead to tragedy.

The first meeting to take place was informal. It was in Seamus Reilly's sitting room, and was attended only by Reilly himself and the Commander in Chief of the Provisional IRA. The atmosphere was very relaxed, both men sipping their drinks, smoking, talking quietly, giving no indication of the turmoil and bitterness that had taken place the night before. True, the Commander was a little edgy to begin with, his sharp bespectacled eyes darting restlessly about the room, but this was attributable to his natural nervousness, a sort of fidgety discomfort he always felt outside his familiar territories.

'You handled that very nicely, Seamus,' the Commander said, reaching out and tapping the bowl of his briar pipe in the glass ashtray.

Seamus Reilly spread his hands demurely, as if to suggest it had been quite a simple task and that such praise was unwarranted. But he was clearly pleased.

'No. I think you handled it very well indeed. It's never pleasant having to expel old colleagues from the Organization.'

Reilly shrugged. 'It had to be done.'

The Commander nodded, accidentally blowing into his pipe and sending up a cloud of blue smoke which he waved away apologetically, a hint of a grin on his face like a schoolboy attempting to forestall chastisement.

'I know,' he said finally. 'But it's never pleasant.'

'True,' Reilly agreed, adopting an appropriately mournful look. 'But they gave us no option.'

'I suppose not.'

'There's no supposing about it, Commander. They were given every chance. The whole success of our campaign depends on discipline. This willy-nilly killing can no longer be tolerated. It does us nothing but harm.'

'And you think they will stop?'

Reilly shook his head after a moment's thought. 'No,' he said grimly.

'Even though we have warned them they risk being shot?'

'Even so. They'll fight us. They think we're getting weak. Or jaded. Or both. They believe our move into the political arena is a sign of submission. No, they won't stop. They'll fight us all right. And they'll have their supporters both here and in Dublin. We're the doves now, don't forget, and the symbolism of dovery makes them puke.'

The Commander allowed himself a wry smile. 'I would never have considered you as a dove, Seamus.'

Unexpectedly, Reilly took the observation seriously. He frowned. 'Things change. People change. Continuous, useless killing is bound to affect us, don't you think?'

The Commander nodded in tentative agreement, and set about refuelling his pipe. 'Of course.'

Seamus Reilly watched the operation with interest, wondering why on earth anyone would bother to smoke a pipe if it required such elaborate preparation. He lit one of his small, thin cigars, and closed his eyes as he enjoyed the first lungful.

'They'll blame you, you know,' the Commander went on, still stoking his pipe. 'Not me. You.'

'That's nothing new,' Reilly answered, keeping his eyes closed.

'They might –' the Commander began, but stopped abruptly.

Reilly opened his eyes immediately. 'Indeed they might, Commander. But it wouldn't be the first time someone tried.'

'You'll be careful?'

Reilly feigned shock. 'I'm always careful,' he said.

While he might have appeared to lead a pretty normal existence, nothing that Seamus Reilly did was on the spur of the moment. Everything was most meticulously planned. Every journey he made, be it to another country or just across the city, was monitored, his car escorted by a constantly changing, interweaving selection of bodyguards in fast, if innocuous-looking vehicles; every visitor he received was given inconspicuous security the likes of which would have been deemed excessive by many. His home was under twenty-four hour observation, his car bulletproof. Seamus Reilly was careful all right.

The Commander had managed to get his pipe going, and puffed contentedly for a few minutes, holding the bowl in his fingers and tapping the stem from time to time on his teeth. 'It's that woman I worry about,' he then said. 'She's the one that will most resent the power being taken from her. They always do. Women.'

'I wouldn't know.'

'Just you keep an eye on her, Seamus.'

'I will.'

'You see that you do.'

The second meeting was rather more sinister. It took place in the evening and in some secrecy in the Andersonstown district of Belfast, in a small bare room over a sweet shop, and it was attended by two men and a woman. Although all three knew each other well, there was a tense furtiveness about them as if they were, in fact, strangers.

'Well?' Patrick Moran asked, arching his eyebrows but managing to keep his eyes impassive. He was a small man, running to fat and balding, and he had an air about him that suggested he was suspicious of everyone including himself. 'Where do we go from here?'

Eddie McCluskey coughed into his clenched fist before answering. He was younger than Moran, about twenty-eight, a handsome, swarthy man with the drooping moustache of a Spanish pirate and wide-set, intense eyes enhanced by thick brows that met over the bridge of his nose. 'We carry on as before,' he said, in a tone that implied he had found the question spurious.

Moran gave a thin hissing laugh. 'Oh, really?'

'Yeah. Sure. Why not?'

Moran raised his eyes to the ceiling as though seeking deliverance from some imbecility. 'Why not? Didn't you listen to anything that was said last night?'

'I listened,' McCluskey said, turning sullen.

'Then you heard what Reilly said?'

'Sure I heard. So what? Fuck Reilly. Who the hell does he think he is anyway?'

The obscenity, about par for McCluskey, brought tiny beads of sweat oozing onto Moran's face. Thus far his clashes with Reilly had been wholly verbal and he had always come off second best: the suggestion, albeit only by implication, that he should physically oppose Seamus Reilly was more than he cared to think about. It was a measure of his very real dread that 'Watch it,' was all he could bring himself to say, and that in an awed, frightened whisper.

McCluskey, ever brash, gave a scoffing snort. 'Shit. Reilly's a nothing,' he sneered.

Not that he meant it. McCluskey, too, was scared of Reilly's awesome powers, but he had an aptitude and penchant for tiresome bravura, a cockiness found in mindless men, displayed, like a peacock's tail, only when secure in the knowledge it will neither be challenged nor, indeed, overheard by the subject.

'If you believe that, it's the biggest mistake you'll ever make,' Moran warned. 'It's a mistake a lot of fools have made only you won't find any of them about to tell you. Reilly has more power than you could ever imagine. Believe me, what he says goes.'

'Big deal. So what do we do? Sit on our arses and do nothing?'

'I didn't say that. We just have to be careful. Very bloody careful. When Reilly said he would have us shot if we didn't keep in line he meant it. Reilly doesn't joke. I don't want to find myself dead in a ditch some night if you do.'

'So what do we do?' McCluskey demanded, running the tip of his tongue over the ends of his moustache as he always tended to when frustration was getting the better of him.

'We carry on our campaign as before only we concentrate on England. And we make damn sure those bloody doves know nothing about it until we're good and ready.'

It was the woman who spoke: her voice calm and cold and certainly educated, almost English. She was a most unlikely-looking terrorist: tall and blonde and beautiful, her slim and graceful body a far cry from the squat, butch, cropped females beloved of television plays about the Troubles. Only her curiously oriental, almond eyes gave any hint of the fanaticism that made her dangerous. Sometimes, behind her back, men called her Pussy Galore but she had little in common with the Bonded lady: it was a nickname that simply did not apply, but caused chauvinistic amusement none the less. 'What we have to do is to give Reilly and his lackies enough to think about over here, plan and execute a proper campaign in England, and then, if need be, take out Reilly himself.'

McCluskey really liked the sound of such an approach but Moran objected. 'We can't. We'd never get away with it.'

'We will if we're careful,' the woman insisted, her voice subtly patronizing now that she had one of the men on her side. 'Of course, if you want out, Moran, there's nothing to stop you going,' she added. 'One good coup in England is all we need, then we'll get enough support from here and Dublin to get rid of the shits and appoint leaders who see things our way.'

Poor Moran was still not convinced. He shook his head dejectedly. 'Reilly will find out. I know he will. Jesus, he'll have us as mincemeat before we – '

'Not if we're careful,' the woman insisted.

Still Moran was unhappy, and it was a sign of his intense dissatisfaction that he continued to protest, something which, as a general rule, he was terrified to do. He was, in a sense, a battered man, perpetually nagged by his far younger, far more intelligent wife, his slow mind plundered of any calmness by the continuous screaming and crying of his children. 'It doesn't matter how damn careful we are,' he argued, flinching at his boldness. 'Reilly will know. He knows everything that goes on. He knows most things before they even happen.'

'Then we'll have to make certain this is the first time he doesn't know, won't we?'

Moran found this simple logic irrefutable. He stood up and started to pace about the small room, measuring his strides with some precision in the manner of a man used to taking what exercise he could in a prison cell, and continually glancing towards the window as if reckoning it as a possible, if inadequate means of escape. Finally he stopped and faced his two colleagues. 'I'll have to think about it,' he told them hesitantly, relieved when the woman smiled pleasantly enough and nodded: 'Fine,' she agreed. 'Take all the time you want, Patrick.'

Sensing his winning streak might end abruptly, Moran said: 'I better be off. It'll be the wife who murders me if I don't get home soon.'

'Sure,' the woman agreed again. 'You get on home. We'll be in touch.'

'He's trouble,' McCluskey diagnosed as soon as Moran had gone. 'As sure as hell he'll be trouble.'

The woman shook her head and pursed her lips. 'No. No, I don't believe he will. In fact, Eddie, I think he'll be very useful.' She smiled. 'If things go as I hope Reilly will suspect us for sure.

13

Well, we might just throw him off the scent for a while if Moran happened to turn up dead.'

'Jesus, you don't – '

'It's up to him, isn't it? If he sticks with us he'll be useful – if he doesn't, well – ' she shrugged, ' – we'll simply have to make use of him. That's all.'

McCluskey shook his head in wonderment. 'Christ above, you think of everything.'

'Someone has to.'

'I'd hate to get the wrong side of you.'

'Then don't.'

Brigadier Brazier drummed his fingers on his desk, approximating the rhythm of the Sousa march. From time to time he stopped and sat quietly, cocking his head to one side, listening, waiting for Major Fisher. The Brigadier gave a noisy, vulgar belch, and glanced at the clock on the wall: three minutes to go. In about two minutes the thump of the Major's steel-tipped shoes across the landing would announce his arrival; Fisher's slow, methodical walk, the dogged strides of this obstinate Yorkshire miner's son, his measured, labouring walk, approximated his cumbersome way of thinking, his complete acceptance of the stultifying military code. He had achieved a rank far above his expectations, was fearful that any novel idea might be seen as some intolerable impertinence.

'Come in, come in,' the Brigadier now called, smiling to himself as he noted the knock had come dead on time.

Major Crispin Fisher came in. 'Sir.'

'Come in, come in,' the Brigadier said again, waiting for Fisher to walk across the room, eyeing him somewhat warily as he stood smartly to attention in front of the desk. 'Relax, man,' he added, somewhat testily. 'This is quite informal. Do sit down like a good chap.' Fisher sat very erect, his hands resting primly on his knees.

'I take it you've been briefed?'

'Yes, sir.'

'Good, And?'

'Sir?'

The Brigadier swallowed his annoyance. 'You think you can handle it?'

'Yes, sir.'

'Hmm. Excellent. You – you've been made aware of the risks?'

'Yes, sir.'

'And that you are not being ordered to undertake this?'

'Yes, sir.'

Brigadier Brazier looked away, for the moment feeling a rare twinge of guilt. The Major's unequivocal subordination irked him: was he simply a moron or had he been brainwashed? It was, he now thought, not impossible that he had been chosen precisely for his simple unquestioning loyalty, 'I don't want to appear rude,' the Brigadier went on, genuinely not wanting to, 'but you have thought this thing through carefully, haven't you? I mean, it is a very risky undertaking, you know. And if anything should go wrong you will be entirely on your own.'

Perhaps sensing his superior's tetchiness, Fisher slightly altered his response, preceding it with a steady, positive nod. 'Oh, yes, sir. I've thought it through carefully.'

Which was more or less true. He had certainly thought about it, if never in the light of refusal: he saw this unexpected mandate as the ultimate recognition of his obedience and submission to military discipline. Indeed, he was flattered that he had been volunteered, and managed, in the days that followed, to enhance the possible sacrifice of his life with a certain nobility, thus giving his dull, lonely, secretive existence a meaning and purpose it had never before achieved. Somehow, although forbidden to mention it to his colleagues, the option of probable death set him apart, and, had he thought about it further, he might have admitted that he would be almost disappointed if he were to come out of this affair alive.

'I'm glad to hear that,' the Brigadier said, and he was, immediately shifting responsibility onto the Major's shoulders. 'You're a brave young man, Fisher.'

Fisher blushed and moved uneasily in his chair.

'No, I mean it,' the Brigadier continued. 'It isn't everyone who could be entrusted with such a mission. Those IRA boys don't mess about, you know. If they find out – well, let's just hope they don't.'

Fisher smiled again, his smile enhanced by a curious lopsided charm, or perhaps it was cunning. 'Yes, sir.'

'One great thing in your favour is that they're pretty desperate just now, and this rift in their ranks is just the break we've been looking for. And God knows, we need a break.'

'Yes, sir.'

'The fact that they've helped two – eh – genuine – ' the Brigadier underlined the final word with aggrieved distaste, ' – deserters in the past month will have made them less suspicious, I suppose.'

'Yes, sir.'

'Although that won't mean they'll relax their vigilance.'

'No, sir.'

The Brigadier stopped for the moment. He sensed, even now, before the covert operation had properly got under way, that it was all going to go disastrously wrong. 'You're quite certain you can cope?' he asked in a quiet voice, his tone coaxing as if hoping the Major would retract his assurances. 'No second thoughts?'

'None, sir.'

Lest he should change his mind the Brigadier stood up abruptly and held out his hand. 'Well, good luck to you Fisher.'

'Thank you, sir,' Fisher said, shaking hands, managing to make even this gesture deferential, and then made for the door. As he reached it he turned. 'One thing, sir – '

'Yes, Major?'

'If – if by some chance something *does* go wrong and I don't – I don't get back – will you explain everything to my father?'

The Brigadier nodded, his eyes unsteady. 'Of course,' he lied.

'It's just that he's very proud of me, sir. I'm the only one he has left and it would kill him if he thought I really deserted.'

'You need have no worries on that score. I'll see to it

personally that he is told the truth,' the Brigadier confirmed, shocked that he could lie so glibly. 'In any case I have no doubt you'll be back to tell him all about it yourself.'

'Thank you, sir.'

For some time after the Major had gone the Brigadier kept his grey, watery eyes fixed on the closed door, the pathetic, time-worn phrase 'lamb to the slaughter' bleating in his mind. Then he reached for the telephone. Carefully he dialled, using a pencil, and then tapping it like a drum-stick on the desk as he waited for his connection. Then:

'I've just seen Fisher.'

'And?'

'He seems all right.'

'He is. He's perfect.'

'He's a bit – '

'Dumb? That's just what we want. The bright sparks are no damn good. They tend to have consciences. And they ask too many questions.'

'I was going to say helpless.'

'So much the better. Far less chance of our – helpless – Major being suspected.'

'I – '

'Don't worry, sir. We know what we're doing.'

'I hope so. I certainly hope so.'

A cackle reverberated down the line. 'We do.'

'You said that about Colonel Sharmann, and I need hardly remind you what a fiasco that turned into.'

The voice coughed. 'We all make the occasional mistake. Anyway, this is quite different. This will work.'

'You really think so?'

'We know so, sir.'

'I wish I had your confidence.'

'Just leave it all to us. You'll see.'

'You'll keep me fully informed?'

The voice sounded surprised. 'Of course.'

'I mean *fully* informed.'

'Of course.'

Myles Cravan popped his head round the door of Declan Tuohy's cramped office. 'Sorry I'm late. Got held up.'

'Traffic or politics?'

Cravan grinned. 'A bit of both.' He sat on the corner of the desk, swinging one leg. 'Had a chance to read that report?'

Tuohy nodded. 'Yes. I've read it.'

'You think it's true?'

Tuohy shrugged. 'Probably. There have been rumours of a split for some time now. You know – the bullet versus the ballot box and all that crap.'

'So what'll happen?'

'Christ knows.'

'You must have some idea – as our resident expert on Irish affairs,' Cravan said, hoping the mild flattery would work as it so often did with what he liked to think of as his little band of temperamental reporters.

'It depends on what support the hawks can muster in Dublin. If they can't get enough I wouldn't give much for their chances. Seamus Reilly and Co. won't take kindly to being opposed.'

'And if they can get support?'

'Then one side will have to back down, and I don't see either doing that without a fight. Reilly certainly won't.'

Myles Cravan used his middle finger to move his rimless spectacles more comfortably up onto the bridge of his nose. Despite his friendly, almost nonchalant behaviour he was a shrewd man, aware of his limitations, recognizing the fact that his genius lay in organizing rather than actual reporting. If this disappointed him he never showed it, seldom interfered, and had the enviable reputation for fighting the ditherers within the system when he believed his reporters were in the right. With these attributes it was not difficult for him to gather together a team of the highest quality, always willing to draft in new talent from outside television as, indeed, he had done with Declan Tuohy. 'You seem very sure of that.'

Declan leaned back and rocked himself sideways in his

swivel-chair, his hands clasped behind his neck, a slightly mocking look in his eyes. Of course he was sure of it! 'Oh, I'm sure of that all right,' he asserted, somehow giving the words a sinister connotation as though his surety was culled from some inside, secret knowledge. Which, in fact, it was – well, up to a point. 'I've known Seamus Reilly all my life. Even at school he would fight like a demon to get what he wanted,' he went on, his voice softening, perhaps the memory of childhood something he liked to recall, something that held pleasant episodes he had a special fondness for. He laughed. 'Seamus Reilly is probably the most honest, most dangerous man I've ever met, or am ever likely to meet,' he said.

'An odd combination,' Cravan said, letting the statement hang like a question.

'Yes,' Tuohy agreed. 'He's an odd man. An orphan of terror – that's what he once called himself: he has a penchant for enigmatic phrases. He'll quote Blake to you by the hour – very into Blake is Seamus. You can never really tell what he's up to. One minute he's being transported to another world – another of his phrases – by Bartok, and the next he's ordering the murder of someone who has stepped out of line. Of course,' Tuohy added, smiling sardonically, 'maybe Bartok does that to you.'

'Maybe,' Cravan agreed, the word tossed in like a goad.

'One thing you can be sure of – if Reilly says he'll do something, he'll do it and damn the consequences. If he gives you his word you can truly believe him – that's what I meant by his honesty. If you give him your word and break it he'll deal with you as ruthlessly as only he can, no matter who you are or how much he cares for you: that's being dangerous. You know, he even had his own brother shot for informing?'

'You told me.'

'Anyway, I can also tell you that he's sick and tired of all the violence. He sees the future of the IRA in politics, and, believe you me, he won't let the hawks have the last say if he can prevent it.'

'So?'

'So – there are rough days ahead, Myles. You can bet your life there'll be an escalation of the killings. Whoever is the better organized will come out on top.'

'Tell me, Declan – how well do you know Reilly? I mean, apart from knowing him all your life – how *well* do you know him?'

Declan Tuohy smiled ruefully. 'Very well. I might even know him better than anyone else. We were very close – still are, I suppose.' Declan paused and thought for a moment. 'Put it this way: if I ever had a problem, any problem, I would probably think of talking it over with Seamus first.'

'And you're certain he wants to see an end to the violence?'

Declan shrugged. 'He wants a stop on what he calls "useless violence" but I wouldn't wager that he means all violence by that.'

'Do you think he'd talk about it? Openly – on television?'

Declan Tuohy hooted with derisive laughter. 'You're joking of course. Seamus Reilly on telly? Not in a million years.'

'Why not? He'd have a chance to – '

'Come off it, Myles. There's a thing called Reilly's law, and the first commandment is self-preservation. If Reilly even hinted he was about to give an interview he'd be dead meat within minutes – regardless of his power. Anyway, it's not his style. He operates from the shadows. That's why he has the power he has. Nobody can ever quite pin anything on him. You'd never get a man like Reilly to expose himself. You'll have to think up some other ruse to boost the old ratings.'

'You wouldn't even ask him?'

'It'd be a complete waste of time. I can just see him. Jesus! He'd probably die from apoplexy. He wouldn't do it, Myles. I'm telling you. He'd think I'd gone mad.'

'You don't know until you try.'

Declan Tuohy shook his head in amazement at the editor's persistence. Yet, of course, there was something fascinating about the possibility. 'Okay,' he said. 'Okay. I'll try.'

Craven beamed. 'Good man.'

'We'll give it a week or two and see if anything breaks over there – if the rift is as serious as we're making out. Then if there is a story I'll see how Seamus feels about it.'

'That's all I ever ask. Try.'

'Yea . . . by the way – if by some miracle Seamus does agree he'll want guarantees.'

'Promise him anything you like.'

'But will you back those promises?'

'All the way.'

'I have your word on that?'

'Yes. You have my word. Just get him in front of a camera.'

'I'll try.'

'Like I said – that's all I ever ask.'

Word of the split in the leadership of the IRA spread rapidly throughout the Catholic areas of the city, spearheading a renewed fearfulness. Immediately neighbours were less open, less friendly towards each other. They spoke less, more reluctant than ever to take sides, speculation of the outcome only discussed in secret with immediate relatives, and even then with caution. The tension was almost tangible. Everyone just waited.

· THREE ·

THE STOLEN DARK-BROWN Volvo moved at a respectable pace through the darkened streets. Patrick Moran drove: when there was a job to be done that involved transport he always drove. Surprisingly, for a man who jittered and twitched like someone in the last stages of Parkinson's disease, he became nerveless and calm when behind the steering wheel. Beside him Eddie McCluskey chewed on his finger nails, tearing off jagged shards with his teeth and spitting them out. 'Why not cut through there to the left?' he asked now, between titbits.

'Too quiet. The more traffic you have about you the less likely you are to be noticed,' Moran told him, sounding superior. 'That's the first principle of this job, Eddie. Don't be noticed. Keep in the thickest traffic and remember the rules of the road.'

'Huh,' McCluskey grunted. Oddly, for the moment, it was he who showed the most uneasiness, yet he knew that once the car stopped and he had the gun in his hand, the cold metal would transmit an awful peace to his mind, and he would kill without the slightest qualm. That was the first principle of his trade, he thought: no feelings.

The car slowed down at the intersection, allowing the armoured trucks to pass, their engines growling. Moran voiced his own resentment. 'I don't like taking orders from a woman,' he said, but tentatively, as if testing his companion's feelings.

McCluskey looked sideways at him, but said nothing.

'You think she knows what she's doing?'

'She knows,' McCluskey confirmed. 'Anyway, who else is there? You?'

Moran shook his head and started the car moving again. 'There's you, Eddie. I'd sooner take my orders from you,' he said, knowing that this would appeal.

Eddie McCluskey smiled pleasurably. 'Yea. Well, she's the boss for the moment.'

'But she didn't even consult us about tonight. She should have at least asked us what we thought,' Moran insisted, suddenly democratic.

'Just standing there and telling us we *have* to do it. I don't like it, Eddie. Another thing: why didn't she come with us?'

'She's got other things to do. Anyway, three's a crowd.'

'Like what, for Christ's sake? I bet she's just sitting on her arse waiting to see if we come back safe.'

'She's all right.'

Moran took his eye off the road for a moment and glanced at McCluskey. 'Hey – you fancy her, don't you?'

McCluskey glowered and kept silent.

Taking this as confirmation Moran went on: 'You really do fancy her. Been having it off then?'

'Fuck off.'

'Come on. Tell us. What's she like in the sack?'

McCluskey blushed furiously and, ignoring the question, stared out of the window.

'Jesus – it must be like shagging a bloody Amazon. I suppose she tells you what to do in bed too?'

'Just drive and shut up.'

'Touchy, are we?'

Yes. Eddie McCluskey was, indeed, touchy on this particular subject. It was an understatement to say he fancied the woman: he lusted after her. Each night, alone and frustrated, he stripped her roughly, threw her on his bed and raped her, ignoring her cries of pain, smiling exultantly to himself as she succumbed, finally, to his sexual prowess, pleading for more. It was one of the contradictions in Eddie McCluskey: these wild erotic chimeras were hobbled by an equally fierce determination to adhere to the narrow sexual precepts of his religion, the archaic doctrines of which (hammered into his brain by family and the Christian Brothers) stultified his manhood and, in a terrible sense, made him afraid of women. 'Jesus, Eddie,' he heard Moran saying, ' 'tis a brave little lad you are putting your dickie-dock at risk like that. Christ above, she'd devour you for breakfast.'

'Very bloody funny.'

Having taken a long, circuitous route through the city, Moran now drove the car along a pleasant, tree-lined avenue in what he always enviously regarded as one of the 'nobby' parts of Belfast. He longed for a house with a garden but was unlikely ever to achieve it, lumbered as he was by a wife and seven children, a crippling rent, and his lack of ambition. Conveniently, he was a great believer in fate. It was at all times handy and there to be blamed for his continuous failure. Fate, he told himself, was either with you or against you. It was responsible for his ugliness, for his sweaty hands and feet. It was fate that had made Mary pregnant at seventeen and thus forced him to marry her, pinning him irrevocably to a domestic drudgery from which he was all too glad to escape. So, he had decided, it was fate that had driven him from the house and into his involvement with the Provisionals. For this he was thankful, feeling important for the first time in his life. He responded with a willingness to please that soon came to the notice of the hierarchy. He was given assignments of considerable trust and these he executed with dedicated efficiency; so much so that within a couple of years he was voted onto the Council: fate had done him a good turn. Then he blew it.

'Slow down,' McCluskey whispered. 'That's the house over there. You don't want to park right outside.'

'I can see it,' Moran answered gruffly, irked by the slight.

'Well pull over then. I'm not just calling in for tea.'

Patrick Moran eased the car to the side of the road, and switched off the lights. He took his time about killing the engine, but finally reached forward and turned the key. Immediately he began to shake.

'For Christ's sake will you stop that jittering about,' McCluskey told him.

'It's nerves.'

'I don't give a shit what it is – just stop it.'

'I can't.'

Nor could he. His entire fat body twitched and perspiration oozed onto his face.

McCluskey swore silently to himself.

'I'll be all right,' Moran assured him. 'Just you go in and get it over. Once I can get the car started again I'll be fine.'

'You bloody well better be. When I come out I want this heap moving before I close the door.'

'I'll be okay,' Moran insisted.

'Shit.'

McCluskey left the car and, for a second, stood beside it, breathing deeply, suffocating the dancing nerves that now attacked his stomach. There's nothing to it, he told himself. Just walk up to the door and press the bell. Kelly would answer the door himself and – bang. Then back to the car and away. Nothing to it. Only there was a lot more to it. This was special. He knew if he messed this one up he was certain to be killed himself. One didn't execute one of Seamus Reilly's men and live very long after it. For an instant, the horror of Reilly's absolute retribution struck him, and he hesitated before resolutely crossing the street, his stride swift and soundless. This was it, then. The declaration of war, he thought. No turning back after this. He moved quickly along the length of the cropped privet hedge, and slid sideways through the wrought-iron gate that someone had left half-open. The house was in darkness apart from an eerie, flickering light in a downstairs room. Television. McCluskey crept up the short driveway, crouching, one hand outstretched, using the side of the silver Austin Ambassador to keep his balance. He felt his feet sink into the soft earth of the flowerbed under the lighted window, and instinctively he scuffed his shoe-marks, making them unidentifiable. Then, raising himself slowly, he peered in, smiling with relief as he noted Tom Kelly alone, slumped lazily in an armchair, watching what was almost certainly a cowboy film. Easy.

McCluskey moved quickly now, jumping back across the flowerbed and onto the concrete driveway, running to the front door. He shoved his right hand under his khaki jacket and grasped the gun, pressing the doorbell with his left. Licking his lips and moving from foot to foot he waited. He pressed the bell again impatiently. A door inside the house slammed and an outline appeared on the frosted-glass panel of the hall door. He tightened his grip on the gun. As always in situations like this he controlled his breathing, inhaling deeply, purposely relaxing himself, widening his huge eyes to an expression of innocence, and steadfastly maintaining these attitudes as the lock clicked and the door opened. An amber light streamed from the hall onto McCluskey.

'Eddie!' Tom Kelly exclaimed, surprised, but pleasantly so.

'I need a word, Tom.'

'Sure. Sure – come in,' Kelly stood to one side.

McCluskey smiled and nodded and stepped into the house.

'In there,' Kelly went on, indicating the room he had just come from with his newspaper.

'A private word,' Eddie told him, standing his ground.

For a moment Kelly looked puzzled. 'Oh. Yea. That's okay. In there. I'm alone.'

'Ah. Good,' McCluskey said, cleverly, he thought, making himself appear nervous, giving the impression by cowering slightly that Kelly was the only one who could solve some immense problem. 'Nice room, Tom.'

'Thanks. Grab a chair,' Tom Kelly invited, making his way to his own chair and flopping into it comfortably. When he looked up he saw the gun pointing at him.

26

Perhaps significantly, as though acknowledging that the inevitable outcome of terrorism was sudden and unexpected and violent death, Kelly showed little surprise. Indeed, if anything, his eyes showed only a mocking defiance tinged with curiosity; possibly, also, a hint of annoyance with himself for being so gullible and stupid and unprepared. 'You bastard,' he said flatly.

McCluskey shrugged. 'It comes to us all.'

'You little bastard,' Kelly repeated.

Since repetition seemed to be in order, McCluskey gave another shrug. 'It's nothing personal, Tom. It could have been any one of Reilly's men. You just happened to be handiest.'

'Jesus! You're more of a moron than I thought you were, McCluskey. Setting yourself up against Seamus Reilly, are you?' Kelly asked before bursting into a great roar of laughter. 'Christ, even you could surely have picked an easier way to commit suicide. I'll give you twenty-four hours before Seamus finds out and cuts your goddam balls off for starters.'

McCluskey smiled thinly. A tiny jumping nerve in his temple showed that the remark had hit home. He tightened his finger on the trigger and fired. Pffffft.

Rapidly now McCluskey unscrewed the silencer and slipped it into his jacket pocket. He tucked the revolver into his belt, blowing on it first, perhaps in homage to the rampaging cowboys who thundered and yoo-hahed across the small screen behind him, all the while watching Tom Kelly twitch away from life.

'Tommy?' a shrill woman's voice called from upstairs.

McCluskey froze.

'Tommy? In heaven's name will you turn down that telly. I can't get a wink of sleep.'

McCluskey moved across the room in three strides and turned down the volume.

'And come to bed yourself,' the voice went on.

McCluskey waited.

'Did you hear me?'

McCluskey produced a loud, meaningless grunt from the back of his throat.

'Well, come on then.'

The sound of footsteps in the room overhead and a door closing made McCluskey release his breath in a long, hissing sigh. He gave Tom Kelly a final, uncaring glance, and left the house, taking pains to close the front door silently behind him.

True to his word, Patrick Moran had the engine ticking over. 'What the hell kept you?' he demanded.

'We had a chat,' McCluskey told him, injecting a swagger into his voice.

'Oh lovely. I'm out here sweating like a pig and you're in there having a little chat.'

'Get this thing moving.'

Moran put the car into gear and drove sedately down the road. 'What did he say?'

'Not a lot.'

'Some chat.'

McCluskey chuckled. 'There wasn't a lot he could say. He *did* say Reilly would have our balls off within twenty-four hours.'

The Volvo lunged as Moran's foot slipped on the accelerator. 'Oh shit,' he whispered, and changed down a gear, glancing sideways at McCluskey. 'You think he will?'

'Sure to,' Eddie said, nodding, clearly enjoying the very real terror his news had inspired. 'Do you no harm. All those bloody kids you have. High time you were gelded.'

Moran was not amused. He was sensitive about the size of his family, feeling, he knew not why, that there was something a bit dirty about fathering what amounted to a litter. In fact, he had gone to some lengths to prevent his last two children being conceived, but, as usual, things had gone wrong. Apprehensive of the sinfulness of contraceptives they had stuck to the rhythm method, but his wife had missed the beat and together they had waltzed into another pregnancy; dismayed, he had stared sin in the face, and tried a Durex: alas, it had burst, and one more little Moran was soon on the way. 'At least I can bloody well do it,' he said.

'Fuck you,' McCluskey muttered, and immediately regretted the words, aware that he had left himself open for Moran's scathing: 'I doubt if you could.'

They headed back into the city in silence, Moran suddenly feeling quite cocky, McCluskey fuming. As they neared St Enoch's 'Where you going to dump this?' was all he wanted to know.

Moran thought for a second, screwing up his face. 'The docks probably.'

'Well, you can let me out here then.'

Obligingly, Moran pulled over to the side of the road. 'Eddie,' he said. 'About what I – well, shit, there's no point in us squabbling.'

'Forget it.'

'I'll see you tomorrow?'

'Yea. Ten as arranged.'

'Sleep well.'

Moran watched Eddie McCluskey saunter away from the car, his stride nonchalant, for all the world a man without a care in his head: certainly not one who had just committed murder. Briefly Moran felt a twinge of pity for him: some day, he thought, some day the awful ghosts of those he had killed would rise up against him. Moran shuddered, his eyes still following the slight figure as it swaggered away into the gloom.

· FOUR ·

Seamus Reilly was seething with fury. Not, it must be said, so much that one of his most reliable and long-standing henchmen had actually been murdered, but that he had clearly been killed by someone he knew, someone Kelly had permitted to enter the sanctuary of his own home, someone familiar enough to be able to lull him into such a state of unreadiness that he could be shot between the eyes without any trace of a struggle: all of which ruled out any 'acceptable' protagonist, and pointed to someone within their own ranks. Of course, Reilly had been expecting some brutal retaliation (one didn't expel members from the Organization without some ill-feeling, did one?), but the speed with which the revenge had been levied certainly surprised him. This, coupled with his awareness that Kelly's death was but a foretaste of yet more violence to follow –a vile aperitif, he was to call it later – filled him with disgust and deepened the foulness of his humour. Therefore, instead of his usual pleasant greetings to his driver, he grunted sourly, slamming the car door behind himself, and puffed vigorously on one of his short cigars. As the driver carefully twiddled the rearview mirror, Reilly's patience snapped. 'For heaven's sake move. I'm late enough as it is.'

'Yes, Mr Reilly. Sorry.'

'Well move then.'

In fact he was not late. He was almost never late. His manic fastidiousness about punctuality was all but proverbial, so much so that on the exceptional occasion when he was not dead on time those waiting tended to regard their watches as somewhat less than reliable.

As he was driven through the streets along a predetermined route and monitored throughout by his own security, Seamus Reilly began to relax to the extent of mildly upbraiding himself for allowing his vexation to become obvious: he abhorred emotional demonstrations of any kind, particularly in himself. But like most things in Seamus Reilly this abhorrence was contrived: over the years his position as head of the IRA Punishment Squad, and the sinister title of Godfather that went with it, had forced him to suffocate any generous feelings he might once have had, so that now he could issue orders for the assassination of what he termed 'troublemakers' and arrange for the support and care of their wives and children with equal equanimity and objectiveness. Or, at least, up until recently he had been able to. He sighed deeply. The strain of it all must be getting to him, he conceded. Small wonder. Drastic change could hardly be expected to take place without leaving its mark, and the changes in Seamus Reilly's life, slow and unnoticed by anyone but himself, had undeniably been drastic. As the Organization splintered and bickered within itself, as successive British governments had vowed to wipe them from the face of the earth, what had started in early manhood as the dramatic and patriotic continuance of an unfortunately violent bequest with clear-cut ultimatums and a clear goal had deteriorated into a struggle for personal survival, and the passionate hope of peace receded.

Reilly lowered the car window an inch and dropped out his finished cigar, opening his fingers slowly and watching the smouldering butt being whisked away. Just when things seemed to be on the point of solution, all hope would be whisked away by an inopportune remark, some stupid harassment, or a wanton killing. He rolled the window up again, carefully, with one hand, replacing the few strands of his hair that had been ruffled by the breeze. He gave a small shudder. That, of course, was the rub: despite his reputation for cold-bloodedness, despite the easy, dispassionate way he had administered death and the brutality and fear that he had used to keep his more recalcitrant men in line, Seamus Reilly had, finally, grown tired of violence. The steady pounding of bombs, the sheer and utter wastefulness of death had come, strangely and quite unexpectedly, to sicken him. That did not mean to say he would not, still, order the extermination of anyone foolish enough to oppose him: he most decidedly would, and ruthlessly: but he would prefer it if the occasion did not arise. The visions of heroic battle leading to the freedom he desired for his country no longer lured him inexorably, no longer either did the prospect of dying for one's beliefs seem all that attractive, perhaps because he now realized how little time was left at his disposal at any rate. The thought brought a wry smile to his lips. Whereas not so long ago he had fancied himself as being remembered for having died – by the bullet, by hunger strike, by bomb it mattered not – now he dreamed of being a sort of elder statesman, negotiating wisely at the table, impartially bestowing the fruits of his vast experience. And to some extent he was on the road to achieving this, for he had gently been leading the Executive round to his way of thinking, by a word here and a phrase there coaxing them towards a political solution, cajoling them into standing for office in elections, gleefully watching them win seats.

Alas something always happened to upset the apple-cart. Some politician, bereft of attention and craving promotion, would issue some ludicrous statement to the effect that the IRA were being soundly trounced, were on the point of abject surrender, and lo and behold, the bombing and killings would start again just to deprive the idiotic pronouncement of veracity; or, more deadly still, the brainless element within the ranks who saw power as emanating only from the barrel of a gun would rebel, as some had only recently done, would be expelled, would slide away and set up their own little covens, creeping out in the darkness to shatter the uneasy stillness with yet more violence.

'We're here, Mr Reilly.'

Reilly jumped. Slamming the door behind him, he walked briskly across the footpath and into the safe house, noting, from the corner of his eye, that he was well and discreetly protected.

The quiet murmur of voices ceased immediately as Reilly appeared in the doorway. For a moment he paused, staring about him as if displeased, wrinkling his nose. The room was almost bare, with only a long, scrubbed, kitchen table and seven chairs as furniture. It was uncarpeted and unadorned, although someone had put a red rose (an Enid Harkness by the look of it) in a jamjar and placed it on the mantelpiece. He turned his attention to the three men waiting for him to speak, all of them standing respectfully. With almost ceremonious decorum Reilly nodded a greeting to each of them in turn, and waved a hand by way of invitation for them to be seated, now ready to preside over this emergency meeting of his nefarious executive. It was responsible for the day to day running of the Belfast branch of the Organization as well as the enforcement of the banning of drugs from the Catholic areas of the city, the collection and distribution of donations, and the sometimes dire punishment of those who stepped beyond the proscribed lines of conduct. Most importantly Reilly's executive was also charged with the investigation of the deaths of any of the Organization's members other, of course, than those they had instigated themselves, although even these were later scrutinized in some detail since there was always something to be learned.

Nobody seemed anxious to begin so Seamus Reilly coughed again and said: 'I presume you've all heard about Tom Kelly?'

All three men nodded, keeping their eyes fixed on Reilly's face, one of them going so far as to open his mouth as if to speak. Reilly spotted this. 'Yes, Regan?' he asked sharply almost as if demanding an interruption.

'I was just going to say, Mr Reilly, we – me and Jim here, have been over to his house this morning.'

'Ah. Good. And?'

Regan looked uncomfortable, glancing at Jim Dowling for help. Not getting any he was forced to admit: 'Nothing, Mr Reilly.'

'What do you mean nothing?'

'Just that, Mr Reilly. Nobody saw anyone. His wife called down to him to tell him to turn down the telly. He turned it down and his wife went back to bed and fell asleep. She found him dead in his chair in the morning,' Regan explained. 'With the telly still going,' he added as if it might be important.

'She didn't hear the shot?'

Regan shook his head. 'She heard nothing.'

'And there was no sign of a struggle?'

'No. Nothing. It must have been someone he knew.'

Reilly nodded.

'I think that it was done to get at you, Mr Reilly.'

Reilly raised his eyebrows, more in surprise at this astuteness than in mockery. 'Do you now? And what would make you think that?'

'Well,' Dowling frowned as he sought to explain his thoughts, 'there's a lot of people have it in for you, Mr Reilly, and they know they can't get at you yourself, so they have a go at those – well, those close to you.'

Reilly conceded this with another nod.

'Or it could be,' Dowling went on, uncharacteristically emboldened by the success of his first explanation, 'it could be that someone wants to take your attention away from something else that's being planned. Using Kelly as a sort of diversion, if you know what I mean.'

Reilly knew exactly what he meant: the diversionary tactic was one he had employed himself several times. A bomb in the city would occupy the minds of the Security Forces while an ambush on the outskirts could go unhindered and leave several soldiers dead or maimed – the mutilated unfortunate shekels of war as one over-zealous magazine had called them. 'And from what,' Reilly now wanted to know, 'do you think they might be trying to divert our attention?'

Dowling shrugged. 'You know there've been rumours, Mr Reilly.'

Reilly gave a tight smile. 'There are always rumours.'

'Yea. But this time it's a bit different.'

'Indeed?'

'He's right, Mr Reilly.'

For an instant Reilly showed a flicker of annoyance. 'I seem to be the only one who hasn't heard them,' he said. 'Maybe one of you would enlighten me?'

The three men took it in turns to look at one another, none of them keen to enlighten. Not surprisingly. It was definitely tricky, for in recent months Seamus Reilly could be easily roused to anger, and only a fool would offer himself to bear the brunt of his rage.

'Well?' Reilly persisted impatiently.

Perhaps because he was feeling left out of things, or perhaps because he was just the most foolhardy, Sean O'Neill decided to speak. 'The rumour is that some of the boys you had expelled are planning something big in England,' he said bluntly.

Reilly froze, the blood draining from his face. 'I see,' he whispered hoarsely. He pointed the two fingers holding his small cigar at Regan, wagging them up and down, ignoring the ash that dropped onto the table. 'I want you,' he said very deliberately, 'to follow this up. Find out more about it. Find out every damn thing you can. I want to know who's involved, who's setting it – whatever it is – up. And I want to know soon.'

'Yes, Mr Reilly,' Regan agreed. 'But I – '

'There's nothing more I want to say about it for the moment,' Reilly interrupted. 'Just you find out what exactly is going on – if anything is. Then we'll talk some more.'

'Yes, Mr Reilly.'

'And be discreet, for God's sake. If something is planned I don't want them to know I suspect anything.'

'Right, Mr Reilly.'

Seamus relaxed. Carefully he wiped the ash from the table with one hand, catching it deftly in the other and tipping it into his ashtray; then blowing on his palm to remove any traces.

This done he pushed the ashtray a little further from him, folded his hands, interlacing his fingers and studying his neatly manicured nails for a few seconds. 'Now,' he said finally. 'Any other business?'

'I did get a bit of information that could be useful,' Regan told him.

'Not, I hope, another rumour?'

Regan smiled apologetically. 'No. A little more solid than that.'

'Ah.' Reilly sounded relieved.

'It seems the Brits are about to try the old defection trick again. I'm told they have – or are about to – move someone in with orders to desert and have us help him.'

'Your source?'

'London. My own contact. Usually very reliable.'

'So you alone are aware of this?'

'I would think so.'

'Hmmm. No names, I suppose?'

Regan shook his head. 'Not yet.'

'Pity.'

'Yes. Still, I'll get it later.'

'And you don't know if this – this deserter is actually here yet or not?'

'No.'

'But you say your contact will be able to let you know?'

'I hope so.'

Reilly frowned. 'Well, that's something. Not to worry. Better keep this strictly to yourself, Regan. I've a feeling we'll be able to use it to our advantage in more ways than one. And you two haven't heard it.'

Reilly stood up and put his chair back against the wall tidily. 'If anything comes up either about those rumours or about the deserter let me know at once,' he said to all three as he made his way to the door. 'Fine. Well, take care,' this was said as a sort of benediction. 'By the way,' he added, turning and pursing his lips. 'Did you deal with that pusher from Derry?'

'Brannigan? Oh yes, Mr Reilly. We dealt with him all right.'

'He won't be peddling his drugs here any more then?'

Regan beamed wickedly. 'Not unless he does it from his wheelchair.'

'Ah. Good. Excellent. It's the one thing I cannot stand and will not tolerate,' Reilly announced self-righteously, and left the room.

Major Crispin Fisher sat on the edge of his bunk, his elbows resting on his knees, his head in his hands, thinking under the watchful eye of Christ crucified nailed defiantly to the wall. Or rather, remembering, and wishing he could go back in time. He was aware, if not fully, of the hazards that lay ahead of him though strangely, three weeks in Belfast, three peaceful enough, uneventful weeks made it rather more difficult to admit the dangers of his mission, and, more than once, he had found himself being lulled into a perilous state of well-being, even finding himself wondering if his superiors had not exaggerated the power and evilness of the enemy.

Now, sitting there, among the familiar and comforting stink of stale sweat, and denim and leather, the grunts and groans and restless shiftings of his sleeping colleagues assailing his ears, he quietly mourned his past: the day his brother – hopeless, demanding, moronic – finally died. He died at eight o'clock in the morning. On Sunday. He was fourteen. There was no breakfast. Nothing but mugs of tea that Dad made while Mam drifted aimlessly about the house, like a lost spectre, closing the curtains (to keep the devil from setting eyes on the dead, she had once explained). It was probably at that point that Chris, already seventeen and about to join the army, wondered if death was the only way to attract the affection and respect he longed for. It was a ridiculous notion: a macabre, perverted fantasy, but it had stayed with him, shimmering in his mind, making death curiously desirable.

He stood up and automatically smoothed the blanket on his bed. Well, perhaps he would find out: perhaps fate, whatever that was, or Christ or some not too preoccupied guardian angel would provide the answer.

'What do you mean she's not coming?' Moran demanded angrily.

McCluskey stared at him complacently. 'She's not coming,' he repeated.

'Shit. She said we were to meet here this morning.'

'Yes. Well, she phoned me last night. She's gone to Glasgow.'

'Glasgow? What in the name of hell has she gone to Glasgow for?'

'I didn't ask.'

'When's she coming back?'

'She didn't say.'

'Christ,' Moran swore, eyeing distastefully McCluskey's persistent chewing of his nails. 'Didn't she ask about Kelly?'

McCluskey shrugged, taking the time to nibble a tricky sliver before saying: 'Just asked how it had gone.'

'That's all?'

'That's all. Stop worrying. She'll be back soon enough.'

'I bloody well hope so.'

The Security Officer at Glasgow airport smiled indulgently at the six young children being ushered along by the tall, attractive woman. 'Quite a handful,' he said pleasantly.

The woman returned the smile. 'Yes.'

'Not all yours?'

The woman widened her smile. 'Oh no. None of them, in fact. Just bringing them over for a few days break. Away from – well, you know.'

'Ah,' the officer sighed sympathetically, patting one of the children on the head, only to be rewarded by a sideways, suspicious look. 'Of course.'

· FIVE ·

I T WAS GETTING on for midnight when Seamus Reilly heard the car door slam outside his house. He had been sitting in the dark, listening contentedly to *Das Lied von der Erde*, but now he reached out and switched on the lamp beside his chair, looking about the room, making sure everything was neat and tidy, frowning like a nervous hostess. He heard his driver insert the key in the front door, the murmur of voices. He was on his feet and moving forward with perfect timing, one hand outstretched, when Inspector Asher was shown into the room. 'Ah, John,' he said. 'You're welcome. It must be mighty important.'

'Seamus,' John Asher acknowledged with a curt nod of his head, shaking hands.

One might have supposed from the civilized greeting that the two men were friends, and in an obtuse way they were, bound by a steely, unwavering patriotism. True, their views were different, but both were totally Irish; both found the military presence insulting and provocative; both smarted under the dismissive arrogance of successive British governments; and while one warred constantly against the invading forces, using

39

violence and intimidation as his weapons, the other waged his battles rather more subtly – but none the less effectively – by upholding law and order by any means, even, on more than one occasion, calling upon the co-operation of the IRA, through the auspices of Seamus Reilly, to further his ends. Both admitted now, after years of struggle, and only to each other, that their prospects of ever reaching a satisfactory outcome to their dreams were slim. It was probably this almost inevitable sense of pending failure that threw them together, attempting to maintain an uneasy peace, yet always bearing in mind that the other was, to use Asher's phrase, a 'ravenous ally'. The dubious friendship was emphasized by the use of Christian names when they met privately, while the distrust remained clearly displayed in the cold weariness of their eyes.

'A drink?' Seamus offered, already making his way to the small table.

'Thank you. I could use one.'

'Ah. That sort of day.' Seamus Reilly sounded as if he understood, and generously added an extra measure to the tumbler.

'That sort of day,' Asher agreed, taking the drink, raising his glass by way of thanks and toast, and swallowing a mouthful of Teachers.

Reilly returned the toast and sat down, waiting. The fact that Asher had asked to see him, had come to his home in the dead of night, had scorned the use of normal security, meant, clearly, that he had something urgent to discuss and for that he liked to be given time to feel his way and select his words. So, Reilly waited, sipping his drink, comfortable in the knowledge that when he was good and ready his visitor would come straight to the point.

Asher had all but emptied his glass before he spoke. 'Seamus, I need your help.'

Reilly inclined his head graciously. 'Of course. If I can.'

'Our intelligence says something big is brewing. Ever since you expelled certain members from your Organization, there have been reports of – well, of activity the likes of which we haven't seen for many a year.'

Reilly raised his eyebrows, but maintained an interested silence.

'The trouble is,' Asher went on thoughtfully, 'the trouble is, Seamus, that our information is that another campaign against mainland Britain is being plotted,' he said, allowing his voice to rise half an octave over the last few words to form a question.

Reilly said nothing, purposely not reacting.

'Are you involved?' Asher demanded bluntly.

'No.'

'Do you know who *is* involved?'

Reilly shook his head, frowning.

'Have you heard anything about it?'

Reilly continued to shake his head. 'Nothing directly.'

'Indirectly?'

Reilly placed his glass on the table beside him, and spread his hands in his curious little Jewish gesture of humility. 'We've had rumours circulating. Nothing definite.'

'I see.' Asher indicated he was not convinced. 'You know what repercussions such mindlessness will have on us here?'

'Of course I do, John.'

'You would tell me if you knew anything?'

Reilly retrieved his glass and took a long, steady drink, keeping his eyes on the bottom of the glass, using the exercise to consider if (if, indeed, there was anything definite to reveal) he would confide in Asher. It was a moot point. Jaded and sickened he might be by the continuous violence, but the good of the Organization would, he knew, always come first. On the other hand, if some plot was being hatched that was detrimental to, and without the sanction of the Council, a plot which would nullify his own efforts to 'calm things down' as he was fond of saying, he would certainly join forces with Asher in an effort to scupper it. 'Of course, John,' he said at last.

'And if you hear anything – definite – in the near future you will let me know?'

Reilly smiled. 'Probably.'

41

Asher seemed satisfied with that: he relaxed, and settled more comfortably into his chair, sipping contentedly at his drink. In the silence he grinned wryly to himself as it dawned on him that here, in the heart of what should have been hostile territory, he was safer than anywhere else in the city. Reilly's security, usually invisible, was better even than his own, better, probably, than any security in the province. Which brought another thought to mind: 'That Kelly – one of your lot wasn't he?'

'Yes.'

'Careless, don't you think? Not like your disciples to get themselves killed so easily.'

'You've had a report?'

'Yes.'

'Anything I should know?'

'I only glanced at it. Nothing significant in it. Nothing in it at all, in fact. Just that he was shot. It *did* strike me that it could be internal . . . ?'

'Perhaps it was, John. We are almost certain it was – well, let's just say it could tie in with what you were asking me earlier.'

'Oooh,' Asher said as if he appreciated the significance.

'We'll find out, though, never fear.'

'And then you'll tell me, of course.'

Reilly found himself forced to grin. 'Of course. Now you tell me something: you're not party to any army skullduggery, are you?'

Asher looked genuinely surprised. 'Like?'

'Only another rumour.'

'About?'

'Something to do with a plant being sent to desert.'

Asher grimaced. 'No. I've heard nothing. Not, mind you, that I would be all that likely to. The army don't confide their dirty tricks in us. Don't confide much at all.' Suddenly Asher snorted. 'We have as much trouble with the army as we do with you.'

Seamus Reilly liked that. 'Poor you,' he chuckled with mock sympathy.

'Yes. Poor me.'

The woman, wearing a long tweed overcoat and a floppy hat, the brim of which she held in one hand, keeping it low over her face, walked briskly along the road, making for a flat in James Gray Street, Glasgow. It was dusk, and the street lights had not quite reached their maximum, glowing an orange-red, giving the high, dour buildings a warmness and comfort they scarcely merited. From time to time she slowed her pace and listened, never stopping but altering her speed as if testing anyone who might secretly be keeping step with her.

When she reached the flats she took off her hat and shook her hair free in a prolonged, circular gesture, using this extravagant action to scan the road down which she had come. Satisfied, she went in and made her way upstairs, wrinkling her nose at the stench of urine, boiling vegetables and rotting woodwork that assailed her. Then slowly, all the while looking upwards, she mounted the stairs. At a door on the third floor she stopped, glanced back down, then knocked. There was a scuffling sound from inside before someone came close to the door and asked in a low, gruff voice: 'Who is it?'

'Me.'

The door opened a fraction, and an eye peered out suspiciously. Then it was thrown wide. 'You're late.'

'You try getting six kids to go to bed.'

'Come in.'

The woman entered, and instinctively started to size up the room. It seemed perfectly ordinary: a glorified bed-sitter: one large room with a tiny kitchenette off it, and a bathroom the size of a cupboard. Along one wall a divan doubled as bed and sofa. There were a couple of armchairs and a table with a red formica top. A light with a paper shade dangled from the low ceiling. The centre upright of the gas fire spluttered. A pale green fitted carpet, stained and balding, covered the floor. Most noticeable, however, despite the attempted cosiness of the fire, was the atmosphere of disuse: it was as though the room, confused perhaps by an ever-changing occupancy, had long since abandoned any attempt to acquire a character.

'Want a drink?' the man asked, already opening a can of beer.

She shook her head.

'Well, sit down. Sit down. How are things?'

She shrugged. 'Rough.'

The man nodded understandingly. 'Yea. Bound to be, I suppose.'

For a while they were silent, the woman seeming to think, the man sucking noisily on his beer, standing, swaying from foot to foot. He was in his late twenties, tall, with sandy neatly-cut wavy hair, and curiously bulbous eyes. He looked tired.

'Well, Dermot, what did you think of my idea?' she asked finally.

'Terrific – if it works.'

'Can you make it work?'

'I think so. I'll need the right equipment.'

'Can you get it?'

Dermot grinned. 'I can get anything if I have the money.'

'You'll have the money.'

'Joe and Peggy have already been down to Brighton. They stayed one night in the hotel. They say there's no problem as long as we can plant our explosives soon enough.'

'How soon?'

'Six, eight weeks before the Convention.'

'That gives them too much time to find them.'

Dermot shook his head. 'They won't find them. I know my job. They won't find them.'

The woman stared at him as if trying to detect a chink in his assurance. 'You'll have the necessary money within the week.'

'Good. That's what I like. No messing.'

'You know what will happen if it goes wrong?'

Dermot laughed. 'The same as will happen if it goes right.'

Two steets away, also in Shawlands, in a flat even smaller than

44

the one where the woman had been speaking to Dermot, Joe Mulcahy and Peggy Dunne lay naked together in bed. They had just made love, although anything amorous had been purely incidental: it had been a dispassionate, mechanical exercise, each seeking comfort rather than satisfaction from their act. Now, still in each other's arms, Joe smoking, they had an air of desolation about them, a sense of inevitable abandonment. As 'sleepers' they were under constant pressure, but pressure of a strange, haunting kind. It was one thing to be hunted for actually doing something: it was quite different to know that one would be the subject of intense investigation if one, for a single moment, ceased to remain faceless. To preserve their anonymity they seldom went out except at night when the darkness blurred their features and hid their anxiety. And there was something else that weighed upon them: the frightening loneliness of waiting. Away from everyone they knew and cared about. Just waiting to be useful. Wondering, from time to time, if they had simply been forgotten.

'Why do you think Dermot wanted all those details about the Grand?' Peggy asked, pulling Joe's hand towards her and sucking a lungful of cigarette smoke.

'God knows.'

'It seems funny he's interested in Brighton.'

'He'll tell us if he wants us to know.'

'What do you think?' Peggy insisted.

'I don't. It's better not to. All I want is to get out of this place. Christ – I hate fucking Glasgow.'

Peggy sighed but did not reply. Although none too keen on Glasgow herself, for her it had its compensations. Plain and dumpy, shy and easily embarrassed, she had, at least, the companionship of a man – something she knew she would have found difficult to procure at home. Aware though she was that any attention he paid her was because of the restrictions of their occupation she managed, in the way lonely women have, to make of him considerably more than he was. 'I'm sure they'll move us soon,' she whispered by way of comfort.

'I hope to Christ they do.'

'They will. They never leave anyone in one place too long.'
'We've been here too bloody long already.'

Declan Tuohy could not sleep. He was exhausted, but sleep simply would not come. He tossed in his bed, sitting up and thumping his pillows every so often, seeming to wreak revenge for his insomnia on the feathers. Of course it was that damned Seamus Reilly who kept him awake; or rather the possibility of getting him to speak. He threw back the blankets and got out of bed, groped about for a cigarette, lit one and puffed for a few minutes. He made his way into the kitchen and poured himself a glass of milk, dolefully eyeing the emptiness of his fridge. One never knew with Reilly. It was not that he was in any way unpredictable: far from it. Anything Seamus did or said had a definite if circuitous logic.

Declan finished his milk and padded back to his bedroom. Somewhere outside a clock struck, and he glanced at the glowing dial of his radio-alarm: one o'clock. Regardless of the hour he stood up and stretched, stubbed out his cigarette, and made determinedly for the telephone in the next room. It would do Reilly good, he thought wickedly, to be woken up. He checked the number in a small book, dialled it with the code for Belfast, and waited.

Only a second. After one ring the phone was snatched from its cradle. 'Yes?'

'Seamus? It's Declan. Declan Tuohy.'

There was, Declan imagined, a small gasp. 'Just a minute,' Seamus said.

It was difficult to surprise Seamus Reilly, but the sound of Declan's voice left him little short of amazed. He put the receiver on the table beside his bed and set about making himself comfortable, folding his old-fashioned bolster double and propping his pillow against it. He reached out and took his dressing-gown from a chair and wrapped it about his shoulders, instinctively letting his fingers feel the old bullet wound in his arm not because of any pain but probably since it was Declan's nephew who had put it there. 'Sorry. This is a surprise.'

– Yes: without doubt it is, Delcan thought. To get a phone call out of the blue at one o'clock in the morning from someone who had not been in touch for the best part of two years was bound to be a surprise. Oddly, despite the bloody and tragic outcome of their last encounter, Declan felt guilty about his long silence, the more so since Seamus had made several efforts to contact him, presumably to heal the rift.

Their relationship had always been touch and go. Childhood had been equitable enough: two small, Catholic boys, bright and romantic, laughing and conning their way through school, snickering at how innocent the priests thought them to be. Adolescence had been tricky: both young men finding themselves inevitably caught up in the horror of sectarianism and the rampant seduction of patriotism, and both with disparate views as to what should be done: Seamus, heir to the military tradition of Collins, raging about fighting to the death; Declan coyly insisting that the pen was indeed mightier than the sword. But it was adulthood that brought about the real trouble: Reilly firmly ensconced as Godfather glorious of the Provisional IRA, constantly wheeling and dealing, plotting and planning, gleefully thwarting the efforts of the Security Forces to subdue his activities; while Declan, rejecting Reilly's pleas to join him, and after a somewhat overblown success with a book of poetry (dedicated to Reilly) that had the pundits scrabbling for superlatives, had turned his back on Belfast, gone to London and receded into dispassionate journalism. Yet they had always written to each other, frequently at first, then less so, until finally it had dwindled to a Christmas card.

'I'm sure it is. How are you?'

Seamus chuckled. 'Never my best at one in the morning. Apart from that I'm fine. And you?'

'Can't complain. Working hard.'

'So I hear.'

'Oh?'

Reilly chuckled again. 'Been keeping an eye on you.'

'I see,' Declan said, sounding none too pleased.

'I like to know what my friends are up to,' Reilly explained. 'Just in case I can help,' he added.

Declan knew that was perfectly true. Whatever else, Seamus was fiercely loyal to his few friends, often aiding them without their knowledge, clearly embarrassed when they found out and thanked him. Indeed, this same man who had ordered the execution of his own brother for informing, could perform acts of extraordinary generosity when he considered them appropriate.

'I'm managing,' Declan told him.

'Yes. Television, no less.'

'You are well informed.'

'Of course.'

'Anyway – the reason I rang: I might be over soon. I'd like to see you.'

Reilly did not reply immediately, and when he did there was a cautious tone in his voice. 'You make it sound ominous.'

Declan laughed. 'I didn't mean to. Just something I want to discuss with you.'

'When are you coming?'

'First week of August?'

'I'll be here. I'm not planning on going anywhere. Ring me when you arrive. I look forward to seeing you again. Declan – is everything all right?'

'Yes. Why?'

'You sound – I don't know – upset.'

'No. Everything's fine. You're imagining things.'

'Perhaps. I'll hear from you then?'

'You will.'

· SIX ·

THE SUMMER OF 1984 thus far had been remarkably sunny. Belfast simmered in the unaccustomed heat. Nerves were unusually taut, tempers controlled on short wires. Towards the end of June, Major Fisher, in casual civilian clothes, made his way on foot past nameless doors and faceless windows into the Old Park district of the city. Although it was still reasonably bright outside, there can have been little light inside the dingy, squalid houses. It was uncannily quiet.

At the end of the street he turned left, crossed the road, and headed for the pub. This was his fourth visit and he winced as he thought of what to expect: the stench of stale beer and acrid, lingering cigarette smoke; the stench, too, of his own fear as he tried to ignore the cold, suspicious stares. Still, the antagonism seemed to be lessening, although this, he conceded, could have been wishful thinking. But the landlord's nod of welcome was real enough. 'Guinness?' he asked, remembering.

'Thanks.'

Fisher took his pint and moved to the end of the bar, propping himself comfortably in the corner. He looked about the room as inconspicuously as he could. It was considerably

49

larger than one would have imagined from outside. There were eight or nine tables, and benches all the way round the walls. At the far end was a stage, a Sinn Fein banner the backdrop. On the walls were photographs of men, some very young, with the legends of their deaths typed beneath their staring faces. Framed slogans proclaimed the need for and the inevitability of a United Ireland. From two rattly speakers on either side of the stage the thin, wailing sound of a ceilidh band emerged, and the twenty or so men already seated nodded away to the rhythm, some of them even as they carried on whispered conversations. Two strips of neon light gave everyone's face a yellow, sickly look, and an underpowered extractor sucked uselessly at the smoke.

Fisher knew he was being watched. Nobody looked at him directly: eyes would flick across him, absorbing him in transit. He knew, too, that some of the men were discussing his presence. Not that he minded. Indeed, it was what he wanted. On previous visits, feigning drunkenness, he had let it slip that he was, to put it mildly, disenchanted with army life; that he, as a Catholic, was ashamed of what he was being forced to do; that he had been misled by biased propoganda. But he had been careful, never being specific, never suggesting that he intended or wished to desert, just dropping hints and leaving the door open for a move to be made.

Suddenly the music stopped: immediately all conversation died. As if on cue the door burst open and four Paratroopers strode in, their faces blackened, their guns at the ready. Despite their harsh training they were all clearly afraid and sublimated this by adopting an almost arrogant strut as they moved about the room, saying nothing, staring at faces, their rubber-soled boots screeching on the linoleum making the only noise. Whatever the exercise was in aid of it was soon over and they left, backing out.

Fisher found himself trembling. That was all he needed: to be arrested for drinking in a Republican pub. Jesus! He stared hard at his drink, trying to control himself by shaking his head.

Perhaps misinterpreting this action the landlord came along

the bar towards him, wiping a glass as he came. 'Bastards,' he said.

Fisher looked up, sensing that some precise retort was now expected. Tricky. He had to be careful. Nothing too derogatory. Nothing out of style. He nodded. 'They're made do it,' he replied.

'Fuck them,' the landlord said, still, it seemed, probing.

'Half of them don't want to. Half of them don't even want to be here,' Fisher replied quietly.

The landlord busied himself stacking the wiped glass on top of several others, forming a precarious pyramid. He stood back and admired his handiwork.

'That's nice,' Fisher volunteered.

The landlord looked at him. 'You could always get out.'

Fisher decided to look puzzled.

'Of the army.'

'Oh. It's not that easy.'

'You've tried?'

'Well – no – '

'Well then?'

'It's not that easy,' Fisher said again, dropping a hint of frustration into his words.

'If there's the will there's the way,' the landlord informed him, and left him to ponder the wisdom, moving back down the bar to pull a pint.

Fisher finished his drink and stood up. It was a good time to leave. No point in forcing things. Perhaps the landlord had meant nothing significant. He buttoned his jacket and made to leave, waving in a friendly way to the landlord who looked as if he was about to return the gesture but at the last minute transformed it into a beckoning for Fisher to come closer. 'I meant it,' he said. 'If you want to get out there's always a way.'

Fisher gave a tiny, wistful smile. 'I'll remember that.' Outside he breathed in deeply, the night air, chilly now, rasping in his lungs and making him cough. Frowning, he set off back to the barracks.

Seamus Reilly made a steeple of his forefingers and tapped them against his lips. Across from him Thomas Regan waited, looking pleased with himself. 'And you're certain he's the one?' Reilly asked.

'Positive. The name came through this morning from London. The description is him to a tee.'

Reilly nodded. 'Good. How often did you say he's been there?'

'Tonight was his fourth visit. I was told after his first and I had him followed there twice more.'

'How's he playing it?'

'Cool, as they say. Not pushing himself at all. Pretending to get pissed and just saying enough to make us interested.'

'A Major no less . . .' Reilly reflected.

'Yep. Hardly looks old enough though.'

'And Sandy has put out a feeler?'

'Yep – '

'Don't say that,' Reilly snapped irritably.

'Sorry, Mr Reilly. Yes. His usual line. Where there's a will there's a way. You know.'

'And?'

'Fisher didn't really react. But he will. He will.'

'We *know* that, Thomas. The thing is how do we get Moran or McCluskey to do the lifting?'

Regan frowned, confused. 'Why would you want them to lift him, Mr Reilly?'

Seamus Reilly appeared to ignore the question, tapping his lips again, already the embryo of a plan forming in his mind. He started to explain. 'I want someone in with Moran, McCluskey and that woman. I want to know if they *did* kill Kelly. I want to know what the hell they're up to. That's why I want them to lift Fisher when the time is right. Get him in there and give him the time to find out what is happening. Then we can take him.' Clearly Reilly liked this and smiled contentedly to himself. 'You go and see Sandy in the morning. Tell him that when he thinks Fisher is ready to get in touch with McCluskey and tip

52

him off to the desertion. Nothing else. He's just to say he has this Brit who wants out.'

'Right, Mr Reilly.'

'And keep an eye on Fisher himself. I want to know every move he makes between now and the time he's lifted.'

'Yes, Mr Reilly.'

'You did well, Thomas.'

'Thank you, Mr Reilly.'

Alone, Reilly poured himself a nightcap, put on a tape of Handel's *Jephtha*, and settled back in his chair, allowing the drink and the music to lull his brain. More and more he treasured these rare moments of tranquillity, more, too, he liked to be alone. – 'Such mighty blessings bring us peace – '. Reilly heard the words of the aria and grunted: there would be precious little peace in the immediate future as far as he could see.

'He's ripe, I tell you,' McCluskey said, almost shouting as if to defy contradiction.

'I don't like it,' Moran said.

'You don't have to,' McCluskey announced, looking towards the woman.

'How can you tell, Eddie?' the woman asked.

McCluskey made a face. 'I can tell. I've seen plenty of them.'

'He could be a plant,' the woman went on.

'Not this one. I've seen him three times in Sandy's place. He's no plant. He's too scared.'

'You can't be sure.'

'I am sure.'

'I still don't like it,' Moran insisted.

McCluskey gave him a scathing look, and turned back to the woman, saying: 'It's too good a chance to lose. You know damn well we could use someone like him if – '

'It's too bloody risky,' Moran insisted, refusing to be put down.

The woman stood up and went to the window. For several

minutes she stared out, seeming to consider the possibilities. 'I suppose he could be useful – '

'Of course he bloody well could,' McCluskey interrupted. 'Jesus, without Reilly it's our best chance of getting info from inside.'

'Have you spoken to him?' the woman asked, coming back from the window and sitting down again.

McCluskey shook his head. 'No.'

'Has Sandy said anything?'

Again McCluskey shook his head. 'No.'

Moran gave a scoffing noise. 'Oh great.'

'Fuck you.'

'Stop it you two,' the woman snapped, vexed. 'Eddie's right. This Brit could be useful.'

'We'll have to move sharpish. We don't want Reilly and his boys beating us to it,' Eddie McCluskey said, pushing his advantage.

The woman frowned. 'I'm not going to be rushed. Just you go on watching him. And keep your ears peeled. When you're certain he's ripe we'll have another meet.'

'We'll lose – '

'Just watch him another while,' the woman insisted.

'By the way.' Brigadier Brazier said as an afterthought, 'What news of Major Fisher?'

There was a moment's silence at the other end of the line. Then: 'Progressing nicely, sir.'

'What does that mean?'

The voice gave a small hollow laugh. 'Just that. Progressing nicely.'

'That's all you have to tell me?'

'That's all there *is* to tell, sir.'

'Well, as long as we don't have another débâcle.'

'We won't, sir.'

'For all our sakes I hope not.'

Dermot Drumm walked the short distance between the two

Glasgow flats, chain-smoking. He looked about him for several minutes before hurriedly crossing the street. He raced up the stairs two at a time. When he reached the flat Joe Mulcahy already had the door open, letting him in without a word, without even a nod of welcome.

'We've got a job on,' Dermot announced, looking about for an ashtray, seeing none and tossing his butt into the empty grate.

Joe Mulcahy and Peggy Dunne looked at each other but said nothing, waiting for Dermot to explain.

'Next Friday I want you both to go to Brighton again. You've been booked into the Grand in the name of Mr and Mrs Clark.' Dermot reached into his inside pocket and took out a brown envelope which he tossed across to them. 'Go out and buy yourselves new clothes. Everything. Shoes, socks, knickers – the lot. Get your hair done. You're newly-weds, you'll be glad to hear, so act a bit dumb when you get there, and look as if you're madly in love. I'll contact you there on Saturday – okay?'

'Okay.'

'They have lots of honeymooners who stay there so they probably won't pay too much attention to you. Just don't attract any unnecessary attention. In fact the less they see of you the better. It'll only seem natural if you stay closetted in your bedroom anyway,' Dermot told them grinning. 'On Thursday I'll bring you a small overnight bag. That goes with you. Treat it carefully.'

The manager of the Grand Hotel, Brighton ushered his assistant into a chair and sat down behind his desk. 'It's been confirmed,' he said. 'She'll be staying here during the Party Convention. Plus most of the Cabinet.'

'Oh boy!'

'Quite. Still, we've plenty of time to prepare. It's not till October.'

'Three months isn't all that long.'

'No, but it's enough.'

'Who'll be handling security?'

'Special Branch, I imagine.'

'They'll want plans of the suites, I suppose?'

'I would think so. I haven't been told, but I'm sure they will.'

'I'll see to that right away.'

'Good.'

'And you'd better see to it that no bookings are taken for the PM's suite from, say, the middle of September.'

'Right . . . . Should we give it a lick of paint?'

The manager smiled mischievously. 'Our rooms are impeccable at all times.'

'Of course.'

· SEVEN ·

ON THE FIRST Saturday in August, Declan Tuohy arrived in Belfast and went directly to his sister's house. He would have preferred to stay in an hotel but knew it was his duty to spend a few days in his old home. Since the death of her husband and son, Rose had deteriorated rapidly, unable to cope with the horror. Now she cocooned herself in a shadowy, haunted world wherein the dead were as real and alive as the living. Neighbours, he knew, dropped in frequently to keep an eye on her, but their visits appeared superfluous: Rose managed remarkably well, keeping her house in sparkling condition, often holding tea-parties for guests that existed only in her mind. And although she had aged she took care of her appearance, always dressed neatly, her hair tidy and nails manicured, just as if she was permanently on the point of setting out for Mass.

He was upset more than shocked when she opened the door to him. True she invited him to enter graciously and smiled a genuine, warm welcome, but there was a wounded wildness in her eyes, and he suspected she did not know who he was: a suspicion confirmed when she asked him politely: 'And you're – ?'

'It's me, Rose. Declan.'

For a second Rose looked puzzled. Then she smiled. 'Of course. How silly of me. Declan. How nice to see you again.'

'I'm sorry to barge in like this, but I had to come over for a few days. I thought you might put me up.'

Rose's eyes twinkled. 'Of course you can stay. Your old room is still where it was,' she said, tittering at her little witticism.

'Thanks, Rose.'

'You just go up and unpack and have a wash, and I'll make us both a nice cup of tea. Have you eaten?'

'I had a bite on the plane. I'm not hungry.'

Declan put his small suitcase by the foot of the bed and threw his jacket on top of it, staring about the room, a curious sense of timelessness sweeping over him. It was as if he had never been away, as if what he had done in the last few years was of so little account the gods had decided to erase it. And perhaps they were right. Of course the window had been mended, and he walked to it and ran his fingers over the new panes. Outside on the street everything was peaceful. A cat preened itself pretending not to notice the party of sparrows near the gutter. Four women chatted, laughing occasionally; three small girls played hopscotch, giggling delightedly as they wobbled on one hopping leg. Declan sighed. It had been just as peaceful the night the bullet had shattered the window, missing him by inches, a bullet, as it turned out, meant for his nephew, Fergal. Everywhere you turned in Belfast reminded you of some tragedy, it seemed. Even the small front garden, so lovingly tended by Rose's husband, was like a horrible memorial to death, its unkempt flowerbeds and overgrown grass, the thistles and nettles, the paper bags, the beer can and two plastic mugs seeming to jeer at the unfortunate man who had been shot in error by the gate. Declan turned away from the window. City of Moloch, he had called it once, much to Seamus Reilly's annoyance – but city of Moloch it certainly was.

When he came downstairs Rose was already in the front room with tea nicely laid out on a tray. 'All settled?' she asked, and without waiting for an answer, went on: 'Now yours is milk but no sugar, isn't it?'

It wasn't, but Declan could not muster an argument. 'That's right.'

'I thought that was it. I remember because it's the opposite to the way Mr Reilly likes his. His is sugar but no milk,' Rose explained.

Declan was astounded. 'Seamus Reilly comes here for tea?' he asked.

'Oh yes. Every week. He manages my money, you know. Some pension fund Tim Pat subscribed to. Mr Reilly collects it for me and brings it round. Then he has a cup of tea and a chat, and off he goes until the following week. Such a nice man. Always cheerful and happy. He *does* make me laugh,' Rose explained, giving a little laugh as if to demonstrate Seamus Reilly's effect.

Declan managed a smile: the thought of Reilly being cheerful and happy was enough to make anyone smile. His smile widened as he recognized the tactful hand of Reilly in Tim Pat's 'pension fund'. Some pension. It was typical of Reilly's delicate humour to disguise the inevitable IRA donation to a member's widow in such innocuous terms. Not that he could have told Rose any different: she would, in all probability, have been appalled to learn that Tim Pat had been in any way involved. True, his participation had been limited: he had been on the quiet list for several years, and the fact that he had just been asked to become active when he was shot (he, too, mistakenly taken as Fergal) was purely coincidental.

'He's a very funny man,' Declan agreed, barely masking his sarcasm.

'And kind,' Rose went on. 'He always brings a little present for me. A few flowers. A pot of honey. Some chocolates. Always some little thing to keep the colour in my cheeks as he says.'

Declan found it difficult not to laugh outright. Although surprised and touched by this new side of Seamus Reilly, the vision of him producing pots of honey by way of offering was somehow hilarious. And the only flowers Declan could reasonably associate with him were the posies he always sent to funerals. 'That is kind,' he admitted.

Rose sighed gratefully. 'Everyone is kind to me,' she told him, for the first time looking at him directly, making him feel uncomfortable, perhaps accusing him.

'I'm sorry I haven't kept in touch more often, Rose.'

'But you have. I remember getting hundreds of letters from you.'

'Hardly hundreds.'

'Oh yes. All those lovely little poems you used to send me – what was it we said? – by the fairy post? Don't you remember?' Rose sounded disappointed. 'When you came home from school you'd slip them under my pillow and tell me they came by fairy post.'

Declan felt suddenly very sad; annoyed, too, that the innocence of childhood should now make him feel so embarrassed; and, stupidly, guilty as if anything so delightful as fairy postmistresses had no place in the hard reality he had so often been accused of avoiding.

'Anyway,' Rose was saying, 'Mr Reilly's been telling me all about you. He always brings me a little snippet of news about what you're doing. It is you who has gone into television, isn't it?'

Declan nodded. 'It is.'

'I thought so. That must be nice.'

For a while they sat in silence, at least Declan did. Rose, on the other hand, although not actually speaking, gave the impression she was fully occupied as hostess, smiling quietly to herself from time to time, mouthing silently, shifting the milkjug and sugarbowl and teapot about the tray as in some elaborate boardgame, or perhaps just needing to touch things to reassure herself of their reality.

At length Declan stood up and put his cup and saucer on the tray. Looking down at his sister he reached out and lightly touched her hair. 'You're a wonderful girl, Rose,' he told her softly.

'Rubbish,' Rose said shortly.

When Declan's flight was some twenty minutes from landing Seamus Reilly was talking to Inspector John Asher. The meeting was at Reilly's suggestion, and took place in a safe house frequently used for such get-togethers.

'There's been a development?' Asher was asking hopefully.

Reilly made a denying grimace. 'I'm not sure,' he told him guardedly.

'Oh.'

'We *have* located the so-called deserter.'

Asher waited in silence.

Reilly, too, remained silent, smiling mischievously.

'He does have a name?' Asher weakened first.

'He does.'

'But I'm not to be told?'

Reilly took a moment to think about this. 'That depends, John,' he said finally.

'On what?'

'On whether we can come to an agreement as to what should be done.'

'We usually do.'

'Yes. We do,' Reilly conceded. 'But . . .'

'But?'

'But like myself you have your loyalties.'

And that was certainly true. Like Reilly, Asher was getting old and tired. Like Reilly he had become sickened by the lawlessness that masqueraded under the guise of 'defending rights'. And like Reilly he wished to God that the fanatics and the politicians and the do-gooders and the meddlers would just vanish and leave the people of the province to sort out their own problems. Not that God had much to do with it as far as Asher was concerned: His ministers – the 'citrus' clergy (as Reilly had once called them) and the tarmac-kissing Polack (as Asher had responded) – were equally laughable, using their religions to pile yet more misery on the community. Yet, while feeling wholly Irish, Asher was sometimes even pompously loyal, in general terms, to the monarch in whose service he was. And while he could and did wheel and deal with the best of them, ultimately, he knew, it was his duty to uphold what remained of law and order.

'So what agreement are we talking about?'

'Let's say a temporary small conspiracy of silence.'

Asher raised his eyebrows.

'We want him left alone, you see. We *want* him to desert – but not to us.'

Asher looked confused. 'No?'

'No. You remember I promised to tell you if I heard of anything big coming down in mainland Britain?'

Asher nodded.

'Well, we are almost certain something of the kind is being planned – without our sanction. We don't know what – yet. We think we know who. And it is to those people we want this man to desert.'

'And then?'

Reilly smiled benevolently. 'And then, when we feel he's learned enough, we lift him, and persuade him to tell us what he knows.'

Asher gave this some thought. 'You know, of course, Seamus, that I should report this?'

'Of course, but then we wouldn't have as good a chance of solving the riddle of what's going on. Besides, you know as well as I do that the army wouldn't thank you for it.'

There was logic in that, certainly. Although supposedly working together to maintain a troubled peace, the army and the RUC were often at loggerheads, the army resenting their role of policing, the RUC resenting the army's usurpation of that role. Indeed, very little information passed between them, each guarding their secrets jealously, each hoping to outdo the other. All of which suited Seamus Reilly.

'I'll tell you what I'll do, Seamus,' Asher decided. 'You give me the name of this soldier, and promise me you'll let me know instantly you have some knowledge of what is being planned, and I'll keep it to myself. How's that?'

Reilly laughed pleasantly. 'Good enough as far as it goes. But I'll need a little more than that, John.'

'Like?'

'Like I'll want all you can get me on our – our soldier friend. There are details you can get at that I can't, and I need to know everything.'

Asher nodded. 'If I can I will. What else?'

'If we find out what is being planned for England I want you to let us handle it. We can always fix it so that you get the credit, but we must handle it.'

'Will you be able to?'

Reilly grinned. 'Oh yes. You see, John, if something is going on we are, like I said, pretty certain who is behind it.'

'Can you tell me?'

Reilly shrugged. 'Why not. You can probably guess anyway.'

Asher decided to guess. 'Moran?'

'And McCluskey and – '

Asher wagged a finger at Reilly. 'You shouldn't have been so lenient with them.'

'Oh they were warned what would happen if they tried anything off their own bat. If we can prove they are involved in something they know what to expect.'

'It might be too late then.'

'It might indeed.'

'And the soldier?'

'Fisher. Chris Fisher. Major.'

Asher looked surprised. 'A Major no less.'

'Quite.'

'I'll see what I can find out. But don't you forget – not a move unless I'm warned.'

Reilly put his hand on his heart. 'Not a move.'

As Declan was drinking tea with his sister, Seamus Reilly was drinking something stronger with the Commander in Chief of the Provisional IRA. He had driven there directly from his

63

meeting with Asher, crossing the border without any problem, arriving in Clones only minutes behind the Commander.

'You look harassed, Seamus,' the Commander observed.

'I am harassed.'

'Ah. That's the first time I've ever heard you admit that.'

'The way things are going it won't be the last,' Seamus told him with a wry smile. 'I hate having to deal with unknown quantities. Give me facts and I can cope, but this "is there isn't there something going on?" business is unbearable.'

'Well – is there or isn't there?' the Commander enquired, swilling his drink in his glass, his eyes dancing good-humouredly behind his spectacles.

'Very probably. Everyone seems to think there is. But we don't *know*. And it's taking too long to find out. *If* something is about to happen I can tell you who's behind it.'

The Commander gave a short laugh. 'You don't have to, Seamus. I warned you that woman would be nothing but trouble. You should have let me have her dealt with there and then.'

Seamus looked gloomy. 'I know. But the repercussions could have been worse. She has support, you know, both here and in Dublin.'

'It wouldn't be doing her much good if she was dead.'

'I'm afraid it's a case of the devil you know.'

The Commander took a long drink, and coughed as the liquid burned his throat. When he next spoke his tone had changed: far less genial, it had a hardness that Reilly recognized all too well. 'It is imperative, Seamus, that nothing happens that will upset the balance of things. The elections are coming soon and we need to win seats if we are ever to deliver this unfortunate country from the horror it suffers. The last thing we need now is some stupidity in England. We've tried too long and too hard to show ourselves as reasonable men to have all our efforts destroyed by these hotheads.'

'I know. I know.'

'Well do something about it for God's sake.'

Seamus held out his hands in a gesture of appeal. 'What?'

The Commander ignored the question, warning instead: 'If you don't find out what they're up to and put a stop to it you will be blamed, Seamus, and even I won't be able to save you.'

'Dammit, I don't even know for sure if *anything* is going on.'

'I presume, at least, you've had that woman watched.'

'Of course.'

'And she's done nothing that might arouse your suspicions?'

Reilly made a little face. 'Not really. She took a party of children to Glasgow for a few days, but she's done that before.'

'Glasgow?'

'Yes.'

'Who have we got there?'

'Eight sleepers.'

'Any who might support her?'

'A couple of hard-liners who might. Dermot Drumm for one. If he supported her then Joe Mulcahy would.'

'Did she meet with Drumm?'

Reilly looked suddenly uncomfortable. 'Not that we know of. She did give our man the slip one evening for a couple of hours,' he confessed.

'So she could have seen him?'

'She *could* have.'

The Commander frowned his displeasure. 'Could they, then, be planning something in Glasgow?' he asked, sounding impatient.

'What in the name of heaven could they be planning in Glasgow?' Seamus asked in return. 'It'd be crazy.'

'Crazy people do crazy things. And crazy people seeking revenge do even crazier things.'

Reilly sighed deeply and shook his head. 'Just leave it with me and I'll sort everything out.'

'I hope so, Seamus.'

'I will. I'm working on it night and day. I've even had Asher agree to help in a way.'

The Commander was forced to laugh. 'You and Asher. The terrible twins. Dear God. If the Brits ever found out about you two being hand in glove all hell would break loose.'

'All hell would have broken loose long ago on many occasions if we weren't.'

'You use whoever you want, but just sort this mess out.

Seamus Reilly was exhausted by the time he got home. He had stripped and was making his way to the shower, a woolly monogrammed towel wrapped about his groin, when the phone rang. 'Damn,' he swore, and tut-tutted his way back to the bedside table. 'Yes?'

'Seamus? It's me. Declan.'

'Oh, Declan,' Reilly said abruptly, trying to orientate himself. 'Where are you?'

'Here. In Belfast. At Rose's.'

'Oh.'

'What's the matter with you? You sound – '

'I'm sorry, Declan. I've had a rough day. I've only just got in. I was on my way to the shower when you called.'

'I'll call back later. I – '

'No it's all right. I'm glad you're here. I look forward to seeing you again. It's been a while.'

'Yes. Can I see you tomorrow?'

'Of course. What time? After Mass?'

'What Mass do you go to?'

'Twelve o'clock, I'm afraid. The flesh and all that. Why don't we have a bite of lunch together?'

'Fine.'

'Right. I'll pick you up at one.'

'I look forward to that.'

'Me too.'

Chris Fisher leaned on the bar, propped in his favourite corner. From the moment he had entered he had sensed that something significant was going to happen. Perhaps it was the more than usual friendliness of the landlord, Sandy: or perhaps it was the fact that not everyone stopped talking when he came in.

'That's a muggy class of a night,' the landlord greeted him, smiling. 'A Guinness as usual?'

66

'Please.'

'And this one's on the house. You're a regular now.'

Fisher drank slowly, and wiped the line of froth from his upper lip with one finger. Without actually meaning to he found himself watching the landlord. He saw him nod to someone in the bar and then jerk his head towards the end of the bar. In the mirror behind the bottles he saw a small man with a moustache get up, place a hand on his companion's shoulder, lean down to him and whisper, and then come across the room towards the corner where he stood. He found himself stiffen in the way (if such was true) that people do when they are about to die.

'You're Chris, aren't you?'

Chris Fisher turned his head slowly and stared the man in the face, noting the wide smile and the cold non-participating eyes. 'Yes,' he admitted.

'I'm Eddie,' the man told him and held out his hand.

When they had shaken hands, Eddie McCluskey said bluntly, 'Sandy tells me you want out.'

Fisher looked about him hurriedly, as if terrified that someone would overhear.

'You don't have to worry,' Eddie consoled him. 'You're safe enough here. Is it true?'

'I don't know,' Fisher said, trying to sound bewildered.

'What d'you mean you don't know?'

'Yes. I want out. But – '

Eddie beamed. 'That's better. We knew you did. We can always tell. You bring your drink and come over to the table and meet a pal of mine.'

Fisher followed McCluskey across the room to the table, aware that every eye in the place was on him.

'Come on. Sit down,' Eddie insisted. 'This is Pat. Pat – Chris.'

Moran looked up and nodded imperceptibly. He was still not happy. Stupid they might think he was but he had instincts about things, and instinct now told him there was something not right about this. Oddly enough it was not so much that he

67

suspected this Fisher of being a plant, more that he sensed, without any conceivable reason, that the hand of Seamus Reilly was behind it, ludicrous though that might be. He had come across Reilly a couple of times since he had been expelled, both times after Sunday Mass, and Reilly's reactions then had been strangely sinister. He had been too disinterested, too non-chalant, dismissing the presence of Moran and what was mobile of his huge family with a bland flick of his eyes as though they did not exist. That was not Reilly. Everything was of importance to him, and he would certainly have been keen to observe what reaction the meeting of their eyes would create.

The three men sat in silence for a while, sipping their drinks, listening to the music, McCluskey keeping time to the rhythm by drumming his fingers on the formica-topped table and occaionally mouthing the words. When the song finished McCluskey said: 'It'll take a bit of time, you know.'

Fisher accepted this. 'Sure.'

'Just you go about your business as usual for the next week or so. When we're ready we'll let you know.'

'Okay.'

'You'll be coming here in the meantime?'

'Should I?'

McCluskey grinned. 'Why not?'

'I thought – '

Moran interrupted. 'We'll do the thinking. Anyway, there are some people you'll have to meet before we do anything.'

'Of course.'

Moran finished his drink, all the while keeping his watery eyes on Fisher.

'I'm off,' he announced putting down his glass. 'You coming?' he asked McCluskey.

Eddie looked a little surprised and peeved, but he said yes.

'You better hang on here for a while after we've gone,' Moran said.

'Right,' Fisher agreed.

'And by the way, don't you ever approach us. If you see

68

either of us in here or anywhere else don't even acknowledge that you know us.'

Outside Moran turned up the collar of his jacket, and stood staring back at the bar, shaking his head.

'What's up with you?' Eddie demanded, determined not to let Moran dampen his expectations.

'I still don't like it, Eddie. We don't need to help the bastard. He can't do us a damn bit of good.'

Feeling suddenly sleepy and not, for the moment, prepared to argue, Eddie said: 'Well, he can't do us any harm,' and started to walk away.

Moran followed morosely in his footsteps, already visions of the harm that the Brit could do clamouring in his mind. 'You're wrong, Eddie,' he said, not caring that McCluskey was too far ahead to hear. 'You're wrong. He'll do us nothing but bloody harm.'

The desk clerk at the Grand Hotel watched Joe Mulcahy sign the register in the name of Mr and Mrs Clark. He gave them the friendly, slightly naughty smile he reserved for newly-weds, and tapped the small brass bell, signalling with his forefinger for the porter to take their luggage upstairs.

His conversation with Declan over, Seamus Reilly made for the shower again. He had almost reached it this time when the phone rang for the second time. Reilly threw up his hands in despair and the towel slipped to the floor. He kicked it angrily out of his way and went naked back to the bedroom. 'Yes?'

'Mr Reilly. It's Regan.'

'Yes, Regan.'

'Sandy just called me. They've made contact. McCluskey and Moran had a drink with him. They stayed together about five minutes then McCluskey and Moran left. Fisher stayed on for a quarter of an hour, then he left too. I thought you'd want to know.'

Reilly sat down on the edge of his bed. 'Yes. Thank you, Thomas. Where did they go?'

'Moran went home. McCluskey went to another bar, stayed twenty minutes and then he went home. Fisher went back to the barracks.'

'Right. I'll have a think about it and talk to you on Monday.'

'Very good, Mr Reilly.'

· EIGHT ·

SUNDAY. THE SABBATH. The day, it is said, that God took a well-deserved rest after His labours. Seamus Reilly frowned at the thought. The way things were going with the world it might have been better if He had spent His Sunday destroying what He had created and starting from scratch again. At least people seemed to act more kindly towards each other on Sundays, like, say, at Christmas, and that, surely, was commendable even if their goodwill was brought about only by their terror of what Christ might make of them when they appeared at His altar for communion.

Reilly clambered out of bed, scattering the newspapers he had been reading onto the floor. Balanced precariously on the small table by his bed was a tray with the remnants of his breakfast: the peel of a grapefruit, crusts of toast, an eggshell. He stretched himself luxuriously, glancing at the clock: 10.45. Just time to shave and dress, have one more cup of coffee before Mass.

At ten minutes to midday he was kneeling respectfully in his pew, waiting for the parish priest to make his entrance. The church was packed, whole families rallying to the latest possible Mass, many left without a place to kneel and cluttering the doorway. Yet in Reilly's pew there was plenty of room. At least four more worshippers could have squeezed in, but no one presumed to infringe Seamus Reilly's right to space. He liked it at the back; for as long as he could remember he had used the same place so that now it was known as Mr Reilly's place, and spoken of with respect. He could see everyone without turning round, and, of course, everyone could see him as they came in. For Seamus it was important to set an example. To be seen. It made him mortal, belying the rumours of his cruel inhumanity. As they came in now people smiled at him timidly, and he smiled back, sometimes giving a tiny wave like a blessing. There was nothing arrogant in this gesture. They were, after all, his people. He protected them and their interests, and he genuinely loved them. Most of all he admired their tenacity to live out their lives in the face of the appalling brutality that surrounded them, content in the assurance that their God was always close at hand.

Reilly bowed his head reverently at the consecration, trying to pray. As ever he failed. His mind would not adapt to prayer: the hypocrisy of appearing to worship a Christ to whom he could not pray disturbed him. He had even spoken of it once to a priest, long since dead, and had been told rather enigmatically ' 'tis your vanity that stands in your way, Seamus. You should follow the admonition of old Ezra Pound and "pull down your vanity" '. His failure irked him, and made him envy the simple, uncomplicated faith of his family, or what was left of it. Even his brother whom he had ordered to be executed had managed a liaison with God denied himself. And his mother . . . Seamus Reilly stared up at the ceiling of the church as though for succour. His mother with incredible blindness had accepted the fratricide as the will of God, had never reproached him, had mentioned it only once, and that when she was dying and too weak to argue. 'That's something between you and Jesus,' she had said. 'If you deserve it, He'll forgive you.' But would He?

Mass over, Reilly blessed himself, sidled from his pew,

genuflected, and walked from the church, nodding appreciatively as a group of men by the door stepped to one side, allowing him to exit unhindered. Outside he set his hat at precisely the right angle on his head, and tucked his missal under his arm. He acknowledged with a single blink the appearance of two men on either side of him and walked towards his car, stopping a couple of times for a word with someone, his hand resting sympathetically on their arm as he spoke, and the faces that had been worried were more cheerful when he left them. Reilly himself felt better that his words had solved their problems. It was what he was there for. He settled back in his seat, and lit one of his little cigars. 'Home first,' he told his driver. As the car moved away he glanced out of the window, and tensed. Patrick Moran, his wife and four of his brood were waiting to cross the road. For an instant Moran's eyes met Reilly's, and a sense of warm satisfaction swept over Seamus as he noted the fear.

Within walking distance of the church that Reilly had just left, in a small house with a pleasant garden, a house neatly and tastefully furnished that smelled of wax and with flowers in nearly every room, the woman, dressed in a scarlet cat-suit, sat in an armchair, one leg curled underneath her. She held a drink in her hand, and each time she moved the ice in the glass clinked. Across the room, in another chair, Eddie McCluskey, wearing what would once have been called his 'Sunday suit', sat smoking, nervously tapping the ash into an ashtray after every drag. Clearly he had just said something that had given the woman something to think about: she had thrown her head back, frowning. McCluskey took to eating his nails. 'Don't do that,' the woman said irritably, glaring at him in disgust.

McCluskey stopped instantly, blushing like a child.

'And you don't agree with Moran? You think he's all right?'

'I'm sure of it,' McCluskey said. 'Sandy thinks so too, and he doesn't make mistakes.'

'We *all* make mistakes,' the woman said, sitting up and sipping her drink.

'Not this time,' McCluskey insisted.

'You think not?'

'I'm certain.'

The woman shook her head slowly, not convinced. 'They've conned us before now.'

McCluskey made a curiously old-fashioned sound. 'Pshaw! That was when Reilly's men handled it.'

'But you know better?'

'Sure.'

The woman thought again for a minute. 'We could use him,' she conceded finally.

'You're damn right we could. He's a Major for Christ's sake.'

'Yes,' the woman agreed but vaguely as though rank was the furthest thing from her mind. 'I won't take any chances, though. He'll have to prove himself first.'

'I can arrange that.'

The woman finished her drink and put her glass down hard on the table, clearly coming to a decision. 'All right. If he proves himself we'll lift him. If he doesn't – ' She shrugged.

McCluskey grinned. 'I know.'

'Pick someone from his own regiment. Someone he's bound to know. If your Major shoots him, okay. If not you shoot him.'

'Right,' McCluskey said, obviously pleased.

'And arrange it soon. I don't want this thing hanging on. I've enough to think about as it is.'

'Do you want to meet him?'

The woman shook her head. 'No. There's no point. Time enough if he's genuine.' She stood up. 'You better clear off. My sister and her husband are coming for lunch. I've the mint sauce to make.'

It had started to drizzle as Reilly and Declan went up the steps into the hotel. As they neared the main door one of the security guards moved forward, one hand outstretched as if to stop them. Reilly removed his hat and fixed him with a furious glare. Instantly the guard froze, and then transformed his act of restraint into a small salute that hinted of respect and brotherhood. 'Morning, sir. Sorry. I didn't recognize you.'

Inside Declan followed Seamus across the open foyer, through the lounge and into the restaurant: as they entered the headwaiter's eyes flickered a warning to an underling and moved forward to greet them. 'Ah, good morning, Mr Reilly. Nice to see you again. I have your table all ready. This way please.'

He led the way across the room to a table isolated from the others in the bay of the window. He snapped his fingers and a waiter glided towards them, his hand already out to accept Reilly's coat and hat.

When they were seated the headwaiter handed them each a menu. 'I'll leave you to decide, Mr Reilly. A drink, perhaps, while you make up your mind?'

Seamus looked across at Declan, cocking an eyebrow by way of invitation.

'Are we having wine?' Declan asked.

'Of course.'

'Then I'll wait.'

'We can have the wine brought now,' Reilly said.

'Fine. I'll have wine, then.'

'Red or white?'

'Whichever.'

Reilly smiled tightly. 'White, I think. Pouilly Fuisse.' He looked up.

'So,' Seamus said, unfolding his napkin and spreading it across his knees. 'You're back.'

Declan nodded. 'I'm back. For two days.'

'A short enough visit. May I ask why?'

'I wanted to talk to you.'

Reilly stared across the table and remained silent.

'Something I wanted to ask you.'

Reilly spread his hands. 'Feel free.'

'We've heard things in London. Something – '

Declan stopped and leaned back as the waiter brought the wine. He poured a mouthful into Reilly's glass and waited for him to taste it. Seamus made a great show of this: sniffing the bouquet, swilling the wine under and over his tongue, a light in his eyes answering Declan's mischievous smirk. 'Excellent,' he said at last.

'You were saying?' Reilly went on as the waiter moved away.

'The grapevine has it that something big is to come down soon in England.'

Reilly sipped his wine.

'Is it true?'

Seamus Reilly put his glass carefully on the table, holding it by the stem, twisting it in small circles. Then he looked up, his face bearing an impish quality, his eyes serious. 'Come now, Declan, you don't expect me to answer that.'

'I hoped you would. You see, the grapevine also says that it's some breakaways who are planning it and that you are – well, none too pleased.'

Reilly gave a small laugh. 'Well I wouldn't be, would I, if it was true?'

Before Declan could answer the headwaiter hovered over them, his little pad at the ready.

'Ah,' Seamus said. 'What do you think, Des?'

'The Dover sole, Mr Reilly. I know you're fond of fish and the sole is very good.'

'Sole for me, then, Des. Declan?'

'The same for me would be fine.'

'Nothing to start with, Mr Reilly?'

'No. And just coffee afterwards. A little spinach with the fish though. And a jacket potato.'

'And you, sir?' the waiter asked Declan, almost as an afterthought.

'The same for me. Thank you.'

The waiter topped up their glasses, whipped the menus away and withdrew.

Declan leaned forward. 'That's my point, Seamus. We hear that you *are* very displeased.'

'You have an imaginative grapevine, Declan.'

'I'm not so sure. Let me put it this way. Off the record as they say. Suppose – just suppose, that the rumours were true. And suppose that you were determined to put a stop to it as I presume you would. And suppose I told you my editor wanted to make a programme giving your point of view which could enable you to put the IRA in a better light. Suppose all that for a minute: would you talk on film?'

Seamus Reilly's eyes narrowed to two penetrating slits. He looked out of the window, looked back again, studied his nails, and finally took to drumming what sounded like a tango beat on the tablecloth with his fingers. Then he looked Declan in the eye. 'Are you really being serious?'

Declan nodded.

The fish arrived, neatly off the bone. The vegetables were spooned onto their plates. The glasses were again topped up. Then they were by themselves again.

Seamus Reilly attacked his meal. He knew he ate too fast, 'gulping' his food his mother had said as if it was the last solid meal he was expecting to have for a long time. It was only when one side of the fish was gone that he spoke, wagging a forefinger at Declan. 'It's certainly an intriguing idea. But tell me: how long do you think I'd live if I did something like that?'

'That's not what I meant, Seamus. There would be nothing underhand about it. You could clear it with your executive. Look, you're trying to become political. If you want to succeed you need the media. You need to drum up sympathy. Let's face it you and I know that everyone in England believes the IRA look like thugs with cabbage ears and broken noses. If you went on and spoke reasonably, perhaps even – '

Reilly was shaking his head. 'It's not me you want, Declan. I'm no politician, nor have I any ambition to be. I can put you in touch with plenty of our men who might consider your proposition, although whether they'd ever be allowed to talk is another matter.'

Now Declan was shaking his head. 'That wouldn't be the same. It's you or nobody.'

Reilly chewed a morsel of sole. 'In that case it's nobody.'

Declan grimaced his disappointment. 'That's a shame.'

Seamus smiled benignly. 'You'll live,' he said enigmatically, making Declan blush slightly, admonished.

They finished their meal almost in silence, once or twice chit-chatting for a couple of seconds, and it was not until the coffee had been left on the table that Reilly spoke seriously again, surprisingly returning to the subject he had dismissed. 'I'll promise you one thing, Declan,' he promised in a voice that suggested his words had already been carefully weighed. 'If ever I feel that your suggestion would be beneficial I'll contact you without delay.'

Declan studied his host's face quizzically. 'That almost sounds as if you think it might be – eh – beneficial one day.'

Reilly beamed. 'Who knows?' Then he leaned forward, his elbows on the table, his eyes suddenly troubled. 'And I'll tell you this as a friend: there *is* considerable friction right now, and we *do* believe something is being planned to discredit those of us who believe in political rather than violent solutions. But you can believe me when I say that I will do anything – anything – to prevent a disruption of a possible chance for peace.'

Declan stared at his friend. How he had changed! Or rather, how he had changed and yet remained the same. Despite his declaration that a peaceful solution was now his desire, his old ruthlessness remained, and he saw nothing ironic in the insinuation that he would cheerfully use violence to ensure that peace.

'Why don't you say that publicly, Seamus?'

'Because it's not for me to speak publicly. I'm only a small cog in the wheel. We have our spokesmen.'

'You? A small cog?' Declan was derisive.

Reilly grinned like a little boy. 'Well – maybe not so small. But nevertheless it's not my place to make announcements.'

'Not even if you got the all-clear? You could ask.'

'No.' Seamus Reilly was adamant.

Later, as Declan was being driven home, Seamus put a hand on his arm. 'I'm sorry you've had a wasted visit,' he said.

'It wasn't a waste. It was good to see you again.'

'We'll talk again before you leave, I hope?'

78

Declan shook his head. 'I'm afraid not, Seamus. I'm off back to London first thing in the morning.'

'Oh,' Reilly said, clearly disappointed, as the car slid to a stop outside Rose Duffy's house. 'Well, at least try and keep in touch a bit more.'

'I will.'

'I know it was hard for you to forgive the things that happened last time you came. But it's the way things are here. Friends and relations die, and they are forgotten almost before we have the time to mourn. You won't believe it but I would sooner have died myself than have your nephew shot.'

'I understand. By the way – thanks for looking after Rose.'

Reilly dismissed this gratitude with a shrug. 'It's the least I can do. Anyway, I'd do the same for anyone.'

Declan laughed. 'You're a terrible liar, Seamus.'

Reilly looked unaccountably sad. 'Yes. I am, aren't I?'

Brigadier Brazier felt replete after his excellent lunch, and glowed in the haze of brandy. He sat, cross-legged and relaxed opposite Colonel Maddox, cupping his glass in both hands. 'That was a most excellent lunch, Matthew. When I asked to see you I didn't expect such royal treatment.'

'It was a pleasure, I assure you. I have so few visitors now, you know. Ancient officers are easily forgotten.'

'You should come down to London more often. Berkshire is all very well but I've always thought the country was strictly for vegetables,' the Brigadier remarked, giving a curious, snuffling laugh.

'Perhaps that's what I've become. Well, perhaps not quite. I read a lot now. Far more than I used to. It's amazing what you can learn from books, you know,' the Colonel observed, smiling inwardly, aware that his little joke would be lost on his superior.

The Brigadier agreed anyway. 'I'm sure it is. May I?' he then asked, producing a pipe.

'Please feel at home.'

The Brigadier went through the mysterious operation of

loading and lighting his briar, puffing a lot, using several matches before getting his bonfire (as Maddox saw it) under way. Finally, he took the pipe from his mouth and, holding the matchbox over the bowl, said: 'No doubt you're wondering why I wanted to see you.'

'It had crossed my mind.'

'Well I'll come straight to the point.'

But he didn't. He decided to take a more circuitous route, thinking of it as 'softening' Maddox. He had, after all, been warned that the Colonel could be tricky, could, indeed, be downright weird, and that the proverbial kid gloves should be worn. 'The trouble with you, Matthew, is that you've always underestimated yourself. We were talking in the club the other night, and all of us agreed that you were the very man to help us with a little problem we have.' He stopped and peered at Maddox through a cloud of smoke.

'Ah,' was all that the Colonel had to offer, but he did lean sideways for a better view of the Brigadier, encouraging him to go on.

'Now there's no one with a better knowledge of Northern Ireland than yourself –'

Colonel Maddox had a fit of coughing. The unexpectedness of the Brigadier's statement took him completely unawares, not least since he knew it to be quite untrue. Admittedly he had done a tour of duty in Belfast, but so had many others, and few tours had ended in such acrimonious circumstances as his. Indeed, his present retirement had been 'suggested'; and Colonel Maddox had been only too willing to comply. Baffled and pained by the duplicity and treachery he had encountered he had withdrawn to his home in Berkshire, only to find himself haunted by the people he had dealt with in Belfast. It could, however, truthfully be said that he had got closer to an understanding with IRA leaders than any of his predecessors, had, in fact, established a crude understanding with Seamus Reilly. But the manipulation of lives had left him scarred and repulsed.

'I'm sorry,' the Brigadier was saying, waving a hand to clear the area of smoke, and continuing blithely, ' – so we want to recall you to duty, temporarily, and would like you to go back to Belfast – just 'till the end of the year.'

Maddox looked aghast. He opened his mouth as if to reply, but nothing emerged, and he hid his discomfort by taking a long drink of his brandy.

Conveniently taking the silence as acceptance, Brigadier Brazier went on, warming to the subject, suddenly becoming quite military, clipping his words and editing his sentences, dropping verbs and adjectives at will. 'Put you in the picture. Trouble brewing, intelligence says. Big. Here. England, dammit. Got a man in, though. Fisher. Major. About to infiltrate. Need you there to liaise.'

The staccato information pinged off the Colonel's brain, making him shudder. He felt, suddenly, as if he was drowning, wave upon wave of remembered intrigue washing over him, and through it all something someone had said to him bellowed: 'if you once put foot in Ireland you will be crucified to it for the rest of your natural days'. But the Colonel was going to have none of that, was he? Certainly not. He was going to protest. 'I – ' That was as far as he got. The Brigadier held up his hand. 'Let me finish. You've dealt with Reilly. And Asher. Handled them well. Bound to be involved. Get them in. Find out.'

Colonel Maddox gave the Brigadier his most doleful look. Already small, menacing *doppelgänger*s of Reilly and Asher were stamping their feet on his mind. He wanted nothing whatever to do with them, nothing to do with their conniving or their treachery. He had almost succeeded in putting the whole bewildering mess behind him and yet here it was, regurgitated again, beckoning him with horny fingers. Dear God, that mad, mad Mr Apple, that crazy mystic, that lampoon who had ultimately been responsible for his downfall, had been right when he said he would be called back from afar.

'I don't think – ' Maddox began.

'You're not going to refuse, I hope,' Brigadier Brazier said, sounding as if a court martial was in the offing. 'We *need* you to

81

handle it. Dammit man, your country needs you,' he added patriotically.

The Colonel wanted to laugh, but, as always, he quietly acquiesced, nodding gently and saying in a whisper: 'Very well.'

'Good man!' the Brigadier exclaimed. 'I knew we could count on you. There's not many of us old-timers left. We have to show the whizz-kids that we still know a thing or two.'

'When do – '

'As soon as possible. The sooner the better. The quicker you can get installed the better for all of us.'

Colonel Maddox smiled wryly.

'You just tell me when you *can* go and I'll make all the arrangements. The end of the week?' the Brigadier suggested, typically usurping the right of choice. 'Can I tell Belfast you'll be there next weekend?'

'Very well. The weekend.'

'Excellent.'

In his bathroom at the Grand Hotel Joe Mulcahy worked quickly and precisely, whistling through his teeth: a cheerful little tune in the manner of a man enjoying himself. Deftly he unscrewed the panelling about the bathtub, laying the screws in a neat, straight line on the floor beside him, making a little pattern by placing them head to tail. Lifting away the panel he leaned it against the wall; then he lay on his back and wriggled his way under the bath, using a torch to see. 'Hey, Peg, bring me in that case, will you?' he called.

Peggy Dunne reluctantly stopped admiring her reflection in the mirror: the new nightdress was, without doubt, the nicest garment she had ever owned: that it had been purchased on the promise of death probably never occurred to her. She primped herself one more time and then collected the case and carried it in to Mulcahy, who, now, was sitting cross-legged on the bathroom floor. 'Very nice,' he said.

'Thank you,' Peggy said, curtsying.

'And very seductive,' Mulcahy added, taking the bag and unzipping it, keeping his eyes on Peggy.

'You just keep your mind on your work,' Peggy told him primly.

Joe grunted. Carefully he lifted out the bomb. Then, methodically, he wrapped it in layer after layer of heavy-duty plastic.

'It doesn't look very big,' Peggy observed.

Joe looked up and grinned. 'Plenty big enough for what's wanted.'

An hour later, the explosive secured to the bath by tape and further kept rigid by being wedged between the bath and the wall, the panelling safely restored, and all trace of interference having been removed, Joe and Peggy lay in bed, both of them perspiring. Their intercourse had been violent and prolonged, Joe's unusually hectic rutting possibly stimulated by the proximity of destruction to his act of creation. Not that he would have thought of it like that: he had one of those opaque minds that could treat sex and killing with equal indifference.

'It's a shame we have to leave here tomorrow,' Peggy whispered, in her naiveté wistfully imagining the whole episode as a true honeymoon, clinging to the illusion of romance for all she was worth.

'Yea. Back to sodding Glasgow.'

'Maybe they'll call us home now.'

'Maybe.'

'Or send us somewhere else.'

'I don't care,' Joe told her. 'Anywhere but bloody Glasgow,' he added and, perhaps to dispel recurring images of the city he loathed, he rolled on top of her again.

It was after midnight when John Asher telephoned Seamus Reilly, awakening him from a deep, untramelled sleep. 'Have I got a surprise for you,' he announced.

Reilly groaned. The last thing he wanted right now was a surprise: to his mind, like telegrams, they meant only disaster and woe. 'God, John, I hate damn surprises – especially at this hour of the night – morning.'

'Guess who's coming to Belfast?'

Reilly groaned to himself again and winced. 'Superman.'

Asher chortled. 'Close. Maddox actually. Colonel Matthew Maddox.'

That made Reilly sit up. He switched on the light by his bed and groped for a cigar with his free hand. 'What for?'

'A message just came through. He's back for six months. Temporary replacement they call it. I've been told to meet him.'

Reilly lit his cigar and gave a short cough. 'It'll be like old times. I thought he was retired.'

'He was. They must have something special in mind to take him out of mothballs. My orders are to co-operate fully with him.'

'When does he get in?'

'The end of the week.'

'I wonder . . . .'

'Wonder what?'

Reilly did not immediately reply.

'Wonder what?' Asher insisted.

'Nothing. Let me think about it. I'll speak to you later. And John – thanks for calling.'

'I thought you'd be pleased.'

And, in a sense, Reilly was pleased. He liked Maddox – 'old Maddox' he always thought of him. He respected the man's integrity, and he was one of the only Brits he had been able to isolate from his Englishness.

Reilly blew a thin stream of smoke towards the ceiling, frowning and looking puzzled. Why on earth would they take the old man out of retirement and send him back? They had been only too glad to be shut of him in the first place. Perhaps they had got wind of . . . perhaps, as usual, they suspected that he, Reilly was involved . . . perhaps Maddox . . . . Oh, dammit, Reilly thought, stubbing out his cigar. He would work it out in the morning. He switched out the light, and settled down to sleep.

· NINE ·

THE SELECTION WAS almost inevitable. Corporal Sammy Wilson, a coward at heart but a bully when surrounded by troops and dealing with unarmed civilians, had long been on the list. For all of the following week McCluskey and Moran watched him themselves whenever possible. There would have been easier victims but they both wanted Wilson, their hatred of him increasing the longer it took to kidnap him. By Friday, the stocky, bull-necked, strutting Corporal had all but driven McCluskey to a frenzy. 'Jeez I want that bastard,' he told Moran.

'We'll get him. They all make mistakes some time.'

Moran was right. At two-thirty on Friday afternoon Wilson made his mistake. Disobeying all the rules, he left the barracks alone to buy a birthday card for his girlfriend in Liverpool. Moran spotted him, despite the anonymity his civilian clothes almost provided, and nudged McCluskey, pointing. 'There's your boyo.'

'Jesus!' McCluskey exclaimed. 'He's thicker than I thought.'

Moran drove the van slowly, keeping well behind the strolling figure, his face breaking into a wide grin as they saw him go into Gerry Carson's newsagents. He indicated and guided the van across the road, parking outside the shop.

'Let's do it,' McCluskey said urgently.

'No. Wait. Let that woman and kid come out first.'

The wait seemed interminable. The woman was dithering, pointing at something then changing her mind. They could see the activity clearly through the shop window, and both men sucked in their breath as they noted Wilson move to the counter, a card in his hand. For a second it looked as though he was going to be served first, but in the nick of time the woman made up her mind and made her purchase.

She had barely put foot on the pavement, dragging the child behind her, when McCluskey and Moran were out of the van and into the shop. With no hesitation McCluskey walked up behind the Corporal and gave him a viscious swipe on the head with a short, leather-covered cosh, catching him as he fell and immediately dragging him behind the counter.

'You didn't see that,' Moran told Gerry Carson.

'See what?'

Moran grinned.

'A Brit?' Carson asked.

'Yea. And a right bastard.'

'Aren't they all?'

'We'll need to leave him here for a few hours,' McCluskey put in.

Carson shrugged. 'There's a shed out the back.'

'Got any rope?'

Gerry Carson stared at them blearily. 'That's what I admire about you boys. So professional. Always prepared.'

'Fuck the crap,' McCluskey shouted. 'Got some rope?'

'There's a ball of strong plastic string in the shed.'

McCluskey and Moran manhandled the unconscious Wilson out through the back door and into the shed. They trussed him up like an oven-prepared chicken, and shoved an oily rag into his mouth, securing it there with a buckleless belt that hung from a nail.

86

The shop was still without a customer when they returned. Gerry Carson looked up from his paper. 'All done?'

McCluskey nodded. 'That back gate. Does it open?'

'It opens.'

'Leave it unlocked for us then. We'll be back later.'

'What's later?

'Later. He'll be gone by the morning.'

'Who will?' Carson asked, and went back to his paper.

McCluskey clasped his hands behind his head and lolled in his seat as the van moved across the city. Now for the bit he liked. Now they'd see if the famous Major was genuine or not. His eyes glazed over with cold, sadistic pleasure.

'You're quiet,' Moran observed.

McCluskey chuckled. 'You ever watch "the A Team"?'

'The kids do.'

'Well, I love it when a plan comes together,' McCluskey told him, finding his quotation hilarious, and bursting into laughter.

At eight o'clock Chris Fisher left the barracks and made his way on foot to what he always now thought of as Sandy's pub. He sensed, as he usually did, that he was being watched, but he knew he was safe enough: he would be safe as long as he was potentially useful. Nothing seemed untoward when he entered the pub: he got the same smile from Sandy; the usual pint was placed before him; none of the regulars gave him a second glance. It was not until twenty minutes later, when Sandy sidled along the bar towards him, that the feeling seemed about to be proven.

'You're wanted outside,' Sandy told him, comically using the side of his mouth.

'Outside?'

'Eddie.'

When he got outside he found Eddie waiting beside the open door of a small, dark-blue car, all smiles and friendliness. 'In you get,' he said, holding the door, and slamming it behind Fisher. Then he hopped into the car himself, sitting beside

Moran in the front. As the car moved off he turned in his seat, resting his arms on the back and his chin on his arms, staring pleasantly at Fisher.

'Where are we going?' Fisher asked reasonably enough.

'You'll see,' McCluskey told him. 'All in good time.'

As they reached the outskirts of the city Moran drove faster, leaning forward over the steering wheel. In ten minutes they were in the country and speeding down narrow lanes with high hedgerows either side, once sending a flock of furious starlings screaming into the sky, their slumber shattered. Then the car turned into a gateway, over some bumpy, muddy ground, and skidded to a halt outside a stone, windowless barn with a corrugated iron roof.

'Right,' McCluskey said. 'Out we get.'

Moran led the way to the barn door. He spent several seconds unlocking it, cursing to himself as the padlock refused to yield. When he finally got it open he signalled McCluskey and Fisher to wait by pushing the flat of one hand in their direction, and slipped in the barn alone. There was a clattering noise from inside as if someone had walked into and overturned a metal bucket; then a glimmer of light appeared. Gradually the light strengthened, and Moran's head appeared in the doorway. 'Come on,' he called.

It took a while for Fisher to accustom his eyes to the light; when he did, he was appalled by what he saw. The floor of the barn was of stamped earth. Four rafters supported the roof and from these three oil lamps, now lit, were suspended, giving the place an eerie, fearful look of sickness. A wooden box had been placed against the wall at the end, and on it sat a man, gagged and tied.

'Ungag the bastard,' McCluskey ordered, and Moran did as he was told.

Instantly the bound man tried to speak, but only an unintelligible squawk emerged. Swallowing hard the man tried to induce saliva into his throat. 'Major,' he cried finally.

Chris Fisher made to move closer, squinting to try and

identify the man. McCluskey grabbed him by the arm. 'You're fine right where you are,' he said.

'It's me, Major. Wilson,' the man called, sounding as though on the verge of panicky tears.

'Wilson! What – ' He rounded on McCluskey. 'What the hell is this all about?'

'It's about trust, Chris,' McCluskey informed him coldly, his familiarity sounded oddly out of place. 'We have to be sure that we can trust you, don't we? So, we want you to do a little job for us. Call it an initiation if you like,' he went on, taking a gun from his inside pocket. He held it out to Fisher, using both hands as if he were a second at some ceremonial duel. 'There's just one little bullet in it. We want you to use that bullet and kill him.'

Fisher felt rooted to the ground. He was certain he was going to vomit.

'I – ' he began.

'Now,' McCluskey went on in a steady matter-of-fact voice, 'in the gun that Pat has there are six bullets. If you happen to miss with your single bullet three of Pat's will go into that bastard, and the other three will go into you.'

Wilson rolled on his box, moaning.

Fisher shook his head. 'I can't shoot a man in cold blood. I – '

'It's up to you. He'll die anyway. We just want to know who's side you're on. I mean, we're not going to take the risk of lifting you if you're not with us all the way, are we? Here, take it.'

Chris Fisher took the gun in his hands, and stared at it.

'Don't kill me, Major. Please, Major. Oh, please, please, Major don't – '

'Shut that fucker up, will you,' McCluskey shouted.

Moran stood his ground. 'Get your man to shoot him – that'll soon shut him up.'

'You've got ten seconds,' McCluskey told Fisher, and pulled his shirt up on his wrist, studying his watch. 'Nine, eight, seven – '

Major Fisher felt himself starting to tremble. A horrible logic

89

screamed at him that Wilson was doomed anyway. Fear screamed that he would die also. The word 'duty' loomed into his consciousness and he grabbed at it, using it to suffocate his fear. He had a mission to accomplish. He raised the gun and pointed it.

'Jesus don't, Major. For Christ's sake, Major. It's me. Wilson. Don't kill me. Please.'

' – three, two – '

Fisher fired. The mingled roar of the gun and Wilson's terrified scream created an appalling crashing wail. Wilson keeled over off his box and lay kicking and shaking pathetically on the ground. Fisher watched, mesmerised. He saw the kicks become little jerks and twitches, heard the gurgling, hollow cry of death. With one final heave, Wilson lay still.

'Just in time,' McCluskey said, tapping his watch, and using a tone that suggested a schoolmaster admonishing a recalcitrant pupil. 'You could have joined him in fairyland in another second,' he added, taking the gun from the Major. Then, sternly, he said: 'Let's get the hell out of here. It gives me the creeps.'

'What about him?' Moran wanted to know.

'What about him? Leave him there. Come on, for Christ's sake.'

In the back of the car, rushing back through the countryside, Fisher fought back the tears. Already shame was penetrating his soul; already the agony of sin was pummelling his mind.

The car came to an abrupt halt, and McCluskey turned his head. 'Here you are, Chris. Back home safe and sound. We'll meet in Sandy's tomorrow. Now that you're with us there's someone you have to meet.'

He clambered blindly out of the car, and trudged away down the street. He had no idea where he was. He did not care where he was. An ambulance raced by, keening, and, immediately the awful wails of Wilson hammered his brain.

'Funny boyo,' McCluskey said, watching the receding, hunched figure. 'He never even said goodnight,' he added, grinning.

'You're fucking evil,' Moran told him, driving on.

McCluskey lay back comfortably in the seat and smiled and smiled. Nice to see a plan come together.

Seamus Reilly listened attentively as Thomas Regan relayed the news. '. . .Waited in the van,' he was saying, 'until a woman and child came out. Then they both went into Carson's shop. Twenty minutes later they both came out. I left Dowling to follow them and checked out the shop myself. Carson was there reading his paper, but the man who went in before them was gone.'

'You're sure?'

'Certain. When Carson saw who I was he got jumpy but I didn't push him. I thought I better check with you first.'

Reilly nodded appreciatively. 'Go on.'

'Dowling followed them back to Moran's house. They stayed there until just after five. Then they drove back to Carson's. They went round the back though, and loaded what Dowling says was a sack of something into the back of the van. He couldn't get close enough to see properly without being spotted himself. Then they took off. That's when Dowling lost them. Evening traffic. It's hell, Mr Reilly.'

Accepting the traffic problems, Seamus Reilly asked: 'This man – the one you think they followed into Carson's – any idea who he was?'

'None. Possibly a Brit. Not from round here, that's for sure.'

'It wasn't that Fisher?'

'Oh no. O'Neill spotted him going into Sandy's this evening. He followed him in. Fisher just had a drink as usual,' Regan said, and then started to shuffle his feet and look uneasy.

Reilly knew the signs. 'Go on, Thomas. Tell me. What happened?' he asked his voice filled with resignation.

'O'Neill went for a pee. When he came out Fisher was gone. His drink was still on the bar. O'Neill went outside and searched up and down the street. Nothing. He must have gone off in a car.'

Reilly nodded. 'That's what I was afraid of.' He stood up and started pacing the room, thinking. He came to a halt by the window, and, staring out he said: 'Right, Thomas. Nine o'clock tomorrow morning I want you to pick up Carson and bring him to the piggery. At ten o'clock tell Dowling to get Sandy and bring *him* to the piggery. I want to find out what's happening.'

'Right, Mr Reilly.'

'And no excuses this time. No traffic problems and no kidney problems.'

'No, Mr Reilly.'

'Good.'

John Asher saw the report minutes after it was passed to the RUC. The unexplained disappearance of any British soldier was a matter of concern and, despite the hostility that existed between them the army always informed the RUC on such matters. Asher's first reaction was to wonder if this Wilson could be the deserter Reilly had mentioned, until he remembered the name given had been Fisher, and that he had been a Major and no mere Corporal. Still, no harm would be done by a word with Reilly: it was always possible (barely but possible) that Reilly had got it wrong: despite his reputation of infallibility he had been known to make the odd mistake.

So, immediately he got home he phoned Seamus Reilly, carefully rehearsing his words as he waited for him to answer. As soon as he heard Reilly's customary monosyllabic 'Yes?' he asked: 'Seamus – you're sure the name was Fisher?'

'Certain.'

'Oh.'

'Why?'

'And you haven't been up to any skullduggery that I don't know about?'

'Probably,' Reilly said. 'Why?' he asked again.

'Soldier gone missing this afternoon.'

'Oh, dear,' Reilly sighed, but not overly concerned.

'Left his barracks at two-thirty and not been seen since.'

'More than likely he's drunk and shacked up somewhere.'

'No,' Asher said. 'At least it's most unlikely. The report says that just before he left he told someone he was just nipping out to get a birthday card for his girlfriend. There's a newsagents just up the road from the barracks. That's where he said he was going.'

Reilly felt a tingle running down his spine. 'You wouldn't know the name of the shop?'

'No. Not off-hand. Why? Seamus – you *do* know something. I can tell.'

'No, John. I don't *know* anything. But – look, can we meet tomorrow afternoon?'

'Yes – no. Not in the afternoon. I've got to pick up Maddox at the airport. The evening?'

'About seven?'

'Yes.'

'The usual place, then. Leave your house at six-forty and I'll arrange security.'

'Right. And I expect you to tell me everything. Don't start buggering me about.'

Reilly laughed. 'Not everything, John. You know we never tell each other *everything*.'

'You know what I mean.'

'Oh I know what you mean all right. See you tomorrow evening.'

' 'Till this evening.'

'Hang on a tick. You couldn't give me a rough description of this missing soldier, could you?'

John Asher thought for a moment, trying to see the report in his mind's eye, trying to recall the image on the small photograph stapled to one corner. 'Mid-twenties. Five foot ten – I think. Clean shaven. Mousey hair. Heavy build. One thing: from the photo it looked like he had no neck.

'Right. Thanks. I'll see what I can have for you by tomorrow night. But don't expect miracles.'

'I never do.'

Seamus Reilly kept the telephone receiver in his hand, using one finger to disconnect the line. Then he dialled another number, nimbly lighting a cigar while he waited. 'Thomas? Seamus Reilly.'

'Yes, Mr Reilly?' Thomas Regan answered, sounding apprehensive.

'The man McCluskey and Moran followed into Carson's papershop – mid-twenties, five foot ten, brownish hair, short-necked – could that be him?'

'It could be, Mr Reilly. I only saw the back of him and he was sort of hunched up. He had one of those zip-up jackets on with his hands in the pockets.'

'I see. But it *could* have been him.'

'It could have been.'

'Right. Now one more thing. Mr Asher is meeting me tomorrow evening. He'll be leaving his home at six-forty. See to it that he arrives at the safe house in one piece.'

'Certainly, Mr Reilly.'

'I'll see you in the morning at the piggery. It's more important than ever now that I speak to Carson.'

'I'll have him there.'

'Good. Goodnight.'

Colonel Matthew Maddox mournfully eyed the suitcase on his bed. It was already packed: only his shaving gear and toothbrush remained to be added in the morning. Beside it was a framed photograph, a book, and a sheaf of papers. Reaching down he picked up the photograph and studied it. How young and resplendent he looked in his ceremonial uniform, how full of hope and promise he seemed, smiling broadly as if the whole world stretched out before him and the young woman on his arm. And how soon it had all collapsed! The childless marriage had been little more than a supreme act of tolerance, and his career – well, the less said about that the better. The trouble was that he had been born into the wrong age. He belonged, he assured himself, to an age of chivalry. And here he was heading for the one place where honour was a dirty word, where intrigue and double-dealing were the norm. Yet he had found a curious contentment in that sorrowful place. It was as though lost souls had congregated there, using each other and the battered streets to play out the desolation of their lives, always hoping that from somewhere peace and happiness would come. That, of course, was what kept everyone sane: the hope. And there was hope was there not? As long as man breathed there was hope.

Carefully he put the papers and the book (a shabby, leather-bound volume, gold-embossed, but with the gilt so wasted the title was illegible) into the case. Then he stood up again and returned the photograph to its perch on the chest of drawers, as though by deliberately leaving the picture behind he was ridding himself of some oppressive obligation.

'How did it go?' the woman asked.

'He did it,' McCluskey told her. 'I told you he was all right.'

'You gave him the gun and he did it. Just like that? No hesitation? No argument?' the woman wanted to know.

'Hell, of course he didn't *want* to do it. I thought he was going to puke all over the place. But he did it. Shit, you should have heard that sod screaming for mercy.'

The information on Fisher's reluctance seemed to put the woman's mind at rest. 'What about the body?'

'We left it there.'

The woman frowned. 'I suppose that's all right.'

'Sure,' McCluskey assured her. 'Nobody'll find it for weeks. Months.'

'When have you arranged to see Fisher again?'

'Tomorrow evening.'

'Good. What time?'

'No particular time. I just said at Sandy's. He's usually there at about eight.'

'I'd better meet him. When he arrives give me a ring at home. Then we can meet here.'

'Right. Hey, what if something happens and he can't make it?'

'That's your problem. He's your baby.'

Chris Fisher awoke from a nightmare wherein he was being clawed to death by a flock of furious starlings, their screams of anger identical to that awful noise the gun and Wilson's cries of terror had made. The light from the corridor outside, permanently ablaze, shone through the small glass rectangle above the door, covering the wall opposite in a dull, yellow glow. Christ on His crucifix cast a shadow twice His size, the shadowy arms no longer seeming to be nailed to the cross but reaching out and down. A heavy vehicle, a Saracen probably, lumbered to a halt outside, its threatening weight shaking the wall, and the shadow moved. Instinctively Fisher recoiled. 'Oh, Jesus,' he moaned. 'Oh Jesus, forgive me.'

· TEN ·

ON SATURDAY MORNING Seamus Reilly was up with the birds. Indeed, their half-hearted, September-time dawn chorus had only just started by the time he had reached the bathroom and begun to shave. He loathed shaving, mostly because he usually nicked himself but he had to go through the routine, sometimes twice a day: his black beard satanic if not shorn to the roots regularly. He chose his clothes carefully: the piggery was not the most pleasant of places, and he dressed accordingly: a roll-neck sweater, a pair of tweed-like trousers, stout shoes. Then he went downstairs, ticking off in his mind the items on the day's agenda. It had all the prospects of being an interesting day.

In the kitchen he went through his morning ceremony: percolating his coffee (a mixture of Kenya and Brazil in equal parts) and toasting his bread, setting a tray and carrying the lot into the sitting room. He was just finishing when he heard his car arrive. By the time his driver inserted his key in the door Seamus Reilly was in the hall, his overcoat already on, his hat in his hand.

'Good morning, Mr Reilly. I didn't keep you waiting?'

'Morning, Danny. No. Timed it to perfection, you did.'

The trip to the piggery did not take long: it could have taken less but Reilly did not enjoy fast driving. He used the isolation of his car as a sanctuary for quiet thoughts, and he illogically felt that the speeding engine would hustle him into making errors. There was, of course, another reason: he liked to be seen by his people as he was driven along. He believed this was important. So many upheavals had taken place within the community over the years, so many people had been arrested, or been killed, or simply disappeared, that his constant visible presence gave a continuum to the Organization. He was seen to be there; there to be spoken to, to be consulted, to give advice, to solve problems. Nobody had ever dared actually stop his car to avail themself of his largesse, but they all felt they could if needs be.

The piggery was about eight miles from Clones, across the border: sixty acres of arable land purchased with IRA funds, and farmed legitimately and profitably by a Provo of un-questionable loyalty. Behind the farmhouse itself, and forming part of a quadrangle of out-buildings, was a long, low building. It was the old slaughter house, no longer used. Inside it stank. Traces of blood from the hundreds, perhaps thousands of pigs that had been killed and disembowelled there were splattered on the floor and walls. A single naked bulb hung from the ceiling, and a long line of vicious meat hooks dangled from a metal rail that ran the length of the shed. The sheer grue-someness of the place had its advantages: it terrified the people who were summoned there, and it was for this reason that Reilly used it when he wanted answers quickly. One such person, already scared out of his wits, was there by the time Seamus arrived.

'Ah,' Reilly said, wrinkling his nose at the stench, 'Mr Carson,' he added politely. 'Thank you for coming.'

Gerry Carson held his tongue, his wide eyes rolling.

'I'm sure you'll want to get back to your business as soon as possible so I'll be brief. Mr Regan here tells me there was a little – eh – a little episode at your shop yesterday?'

Carson glanced from Reilly to Regan, and then down at his feet.

Unperturbed Reilly continued quietly, keeping his voice calm and reasonable. 'I believe three men went into your shop but only two came out. I was hoping, Mr Carson, that you could explain this somewhat extraordinary situation to me.'

Gerry Carson decided to bluff. 'The three of them went out, Mr Reilly. Honest, the three of – '

Seamus Reilly held up his hand. 'No, Mr Carson. Two came out. And immediately after they came out Mr Regan went in. There was no sign of the other man. Now please explain.'

'Maybe – ' Carson started, but that was as far as he got with his hopeful hypothesis.

'Dammit, Carson,' Reilly snapped, 'don't try and treat me like a fool. I haven't all day to waste on the likes of you. Now what happened?'

Foolishly, Carson looked as if he might be about to attempt yet another diversionary tack. Immediately Reilly gave a little flick of his wrist and Thomas Regan moved forward menacingly. 'All right. All right,' Carson said, holding out both hands in a plea for restraint. 'This fella came in. Never seen him before. Then two of your men came in. They hit him on the head and knocked him cold. Knowing they were from you, Mr Reilly, I didn't like to say anything. I mean, I don't interfere where I don't belong. They said they wanted to dump him with me for a couple of hours so I told them they could leave him in the shed at the back. That's all I know. I don't even know when they took him away. All I know is that he wasn't there this morning.'

'The two men who you say were from me, did they say they were from me?'

Carson frowned, thinking. 'Well, no, Mr Reilly. But everyone knows that Eddie McCluskey and Pat Moran are with you.'

'Do they now,' Reilly said ominously. 'Did they happen to mention *where* they would be taking him after they collected him?'

Carson shook his head. 'No. Definitely not, Mr Reilly. I'm positive about that.'

Reilly fixed the man with a withering, prodding gaze. He decided to believe him. 'Right, Carson, you can go. Mr Regan will drive you back. Just one thing – and remember it well: you have not spoken to me. If either McCluskey or Moran should contact you again nobody has questioned you.'

'I'll remember that, Mr Reilly.'

'Do,' Reilly warned. 'Be very sure you do. And also, you get in touch with Mr Regan if they come back.' He turned away and walked across the shed to the enormous wooden scraping block that stood in one corner. 'Take him home, Thomas,' he said without turning round. 'Take him out of my sight.'

Alone, Reilly took to pacing the shed, his head bowed, his hands clasped behind his back. So far so good. McCluskey and Moran were definitely involved in some sort of kidnapping. Seamus felt a cold shiver down his spine. Already he suspected the reason and it horrified him: if correct it was a system of proving trustworthiness that he had always found repellent. And it was usually self-defeating in his experience: even those who could have been trusted veered away and became suspicious as hatred took over from the pangs of conscience, a deep-rooted loathing for those who had humiliated them and shown them their weaknesses, had demonstrated man's bitter attachment to himself even at the cost of another's life.

Reilly stopped for a moment and cocked his head on one side. He heard the car door slam, and he moved back towards the door. He was leaning against the wall, his hands now deep in his pockets, his ankles crossed when Jim Dowling pushed Sandy into the barn before him and into the centre under the light.

'Sorry to drag you here, Sandy,' Reilly apologized from the shadows.

Sandy swung round. He was sweating and he used his two pudgy hands to wipe his face. 'Oh. Mr Reilly.'

'Yes. Sorry about this. A few questions, that's all. This

deserter – Fisher – that we've been interested in . . . we haven't been able to locate him?'

Sandy looked relieved. 'You know, I was going to try and contact you about that, Mr Reilly. I said to myself last night when it happened "I'll have to contact Mr Reilly about that".'

'Very commendable, Sandy. About what?'

'Fisher. He was in the pub last night. Then about a quarter past eight Eddie McCluskey stuck his head in the door and told me to send him out.'

'And you sent him out?'

'I did, Mr Reilly.'

Reilly glared at Dowling.

'Why the hell didn't you tell me that last night?' Dowling demanded.

'I didn't get the chance, did I?' Sandy defended himself. 'You came out of the piss house and you were out the door like a scalded cat.'

'Do you know where they went?' Reilly interrupted.

'No idea, Mr Reilly. But I can find that out for you easy enough if you want me to. Someone's bound to know. Someone knows everything in my pub.'

'Thank you, Sandy. I *would* be obliged. Find out where they went and get in touch with Jim here, will you? I would like to know as soon as possible.'

'With a bit of luck I'll know by tonight, Mr Reilly.'

'That would be appreciated.'

'Anything to help.'

Reilly gave him a sceptical look. 'Take Sandy back, will you, Jim?'

Reilly waited until he heard the car drive away before leaving the shed. His driver was waiting, the car door open. He noted Reilly's satisfied look. 'Everything went well, Mr Reilly?'

'Yes,' Reilly said curtly, getting into the car, waiting until they were heading back along the country road before adding. 'Everything went well. At least, it went well for me.'

From another direction another car was heading for the city. It was a military car but unmarked. Colonel Maddox and Inspector Asher sat together in the back seat, each staring out of his own window. Some moments earlier Asher had asked the Colonel how he liked being back in Belfast, more by way of conversation than anything else, and was waiting for a reply. He had all but abandoned getting one when the Colonel said: 'You really want to know?'

'Well – yes.'

'I feel frightened to death,' the Colonel confessed.

'Things *have* improved since you were here last, Colonel.'

The Colonel gave a short laugh. 'Not that sort of fear, John. Not fear for myself. I am afraid for others. Every time I've been here I have been surrounded by tragedy and sorrow. It follows me. It haunts me. I'm afraid I'm the ill wind that bears nobody good.'

'Nonsense,' Asher said sharply. 'You are – '

' – surrounds you,' the Colonel was saying perhaps to himself.

'I wouldn't let it worry you, Colonel,' Asher said, trying to sound jovial. 'You're almost one of us now.'

The Colonel turned his head. 'That's what does worry me, John. I'm starting to look at death and tragedy through distorted eyes, seeing them as the norm rather than the exception. How *do* you live with it all the time?'

'The same way people live with other afflictions – poverty, disease, racist attacks. After a while you don't notice that they are in any way extraordinary. Indeed, here, when everything is quiet and peaceful we tend to worry since we know it only means the explosion, when it comes, will be all the worse.'

The Colonel was shaking his head. 'You make it sound as though you're fighting a losing battle.'

'Of course we are. Every schoolchild knows that. There is not and never will be a solution here.'

'How sad,' the Colonel remarked. 'How very sad.'

The car braked sharply and turned left: the men swayed in their seat. Suddenly Asher chuckled. 'They've given you your old office back. It will be like old times coming to see you there.'

'As bad as that?'

Asher's chuckle became a laugh. 'They weren't *that* bad, Colonel. I was talking to Reilly the other day and he's pleased you've come back. I'm damned if I know why, but he actually likes you.'

Perhaps Asher's humour was infectious because the Colonel tried a small jest. 'I'm a very likeable chap,' he said. 'How is the dreadful Reilly anyway?'

'As dreadful as ever. Actually, I think you'll find he's mellowed quite a lot. We get on very well together – unofficially, you understand.'

'Of course.'

'We sometimes joke that if the two of us were left alone we could come close to a solution. As Reilly always says, we're just a couple of old sods trying to do what we think is right. I suspect you'll be seeing quite a lot of him.'

'Oh? Why should that be?'

Asher sucked in his breath aware that he had gaffed. Using the driver as an excuse he said quietly, with a jerk of his head: 'Not here, Colonel. We can discuss that later.'

'I don't – '

Asher held a warning finger to his lips. 'Later.'

And later, in the Colonel's office, Asher was forced to return to the subject despite hoping Maddox would have forgotten about it by then.

The two men sat opposite each other across the desk, both with a drink in their hands. It was, indeed, like old times. The Colonel had insisted on going straight to his office, and had produced the bottle from his briefcase, holding it up mischievously. 'We always had a drink together, didn't we?' he asked.

'Nearly always.'

'Well, we better start off on the right foot.'

Now, sipping their drinks they allowed the room to grow dark about them. Asher was feeling rested and relaxed for the first time in ages when the Colonel blundered into his tranquillity. 'Why did you say I'd be seeing a lot of Reilly?' he wanted to know.

'Because we're – Reilly and me – we're co-operating . . . . Look, Colonel, we know quite well why you've been sent.'

The Colonel looked disbelieving and amused. 'Do you, indeed?'

Asher nodded.

'Tell me.'

Asher hesitated, but not for long. 'You've been sent so that a certain – shall we say person? – can contact you with information.'

Maddox now looked less amused.

'In fact, I can tell you quite a lot about what has been going on – all of which Reilly knows. Indeed, most of it came from him.'

Colonel Maddox looked decidedly worried.

'You want me to be frank, Colonel?'

The Colonel nodded.

'Fisher. Major Fisher. Mean anything?'

'My God,' the Colonel whispered. 'You *do* know. Nobody apart from myself is supposed to know about that here.'

Asher beamed. 'Don't look so worried. We've known for months. Fisher doesn't move without being watched. By the way – he's made contact. Things could be hotting up soon.'

Colonel Maddox stood up and clasped his hands behind his head. He stared at the ceiling and demanded: 'What in the name of hell am *I* doing here if everybody knows?'

'*I* can't answer that, Colonel. Mind you, the clever chaps in London don't know that we know.'

'They'll know damn soon,' Maddox snapped, and moved towards the phone on his desk.

John Asher reached out and caught his hand. 'Just before you do that, Colonel, there are one or two other things you should know.'

For what seemed a very long time the two men remained frozen, Asher still holding the Colonel's hand. The Colonel was the first to move: he withdrew his hand and straightened up, keeping an eye on Asher all the while, and then sat down heavily. 'It's starting again, isn't it, John? The intrigue.'

'It never stops, Colonel. Just listen to me a minute. Before you alert London I think you should speak to Reilly. I'll be speaking to him tonight about another matter – about a Corporal who has disappeared – and I can set up a meeting for tomorrow morning. When you've spoken to him if you still want to inform London – ' Asher shrugged – 'I won't try and stop you.'

'Corporal who's disappeared?' the Colonel asked, bewildered.

'Don't concern yourself with that for the moment, Colonel. That's being dealt with. What about Reilly? Will you meet with him?'

Maddox sighed. 'You seem to think I should.'

'I know you should.'

'Very well. Tomorrow morning.'

At four o'clock the patrol moved into the Shankhill Road. Within minutes the area was saturated with troops, toms kneeling and lying in every corner, crouched in doorways, making sure the locals were aware of their presence. Major Fisher was in command of what all the soldiers knew was nothing but another futile, token exercise; they followed a procedure that would yield nothing and make them more hated than they already were. The Shankhill Road today, somewhere else tomorrow, democratically alternating their harassment between Protestant and Catholic so that it would appear they were impartial. It was always the same: line the bastards up against the wall in long rows, their legs spread, keep them there, waiting. The junior officers seemed to enjoy this: they strutted up and down the line of spreadeagled bodies, relishing their moment of power, their superiors not interfering, seeing the random pounding of someone's kidneys as harmless, as 'good training', as toughening the men up.

That afternoon was no different. Major Fisher moved down the line carrying out lengthy P checks and asking detailed questions, hoping someone would say something out of place. They never did. They were either defiantly dumb or exaggeratedly polite, and Fisher could see in their eyes the loathing and contempt, the smirky insolence that was a far cry from the fear and intimidation the military presence was supposed to induce. As he moved down the line he felt a terrible rage building up within him, a hatred for these incomprehensible people, for the army, but mostly for himself. For God, too, who had allowed him get conned into –

'Sir?'

Fisher swung round.

'There's nothing here. Can we let them go?'

Fisher nodded. 'Yes, Lieutenant, let them go.'

'You all right, sir?'

'Of course I'm all right.'

He watched the men straighten up from the wall, rubbing their hands together, filing away. When they reached the end of the street and out of harm's way the jeers and catcalls would come: 'Fucking English pigs youse animals, sons o' fucking bitches! Murdering Brit bastards!' Fisher winced.

And then it was the bumpy, uncomfortable haul back to the barracks, the men yawning and exhausted, talking to each other in undertones about what they would most like to do to the crummy shits who called them names; or just sitting there, their heads in their hands, longing to be far, far away from it all, away from the degradation and insults, away from the stupid wastefulness of it all.

Fisher threw himself on his bunk bed and covered his eyes with his arm. Suddenly, for the first time in his life although he had thought he had experienced it before, he knew the real meaning of loneliness, an isolation penetrated by appalling visions and shattered by terrible screams, his own silent, piercing screams melded with those of a short-necked ghost whose petrified eyes bore into his very soul and focused towards an unhearing God.

Reilly listened to Thomas Regan, his lips pursed, a satisfied twinkle in his eye that the little pep-talk he had had with Sandy in the morning had borne fruit so rapidly.

' – so I went out there with O'Neill,' Regan was saying.

'And?'

'Oh, he was there all right, Mr Reilly. Dead as a dodo. One shot did it. Bang in the heart.'

Reilly nodded. 'Poor bastard,' he said, sounding uncharacteristically sympathetic. 'What did you do with the body?'

'We have that. In the lock-up.'

Reilly nodded again, approvingly. 'Good. Keep it there. I'll tell you what to do with it.'

'That's what I thought, Mr Reilly. I was sure you'd have some use for it.'

Seamus Reilly ignored the statement. He drummed his fingers on his knee, frowning. 'I think,' he said finally, 'I think we better have this Fisher character in. But be careful, Thomas. I don't want them to know about it. Pick him up when you can – as soon as possible, but *do* be careful. They're bound to be buzzing around him now so it won't be all that easy.'

'Leave it to me, Mr Reilly. We're having him watched every time he leaves the barracks. We'll pick our time.'

'Good.'

Later, dressed suitably for the children's concert he had been invited to attend, Reilly met Asher. 'Your Corporal has been found,' he said.

'Where?'

'That's not important, John. He's dead. Shot.'

'Shit,' Asher swore, and made Reilly wince at his vulgarity. 'Where is his body?'

'We have it now. I want to talk to you about that.'

'I'm listening.'

'Not now. Tomorrow.'

'Ah, tomorrow. I've arranged a meet between you and Maddox for tomorrow, Seamus.'

'He's here?'

'You must be slipping. Yes, he's here. Came in this afternoon. It's important that the three of us talk.'

'If you say so.'

'Tomorrow morning. Eleven?'

'Yes. Where?'

'His office, I thought. Bring back memories for you. They've given him the same one he had.'

'You'll arrange things?'

'Of course. You'll be as safe as a match in a glacier.'

Reilly snorted. 'How is he?'

'The same as ever. Older, of course. But just the same.'

'He must be the only one who is.'

'He doesn't live here.'

Reilly gave a short laugh. 'Too true. Well, I must go. I'll see you in the morning. Who knows what will have happened by them?'

'What does that mean?' Asher asked, immediately suspicious.

'Just what it says.'

There was now no turning back; the murder of his colleague had seen to that. Chris Fisher trudged towards Sandy's pub. It had also broken him, wrapping his spirit in dread, his conscience branded and searing in pain. The only redemption lay, he now thought, in seeing the awful business through, if only to give his cruel act some meaning acceptable to whoever judged such things.

It was after eight when he arrived at the bar. Moran and McCluskey were waiting for him at one of the tables. McCluskey waved him over. 'We thought maybe you weren't coming.'

'I'm here.'

'Yea,' McCluskey agreed, staring hard at his eyes. 'You want a drink?'

Fisher nodded.

'What?'

'Anything.'

McCluskey grinned. 'A whisky here, Sandy,' he shouted. 'A double.'

Fisher lowered his drink in one swallow, shivering as the liquid burned its way down inside him, aware that the two men were studying him. It was time to start acting again. He put down his glass and smiled broadly. 'I needed that.'

'Yea, well, we had to be sure,' McCluskey put in. Then: 'Ready?' he asked, standing up.

They left the bar, McCluskey leading the way, then Fisher, Moran bringing up the rear.

As Moran started the car, McCluskey leaned across. 'Just another little precaution,' he said, producing a black scarf from under the seat and tying it securely about Fisher's eyes. 'We still have to be a bit careful, you know. Not that we don't trust you. But the less you know the less you'll be able to tell if the Brits find out.'

They drove in silence for about half a mile, taking a circuitous route into Andersonstown. Once Moran muttered. 'Shit!', his eyes flicking to the mirror above his head, then back to the road, then onto the mirror again. Then: 'It's okay,' he said, sounding relieved. 'I thought for a sec we were being followed, but it's turned off.' Without further incident they reached the sweet-shop and went inside. The door had been closed behind them a matter of seconds when a Range Rover drove past, turned down a side street, and parked.

Fisher blinked in the light, and rubbed one of his eyes, allowing Moran to guide him into a hard-backed kitchen chair. 'This is him,' McCluskey said.

The woman stood up and walked across the room, standing directly behind Fisher. 'So you're the one who wants to desert,' she said, not sounding particularly pleased.

'Yes,' Fisher said.

The woman made a clucking noise. 'What makes you think we'd want the likes of you?'

Fisher turned his head and looked up into the woman's face. 'I just hoped you would.'

'What good could you think you'd be?'

Fisher shrugged. 'I didn't think,' he answered, and made to stand up. 'If you can't – '

'Sit down,' the woman ordered. 'It so happens you might be useful. Stay on at the barracks for the time being. Just do what you always do. When we're ready for you, we'll let you know. You won't have to wait that long.'

Fisher nodded.

Now the woman walked slowly round until she was facing him. She leaned down and looked hard into his eyes. For several seconds she stared, saying nothing, almost as if she was daring him to flinch from her gaze. Still unblinking she said: 'And don't ever try and get cute, sonny,' she warned. 'One hint to me that you're playing us for fools and you're as dead as that bastard you killed yesterday.' Then she straightened up and moved away, arching her back, and caressing the nape of her neck with one hand. 'Take him back, Pat, will you. Let Eddie stay a while. I want a quick word with him.'

Patrick Moran guided Fisher out the door and closed it behind them. But he did not immediately start down the stairs. He lingered by the door, ostensibly to light a cigarette, taking his time about it, his head almost touching the woodwork of the door. Fisher watched him, and instinctively listened. At first there were just a few muttered words from McCluskey: nothing distinguishable. Then the woman took over. She seemed to be pacing the room as her voice came in waves although little of what she said seemed important at the moment. ' – do for Brighton – ' was one thing. ' – toffee Brit accent – ' was another. By then Moran, it seemed, had heard enough and he pushed Fisher ahead of him down the stairs.

'Where d'you want me to drop you?' was what Moran wanted to know.

'Anywhere. Near Sandy's will do.'

Moran obliged and dropped him outside the pub, driving off quickly without another word, without even noticing the Range Rover pulling into the parking space he had just vacated.

Seamus Reilly was peeved that he had to get dressed again. He had thoroughly enjoyed the concert, and had returned home at about nine-thirty, delighted with the opportunity of an early night. Twenty minutes later the phone by his bed rang. It was Thomas Regan. Did Mr Reilly want to see that soldier Fisher right away. Very well. Would he bring him round now? Right, Mr Reilly. Yes, he would take every precaution that the Major had no idea where he was taken to.

By the time Regan arrived, Reilly was dressed again. He had drawn the curtains in his sitting room, put the few family photographs into a drawer, switched on one bar of the electric fire, and poured himself a drink. Not that he wanted a drink: he wanted something for his hands to do. He would, under normal circumstances, simply have smoked, but he was trying to abandon the habit, albeit none too successfully. He opened the front door and signalled Regan to take the blindfolded Fisher into the sitting room by flapping his hand in that direction. Then he followed them in and closed the door. 'Take that thing off,' he told Regan. 'Yes, Mr – sir,' Regan said, and removed the blindfold.

Seamus Reilly studied the man before him. How inoffensive the poor creature looked! And probably, at another time, he was. Despite his innate dislike of the British Army, Reilly felt genuine sympathy for the young man. He was, he recognized, just a pawn. An innocent of sorts. He held out the palm of his hand indicating an armchair. 'Please, Major.'

Fisher looked taken aback, but sat down obediently.

'You've had a difficult few days,' Reilly observed. 'A drink, perhaps?'

Major Fisher shook his head. 'Thank you.'

Not offended, Reilly sipped his own drink for a few seconds, gathering his thoughts. 'Well, now, we have a problem here, do we not?' he asked in a chatty, friendly voice. 'I'm afraid you're rather in over your head, Major. And I'll bet they never told you in London that you might have to prove yourself by shooting one of your colleagues.'

A flicker of consternation passed over Fisher's face.

Reilly beamed. 'Oh you don't have to worry about the fact

that we know,' he explained. 'It's our business to know. It might set your mind at rest to tell you that we had a file on you before you ever set foot in Belfast. Dear me, dear me,' Reilly scolded himself, 'I haven't even told you who we are. Well, Major, let me just say that I am one of your real terrorists. Not one of those petty little gangsters you've got yourself mixed up with. I am the real thing,' he concluded dramatically, smiling happily at his little pomposity, pausing in case the Major wanted to say something, but not at all nonplussed when nothing was forthcoming. 'To come to the point,' he went on. 'As I see it you have two choices. One, you can help me. Two, you can, as they say, prepare to meet your Maker. And I suggest you consider the first as the better alternative. All *I* will want from you is information, and only information about the thugs you were with earlier. Nothing treasonable. You can't call that too unreasonable, can you?'

Fisher looked towards Regan as if for confirmation of Reilly's good intent, and was met with a blank stare. 'How do I – '

Reilly made a pained expression. 'You don't know, Major,' he interrupted. 'But let me put it this way. If I wanted you out of the way I could quite simply have you shot. If I wanted you discredited – well, you can believe me I have enough ways of letting the army know we're onto you to render you useless. And if *I* want information about the army I don't have to rely on someone like you who has just arrived.' Reilly let the message sink in, swirling the drink in his glass. 'For a start,' he finally went on, 'who did you go to see tonight?'

Fisher wet his lips. 'I don't know.'

'That's not an auspicious start, Major.'

'It's the truth. I don't know. Some woman.'

'Ah. A tall lady with long reddish hair, quite pretty?'

'Yes.'

'Excellent. There you are. That wasn't hard, was it? Now, what did she say to you?'

Fisher frowned. 'Not much. She wanted to know why I thought I would be useful to her. Then she said I might be useful and told me to carry on as usual until they were ready to contact me.'

'And that was all?'

'Yes.'

Reilly glanced towards Regan.

Regan nodded. 'He was only in there a few minutes – sir.'

'Did she say anything to the two men while you were there?'

'No – yes – not exactly.'

Reilly made a face to suggest his patience was running out. 'Which is it, Major?'

'Not when I was in the room. When the fat one – Pat – took me out of the room to drive me back he stopped outside the door to light a cigarette. I heard a few words. They didn't mean anything, though.'

'What few words did you hear, Major?' Reilly coaxed, leaning forward, his eyes dancing.

'Two things. The first sounded like "do for Brighton" but I can't be sure. And then "toffee Brit accent". That's all.'

'Now think, Major. Are you certain it was "do for Brighton"?'

'No. I'm not. I just said I wasn't sure.'

'All right. Was it definitely Brighton that was mentioned?'

Fisher frowned. Then he nodded. 'Yes. I'm pretty sure it was Brighton, but the rest – well, it doesn't make sense, does it, "do for Brighton"?'

Seamus Reilly was on his feet now, standing with his back to the fire, staring at the ceiling. Brighton. What in the name of God could be so interesting about Brighton? Suddenly he snorted. The bastards were probably planning a dirty weekend. Herself and McCluskey off to rut. 'Right,' Reilly said. 'From now on, Major, you'll be working for us. This gentleman here will be in touch with you regularly. I want you to carry on your little game with the others but you will tell us everything that transpires. I want to know every single word that you hear. In return we will help you. We will, in the first instance, see that no harm comes to you personally, and we will also allow you to pass on some of the information you glean to your superiors.

That seems fair to me. If you try to double-cross me, however – well, let me say that your lady friend will seem like Saint Bernadette, and her two henchmen as mild and harmless as Tweedledum and Tweedledee. Do I make myself clear?'

Fisher nodded. He was out of his depth and sinking fast. The imagined glories of espionage were rapidly becoming sordid and cruddy. There was no one he could turn to. The promised contact had not yet emerged, and he was suddenly gripped by the fear that he had been abandoned, that *they* already knew he had murdered Wilson and had disowned him. And it was possibly this dreadful sense of isolation that made him see Reilly's pedantic reasonableness in a new light. Somehow, the small, quiet-spoken man sitting across from him seemed totally trustworthy, the more so when he added. 'You can think of me as your guardian angel from now on. Just go about your duties and everything will work out in the end. One thing I can promise you: the end isn't as far away as you might think,' Reilly concluded.

· ELEVEN ·

SEAMUS REILLY WENT to early Mass, and was home again shortly before nine o'clock. He made himself a pot of fresh coffee, and settled down with the Sunday papers before he left for his meeting with Asher and Colonel Maddox. He found it impossible to concentrate, abandoning his reading, tossing the papers onto the floor beside him. He leaned back in his chair, his eyes closed. It was undoubtedly curious how Colonel Maddox and his paths continued to cross: their lives would touch briefly, the one never quite outwitting the other, yet forced, in the end, to call the game a draw. *The end isn't as far away as you might think.* For some reason his words of the night before repeated themselves in his brain. He shuddered. Dealing in death made it no easier to accept the imminence of one's own. He stood up and walked to the window, staring out. That was the saddest thing: death was so constant here, so familiar, that when someone died within days it was as if he had never lived, taking with him into the cold, unfriendly ground all memory of his life so that in the twinkling of an eye his existence was erased from the earth.

His mournful thoughts pursued him as he drove later

through the deserted streets. That was, of course, the most appalling aspect of it all: the wastefulness. The continuous, unrelenting wastefulness of young lives. The unlamented heroes – where had that phrase come from? Reilly looked puzzled for a moment, then brightened. Declan Tuohy. If only he had stayed! What was it he had written?

Like small unwanted creatures of the night
They crawl to hiding places in deep shadows,
There to curl in upon their loneliness and die
Not knowing why their screaming souls fly unheralded
Towards an angry Christ, then driven to an awful place
Devised for unlamented heroes.

'Will I drive in or stop here, Mr Reilly?'
' – ? What?'
'Do you want me to drive in or stop here?' the driver asked again.

Out of the window, Reilly spotted Mr Asher waiting for him on the footpath and noted the absence of obvious military presence. 'You can pull in here.'

Asher came across to the car, rubbing his hands as though to warm them. 'On time as usual,' he remarked. 'Parky this morning.'

Together they walked through the high, metal gates, and past the guards who made no attempt to hinder them. 'Into the lion's den,' Reilly remarked facetiously as they climbed the stairs.

'Hm. A dozing lion, however,' Asher said.

'Let's hope we don't startle him into full awareness then.'

Colonel Maddox, however, seemed bent on lending the lie to their approximation of him. He looked anything but dozy. His eyes were bright and excited. He rose to his feet as the two men came in, tapping the palms of his hands together as though applauding, then motioning Asher and Reilly towards the two chairs drawn up close to his desk. 'The terrible twins,' he observed lightheartedly.

Although not too amused Reilly managed a weak smile, while Asher looked embarrassed, hiding his feelings by lighting one of the black cigarettes he preferred. After a short cough he said, if only to break the silence: 'Not so terrible, Colonel.'

Maddox eyed them for a second. 'Perhaps not,' he conceded. Then, directing his full attention to Reilly, he continued: 'Mr Asher thinks we need to talk.'

'Mr Asher is usually right,' Reilly said.

'Indeed,' the Colonel agreed. 'That's why – that's why we're here,' he added, clearly changing his mind from what he had originally intended to say. He looked from Reilly to Asher and back to Reilly again, waiting for one of them to speak.

Asher took the initiative. Blowing a stream of cigarette smoke towards the ceiling, he spoke very deliberately. 'Well, Colonel,' he began but immediately glanced at Reilly for approval. Reilly bowed his head by way of signalling him to continue. 'I suggested we meet since there seems to have been an unmerciful cock-up at your end. The fact that Mr Reilly and I seem to know more about your reason for being here than you do proves my point. I asked you to refrain from contacting London until we had met because – ' Asher stopped again and turned to Reilly, hopefully implying that he should take it up.

Reilly did. 'Obviously London has recently become aware of something that we have known for a long time. We have had our problems. We have been forced to expel certain members, and some of these people have decided to – how shall I put it? – go it alone. There seems to be no doubt that they are planning some sort of action in England. That, Colonel, believe you me, is the last thing we want at the moment. We are trying to stop any such action, and we believe we are well on our way to doing just that. We've known about Fisher and his proposed activities for quite some time. We know you've been sent over to act as his contact. Quite rightly you feel you should inform London that Fisher's cover has been blown, as they say. But we, as it happens, need Fisher. We know he has been accepted as a deserter by some of our disenchanted brothers, the ones, in fact, whom we believe to be planning the attack in Britain. You didn't know that?' he asked, noting the Colonel's flicker of surprise. 'Never mind. It is a fact. Now I had a chat with Fisher last night,' Reilly continued, keeping his voice casual, enjoying the amazement his information created, 'and I think we came to an understanding.' Reilly grinned. 'I made him an offer he couldn't refuse,' he said wickedly. 'He is going to continue his – eh – relationship with the splinter group but he will also be reporting everything that goes on to one of my men. If you inform London they will simply pull him out and our chances of finding out what is being planned and nipping it in the bud will be greatly lessened,' Reilly concluded solemnly, and filled the awed silence that followed by giving way to temptation and lighting one of his little cigars.

Unexpectedly the Colonel began to smile, shaking his head in something approaching admiration. 'You people never cease to dumbfound me,' he confessed.

'What he says does make sense, Colonel,' Asher volunteered. 'We've – we've been working together on this for some time now,' he went on cautiously. 'It's in nobody's interest to put a spanner in the works just yet.'

Colonel Maddox stood up, paced a few steps, then sat down again, studying his signet ring. 'So you're asking me to sit here behind this desk and do nothing, knowing that an entire operation has been blown?'

Reilly smiled. 'Something like that. We will, of course, keep you fully informed. Indeed, we have to. It may come to it that we will need the might of your influence in the long run. We have very limited resources,' he concluded coyly.

'Why not give me the names of the people involved? I can have them arrested. That would end the matter.'

'Mr Asher could have done that some time ago, Colonel,' Reilly informed him. 'Alas, it's not that simple. It would cause problems, you see. They do have considerable support still both here and in Dublin. The repercussions following any attempt to arrest them could be – well, catastrophic.'

'For you?'

Reilly nodded. 'For me. Whereas if we were allowed to deal

with them in *our* way, the solution would be final and there would be no waves.'

'And supposing you fail? Supposing they do whatever they're planning to do before you find out?'

Reilly shrugged. 'That is a possibility, Colonel. But *you* certainly won't be able to prevent it any quicker than us.'

'You've no idea what they are planning?'

Reilly hesitated. 'No,' he said finally. 'But whatever it is it will have to happen soon. The longer they delay the more face they lose.'

The Colonel put his elbows on the desk and buried his head in his hands. He knew Reilly was right; knew, too, he was about to capitulate; but not, it seemed, without knowing precisely where he stood. 'What is it you want me to do?' he asked.

Reilly raised his eyebrows and spread his hands. 'Why, nothing, Colonel. Absolutely nothing. Just relax and enjoy our fair city. We, Asher and I, will do all that is necessary. I should think that, given a little luck, we should clear the whole thing up within a couple of weeks.'

The Colonel looked at Asher.

'I think he's right, Colonel,' Asher said.

'And I have your word that you'll keep me fully informed?'

'Of course,' Reilly said.

'I was talking to Mr Asher.'

'Of course,' Asher echoed, giving Reilly a smug little look.

'Two weeks?' the Colonel now asked Reilly.

'Give or take a week.'

The Colonel pursed his lips and gave his ring a couple of twirls before coming to a decision. 'Very well. Meanwhile, though, what about Fisher?'

'No need to worry about Fisher, Colonel,' Reilly said. 'He is now under my protection. He's safer now than he would be in his own home.'

The Colonel looked sceptical but nevertheless accepted the assurance. 'How you seem to thrive on treachery.'

'I hope to Christ you know what you're doing, Seamus,' Asher said as they walked down the corridor from the Colonel's office. 'You mess this up and it'll backfire on me. I need my pension.'

'We'll look after you, John. We have an excellent pension scheme.'

'That's all I need.'

'What we all have to do now is the hardest thing of all: we have to wait. Wait for them to move. Wait for them to say a word out of place that Fisher can tell us. Wait for them to make a mistake.'

'Supposing they don't – make a mistake, I mean?'

'They will. Never fear. They will. They're being driven by revenge and humiliation. Anyone with those two things goading them will make mistakes. Damn! I forgot to tell Maddox to call in Fisher. The poor bugger will go scatty if he thinks London has deserted him.'

'Leave that with me. I'll tell him.'

Asher found the Colonel still sitting at his desk looking decidedly forlorn. 'You strike me as a man who could use a drink, Colonel.' Asher told him. 'Shall I?' he asked, indicating the filing cabinet, and without waiting set about pouring two stiff drinks. 'Reilly asked me to come back,' he continued, handing the Colonel his glass. 'He feels it's important that you call Fisher in for a chat in case he feels he's been abandoned. What you tell him and how much is up to you.'

The Colonel swallowed half his drink before speaking. 'Every time I set foot in this godforsaken city I am encircled by perfidy,' he said, frowning slightly, wondering if he had chosen the right word.

Asher sat down, and waited, the Colonel's observation seeming not to warrant a reply. But the poor old chap was right: he did seem to land himself in the midst of turmoil. For months, years on end nothing would happen, and then, out of the blue, some unheaval would occur and the unfortunate Maddox would inevitably follow in its wake.

'Have I done the right thing, John?'

'I believe so, Colonel. In any other place you would probably be mad to even contemplate such a thing, but here . . . ,' Asher let his voice trail away. He took a sip of whisky before continuing. 'Reilly is a shrewd bastard, you know. Devious, true, but very, very shrewd. And he keeps his word. Anyway,' he continued, 'there's no other option. Look on the bright side. It's a far better thing to have Reilly with you than against you. He *has* to work this thing out. It's a question of his own survival as much as anything else.'

'Hah. He's a survivor if ever there was one.'

'That's what I mean, Colonel. Reilly isn't going to let anything happen that would jeopardize his position. God knows he hates the British, hates us, the RUC, too, but he'd side with anyone if he thought he could help his cause by so doing.' Asher grinned suddenly. 'Why not tell London you have the IRA doing your work for you? That should impress them!'

Even the Colonel was forced to laugh. 'I imagine it would. God, John, can you imagine the consternation.'

'The mind boggles.'

'Yes,' the Colonel said, wiping away the laughter, 'I'll have Fisher in.'

'Good. I'll tell Reilly.'

Major Fisher felt the blood drain from his face when he was told Colonel Maddox wanted to see him immediately in his office, visions of a court martial and total disgrace looming into his bewildered mind. Worse still, the thought of his father's shame. Irrational solutions arose: flight or suicide. Immediately they were dismissed. Nothing could be worse than the torment he was currently experiencing. It would be bliss to get it all off his chest regardless of the consequences. So it was a bold, determined Major Fisher who confronted the Colonel, standing stiffly to attention, his eyes fixed on a crack in the plasterwork above the window.

'At ease, Major,' the Colonel told him, sounding tired, deciding the expression was too military, and adding: 'Do sit down, like a good man.'

The Major sat down, hunching his shoulders, his hands

between his knees, wearing the expression of a boy about to be chastised.

And possibly it was this very expression that made the Colonel feel strangely paternal. Unless he saw in the younger man an image of himself, the mind (like the shoulders) hunched against further bludgeoning, the eyes frightened and tired, mocking the brave, self-assured entrance. Another poor fool, the Colonel told himself, caught up in the whims of terrorism. 'A tricky kettle of fish,' he said aloud, giving a little start as though the words had been intended only as a thought.

'Colonel?'

The Colonel gave a weary smile. 'The first sign. Isn't that what they say? Talking to yourself. Have you ever thought about madness, Major?' he asked. 'I suppose not. Why should you? A strange old man once told me – here in Belfast – that madness lurked close to the skin in all of us. He was probably right. Look around you here and you begin to wonder.'

Major Fisher eyed the Colonel anxiously.

'But like every other adversity in life it can be overcome,' Maddox rambled on, or seemed to ramble, although he was trying desperately to get to the point. 'And we all have some lurking enemy to overcome, do we not?'

The Major blinked rapidly: this was a far cry from what he had expected.

'Take yourself, for example – Chris, isn't it? May I call you Chris? Take yourself for example, I hear you have landed yourself in trouble. Amazing. Here I am, not twenty-four hours in this dreadful place and already I know the – '

'Colonel – ' Fisher began, but stopped abruptly.

Maddox raised his eyebrows. 'Yes?'

Fisher shook his head and stared down at the floor.

'Oh for goodness sake don't be so despondent. Everything has been taken care of. We are, would you believe, under the protection of the great Seamus Reilly. Name mean nothing? Surprising. I understand you had a little chat with him last night. A nice man. Deadly as they come, but always the gentleman. He tells me you made an agreement. I've made agreements with him in the past. Very reliable chap. Never goes back on his word.' The Colonel stood up and moved around the desk. He pulled a chair across the room and sat down beside the Major, tapping him on the knee with one finger as he continued, his voice more caring than ever. 'Now listen to me carefully. I know what's been going on. I know why you were sent here in the first place. Believe it or not it's because of you that I'm here. I'm what they grandly call your contact. But be that as it may, there are intrigues taking place the likes of which you couldn't dream of. I know about them. I am being fully informed about them each step of the way. I want you to do what Reilly told you to do. Just carry on as if nothing had happened. See the people you've been seeing and tell Reilly what he wants to know. That's all.'

Major Fisher looked into the Colonel's face. 'But, sir, Wilson,' he blurted out.

Maddox straightened up, bewildered. 'Wilson? Who is Wilson?'

'Corporal Wilson, sir. I – '

A tiny light of understanding dawned in the Colonel's eyes. 'Corporal Wilson,' he repeated to himself. 'Someone mentioned a Corporal to me. Ah. Gone missing. A Corporal gone missing. Would that be the one?'

Fisher nodded, and before he could control himself, he was crying. His whole body shook with uncontrollable grief, a small whining noise created every time he took breath.

Colonel Maddox was mortified. He could, he liked to think, cope with most things, but an officer weeping before his very eyes and for no apparent reason was an experience he had yet to encounter, and, faced with it, was all at sea. He narrowed his eyes and peered through them at the shaking body. He stood up, walked away a few steps, turned and peered again as though by distancing himself it might make a difference. He cocked his head on one side, trying to pick up the mutterings that emerged from the tears. Suddenly he stiffened. He could have sworn the Major had said 'I shot him.' 'What was that you said?' he demanded.

The Major looked up. He took a handkerchief from his pocket and blew into it loudly. 'I shot him, sir.'

Maddox's immediate reaction was to think Fisher had taken leave of his senses. 'Don't be silly, Major,' he said. 'Pull yourself together,' he added more brusquely.

'It's true, sir. They made me. They said it was to prove I wasn't a plant. They said if I didn't they'd kill me and then kill Wilson anyway. I shot him, sir.'

Maddox was appalled. Strangely, however, the death of the unfortunate Corporal didn't enter his feelings. What horrified him was that anyone could be asked to do such a thing, that such savagery could still be countenanced. And there was more to it: forcing a man to murder a colleague was bad enough, but how could they inflict such torment? And what did he, Matthew Maddox, say to the young man now? Don't let that worry you? Just put it behind you? Forget it? Useless, insulting platitudes. 'You poor man,' Maddox heard himself say. 'What can I say?' Well, that was one way of getting out of saying anything. If only he had left it there. But he didn't. On and on he rambled, trying to disguise his own ineptitude in a flurry of words, plucking clichés from the air and tossing them hope- lessly across the desk. And he got confused, kept repeating himself, losing track altogether of what he had hoped to say. It was, therefore, with bemused gratification, that he noted the Major looking at him kindly, and heard him say: 'Thank you, sir.'

'That's better,' he proclaimed stoutly. 'What's done is done. Dreadful for you, of course. But we won't speak further of this. Keep it strictly to ourselves.'

'But – '

'No buts, Major,' Maddox said, gaining control of himself again. 'Nobody else need know. I will take care of this. Or rather, I'll get someone to take care of it. Now, off you go. We'll be in touch soon again.'

Alone, Maddox considered the consequences of what he had just done, and poured himself a drink to drown the unpleasant thoughts that crossed his mind. Best to take his own advice.

What was done was done. He would, he decided, quite simply get Reilly to arrange things, make it look like a simple terrorist killing.

· TWELVE ·

THE MANAGER OF the Grand Hotel, Brighton buzzed about his domain. As far as he could judge, everything was ready to welcome the Prime Minister and the majority of the Cabinet. He had personally checked the Prime Minister's suite, removing a few objects of frippery put there for the honeymooners who normally stayed there, removing, too, tactfully the display of red roses and arranging for a bouquet of blue iris and white gypsophila to be substituted. He had run his fingertips along ledges to be certain the temporary staff had dusted properly: they had. The police had searched the hotel thoroughly; they had brought in their sniffer dogs; there were plain clothes men stationed in the foyer and on almost every floor.

Two streets away, back from the esplanade, in a small but clean guest house, Dermot Drumm lay on his bed, his eyes closed. Frequently he turned his head to study the little travelling clock on the table. The hour hand seemed to drag its way around the dial. Ten past bloody ten. Still far too early for those bloody Tories to be in bed. He propped himself up on one elbow and lit a cigarette, sucking the smoke deep into his lungs, bringing on a fit of coughing. For several seconds he was doubled up, his thin, wiry body racked in pain as he rasped the acrid fumes from his throat. 'Shit,' he said aloud, stubbing out the cigarette in a tin ashtray already filled with partially smoked Consulate. He went to the washbasin and drank some water, slurping it directly from the tap. Then he wiped his face with a towel and stared at his reflection in the mirror, twisting his face into a series of comic and sinister expressions, saying quietly to himself: 'Police have issued a photofit of the man they wish to question in connection with the Brighton bombing.' He was contentedly resigned to the fact that this would probably happen. He expected to be caught eventually. You didn't blow the Prime Minister of England to smithereens and get away with it. Not that it mattered. If they didn't get him Reilly would, and his chances of survival were infinitely better in one of HM's prisons. And prison held no terrors. He had spent more years inside them than out; should be in one now only he had been spirited away from Belfast and across the sea to bloody Scotland in a fishing boat. That had been Reilly's doing. Reilly was all right in those days. Gone soft now, though. Into fucking politics . . . .

At 2.40 a.m. Dermot Drumm shut the front door of the guest house behind him. He had taken the precaution of warning the landlady that he would be leaving very early, paying her in advance, explaining that as a traveller in farm machinery he had to make his calls at an ungodly hour.

'You poor man. I hope they're paying you well,' the landlady had sympathized.

'Not as well as they should,' Drumm quipped.

'They never do. You know my husband, God rest his soul, worked for the same company for the best part of forty years, and they retired him off with a pension that wouldn't feed a canary. Still, I expect you're grateful to have a job at all these days.'

'Indeed I am.'

He crossed the road, swinging his small overnight bag, and unlocked the door of the Audi. He threw the bag onto the back seat, and got in behind the wheel. Then he leaned across and took a small metal device from the glove compartment. He glanced at the clock on the dashboard. He would wait a few minutes. As it turned out that few minutes' wait was to prove, from his point of view, a grave error of judgement.

At 2.53 the Prime Minister left her bathroom, closing the door. Immediately the bomb exploded.

One hour after the bomb had demolished the central section of the Grand Hotel, Seamus Reilly was awoken by the telephone. Without opening his eyes he grabbed the receiver and pulled it into the bed, hearing the rattle of excited words before he got it to his ear. When he finally got it there he heard only the tail-end: '. . . broken loose. Bloody pandemonium.'

'Who is that?' he asked sharply.

'It's me. Regan, Mr Reilly. They've done it. Blown up the hotel in Brighton where Thatcher and the Cabinet are staying.'

For a second Reilly felt he was in the throes of a horrible dream. Quite literally he froze, every nerve and muscle in his body seizing, his brain, still dulled by sleep, unable to grapple with the horrendous news.

'Are you there, Mr Reilly?' Regan asked anxiously.

'Yes. I'm here.'

'Did you hear me? They've blown up the bloody hotel.'

'I heard,' Reilly answered, slowly coming to grips with his thoughts. Regan was babbling on. '. . . least three dead. Christ knows how many injured. Jesus, Mr Reilly, this is – '

'Calm down, Thomas,' Reilly said quietly, aware that the advice was as much for himself as for Regan. 'Calm down,' he repeated. 'Start again. Tell me everything you know.'

'Only what I've told you, Mr Reilly. My contact called me from Brixton. I don't know where he got it from. A bomb went off some time around three o'clock and blasted the Grand Hotel. There's bodies everywhere.'

'Thatcher?'

'No news on that. No names at all. Jesus, Mr Reilly what – '

'Just a minute, Thomas.'

Reilly stared into the darkness. Bloody Brighton. Christ, he should have – 'Thomas. There's nothing we can do right now. Come round in the morning. Early. Eight o'clock. I'll talk to you then.'

'Right, Mr Reilly.'

Within seconds Reilly was dialling the number of his Commander in Chief. The phone rang and rang. He was on the point of hanging up when the receiver clicked and a tired, gruff voice asked 'Yes?'

'Seamus. Reilly. I've just been told someone's blown up the hotel where Thatcher is staying for the convention.'

Silence. The Commander was clearly as stunned as Reilly himself had been; he was also furious as Reilly could tell when he finally spoke, his voice crisp and cold and deadly, making the single word into a sentence of death. 'Who?'

Reilly's voice carried a shrug. 'Your guess is as good as mine.'

The Commander was in no mood for guessing. 'I want to know who,' he said flatly. 'Find out, Seamus. And fast.'

'Very well. I – '

'And deal with them,' the Commander added icily. Then, finally, he exploded. 'Jesus Christ! It's that fucking woman. Seamus I want that bitch hung drawn and quartered.'

'She will be if it *is* her.'

'It's her. I know it is.'

Reilly knew that too. 'Possibly,' he said.

'Meanwhile, I'll issue a statement claiming responsibility. I've got to. If *we* don't *they* will and make us look like incompetent fools who can't keep things under control.'

Reilly was shocked. 'We can't – ' he began to protest.

'We have to. We lose everything if we let them take the credit. They'll have those lunatics both here and in Dublin rallying round. Before you know it we'll be well and truly split down the middle. I've got to prevent that. I've no option. We have to claim responsibility and ride it out.'

Seamus Reilly wanted to protest again, but he knew it would

be futile. The decision had been made; and there was a grim, twisted logic to it. For a man who had always prided himself on his calm, detached, unemotional approach to things, Reilly was surprised and alarmed at the anger he felt rising within him, a hatred he had never before felt. That anyone should reduce his efforts for peace to so much rubble by such a stupid (and, more to the point, unsanctioned) action was more than he could stand. Borrowing the Commander's original tones of wrath he said: 'That decision is yours, of course.'

'Precisely.'

'And when I find out who was responsible I have your authority to deal with them as I wish?'

'You do.'

'Without question?'

'Without question . . . . You sound as though –'

'Without question?'

The Commander was forced to grin. 'Very well, Seamus. Without question.'

'Thank you.'

Seamus Reilly put the receiver back in its cradle and got out of bed. He put on his dressing gown and made for the bathroom. He was trembling. He tried to put it down to his anger but couldn't: he knew it was the sense of foreboding that made his nerves jitter. Again the words 'you are already dead' blundered into his mind. Damn them all to hell.

Five minutes later he was talking to John Asher. 'You won't have heard, John. Someone just blew up the hotel in Brighton. The one where Thatcher was staying.'

For a second Asher said nothing. Then: 'Holy Jesus. Is she dead?'

'I don't know. There are some dead, but I don't know if she's one of them.'

'Holy Jesus,' Asher said again.

'The reason I'm ringing, John, is to tell you that we have – that it has been decided that we must claim responsibility. You have my word we had nothing to do with it, but expediency dictates that we must say we did.'

'I don't under—'

'I can't explain now. Look, I have a meeting at eight in the morning. Can we get together around nine?'

'Yes. Yes, of course. You want me to come there?'

'If you can. I've got to be where I can be contacted.'

'I'll be there.'

'We'll have to move fast and I'll need your help.'

Asher hesitated. 'You're not – '

'You have my word. We had nothing whatever to do with it. I'll explain everything when we meet. We'll also need to see Maddox. I'll need him to . . . . I'll explain that in the morning also.'

Across the city Eddie McCluskey watched the woman anxiously as she paced the room like a cat, from time to time slapping her clenched fist into the open palm of her other hand, muttering to herself 'ring, ring, ring', and frequently stopping to stare at the phone as if she could mesmerize it into action. McCluskey was confused. He had been there since the evening before and had no idea why: he had simply been told that she wanted him there. It had, of course, happened before: several times. He was used to such summary commands. But this was different although he could not quite put his finger on it. Perhaps it was her uncharacteristic excitedness, a sort of semi-controlled frenzy that, to his mind, only made her more sexually desirable. Then there were her long silences when all she did was alternate her magnetic gaze between him and the telephone, seeming to find both equally fascinating. There was the way she kept wetting her lips, flicking her pink tongue in and out of her mouth like an adder. There was the occasional moan, not of pain but of, it struck him, longing. And it was all these with their promise of something that had sustained him through the evening and early morning.

When the phone did, at last, ring, she was across the room in three strides, grabbing the receiver. 'Yes?'

This was followed by a series of curt, chopped words. 'Yes. Yes. Good. How many? Shit. Yes. Right. Good. No.' Then the receiver was slowly, reluctantly replaced. 'We've bloody done it,' she exclaimed without turning round.

Suddenly she was waltzing about the room, her arms clasping herself in a tight embrace, her eyes dancing too. 'We've done it, we've done it, we've done it,' she kept saying, whirling about like a dervish.

McCluskey may have been impressed, but he was also confused. 'Done what, for Christ's sake?'

The woman stopped dancing abruptly. Then she rushed towards him, grabbed him by the hands and pulled him from the chair. She threw her arms about him, pressing her body hard against his. 'We've beaten Reilly, that's what we've done. We've beaten that smug little bastard,' she told him, her voice little more than a whisper but the venom in it screaming.

It was something of an anticlimax when all McCluskey could do was ask 'How?'

The woman stood back, holding him by the hands at arms' length. 'You know those trips to Glasgow?'

'Yea?'

'I was arranging the bombing of all time. And this morning it went off. Right under Thatcher's knickers.'

'Jesus. You *what*?'

'Months ago,' the woman exaggerated, 'as soon as I knew what hotel they were using for their convention, I had a bomb planted. This morning we set it off.'

'Christ Almighty!' McCluskey's mind skirted the horror of the bombing itself: such an enormous undertaking was way beyond his understanding. What took over his whole consciousness was the furious wrath of Seamus Reilly, and of that Eddie McCluskey was petrified.

'You should have fucking told us what you were doing. We'll have to get out – '

'What for?' the woman demanded, amazed.

'What for? Jesus God. Reilly, of course. What the hell do you think he's going to do to us? He'll crucify us, that's for sure.'

'No he won't,' the woman said firmly. 'He wouldn't dare now. He knows bloody well that we have our supporters and that they'll be right behind us now. It will take Reilly all his time to survive himself. He won't have a minute to spare on us.'

McCluskey was not convinced. 'You're wrong,' he told her mournfully, shaking his head. 'You don't know him like I do. You've made him lose face. That's something you can't do to Reilly.'

'To hell with Reilly's face. He's a nothing now. You just wait, Eddie,' the woman told him, moving away, staring into the distance as though in a trance or having a wonderful vision. 'You just wait,' she told him again. 'In a couple of hours when I announce that we did it, Reilly's power will be nil.'

'Yea, well, I'll tell you something. I can give you the names of eight different people who thought they had outwitted Reilly, and you want to know where they are now? Nobody fucking knows! They just bloody vanished.'

'We won't vanish, Eddie. Not us, I can promise you that.'

'Yea. The others said that too.'

The woman moved round in front of him again, and held out her hands. 'Come on, Eddie. Come with me. I *need* you now. Come on.'

Meekly Eddie McCluskey gave her his hands and allowed himself to be led into her bedroom, the aching in his loins for the moment obliterating his fears.

Perhaps significantly, Colonel Maddox was last to receive the news, reaching him through official channels, almost, it seemed, as an afterthought. His reaction was curious. Although naturally shocked and disgusted, he also felt an odd kind of satisfaction as though believing the outrage would inflict on his superiors the sort of unsolvable quandary they had inflicted on him. But he should have known better. That damned conniving Reilly. Lulling him into a false sense of trust while all the while he had been scheming to annihilate almost the entire government. Well, enough was enough. He would fix Seamus Reilly. He had been made a fool of once too often.

It was seven-thirty when Declan Tuohy learned of the bomb-

133

ing. The thirteenth was his day off, his first in quite a while, and he had determined to enjoy it, starting with a luxurious sleep-in. He had taken his phone off the hook, and drunk a little too much. So, it was in something of a haze that he went to investigate the hammering on his door. It went a long way to clearing his head when he saw it was the editor himself who was creating the ruckus. 'Where's the damn fire?' he asked, trying to smile.

Myles Cravan was in no mood for stupid remarks. 'Get dressed, Declan. And be quick about it.'

'It's my day off, dammit.'

'It was. Your friends have really gone to town this time. Tried to blow the whole damn Cabinet up.'

'*What?*'

'That's right. The IRA have claimed responsibility for a bomb that blew the shit out of Thatcher's hotel in Brighton. You get into the office and see what you can find out.'

'God above!'

'So much for your peaceful Seamus Reilly. Little bastard. He – '

'Hey now, hang on a minute. You don't know it was Reilly.'

'It was the bloody IRA, wasn't it? That's Reilly as far as I'm concerned. Come on, for Christ's sake. Throw some clothes on. I'll take you back with me.'

The woman eased McCluskey from on top of her and reached out to switch on the bedside radio . . . THE IRA HAS CLAIMED RESPONSIBILITY. A REPORT NOW FROM . . . That was all she heard. In an instant she was out of bed, wrenching the radio from the table and hurling it against the wall. For a second she stood still, her lips quivering. Then she started to scream. 'Fuck you Reilly,' she screamed, repeating the curse over and over again.

Poor McCluskey was scared out of his wits. He sat up in the bed, his mouth open, gaping. It wasn't until the woman had stopped that he dared ask: 'What the hell has happened?'

The woman rounded on him. 'What the hell has happened?

That fucking shit Reilly has claimed responsibility. He's grabbing the credit! He's making everyone believe they did it.'

McCluskey, for the life of him, couldn't digest the significance of all this. 'So what?' he was foolish enough to ask.

The woman looked as if she was about to physically attack him. Instead, when she spoke, her voice was calm and almost a whisper. 'Get the hell out of here, McCluskey.' Then she closed her eyes and yelled again: 'Get out!'

· THIRTEEN ·

SEAMUS REILLY HAD just turned off the early morning news when Thomas Regan knocked at the door.

'Sorry I'm a bit late, Mr Reilly. Bloody murder out there this morning. Saracens and foot-patrols everywhere,' Regan explained, closing the door and following Reilly into the kitchen.

Reilly dismissed the apology with a small gesture, and filled the kettle with water, plugging it in and switching it on. 'You take tea, don't you, Thomas?'

'I do, Mr Reilly. Thanks very much.'

'What more have you learned?' Seamus asked, sounding curiously vague as if he really couldn't care less, and setting about percolating himself some coffee.

'Not too much yet, I'm afraid. But I will. I've got everyone on it.'

'You've heard we've claimed responsibility?'

'I have, Mr Reilly,' Regan admitted, looking uncomfortable. 'And?'

'And what, Mr Reilly?'

'What did you think when you heard that?'

Regan began to fidget with his hands as his mind fidgeted with his thoughts. 'I didn't think anything, Mr Reilly. It's not my place to question something like that. If that statement was issued it was issued for a reason, and I just accept it.'

Seamus Reilly stared at Regan in quiet amazement, amazement and envy. 'How lucky you are, Thomas, to be able to do that. Ah,' he added as the kettle boiled. 'Your tea. I'm afraid it has to be a bag.'

'Grand, Mr Reilly.'

'Sit down, Thomas. And listen to me. We had nothing whatever to do with it. Nothing. But for – for reasons we had to claim we did. I, now, have been given the task of finding those who really are responsible and dealing with them – in any way I like, I might add.' Seamus paused to let that much sink in.

Regan nodded thoughtfully, adding milk and sugar to his tea, and stirring it.

'Whatever I do I want you to understand that I am doing it for a very good reason. I just want you to go along with me. I'll explain what I can – the rest you'll have to take on trust. The one major problem facing me is this: I cannot execute my orders in such a way that makes it seem we are taking our revenge for something done without our sanction. It will have to be done through other channels. For that reason I will be working with Inspector Asher.' Reilly paused again, and, similarly, Regan nodded again. 'Whatever I ask you to do I want you just to do it. No hesitation. No questions. I can promise you I will see to it that you come out of it unscathed – unharmed,' Reilly put in as he saw the squint of puzzlement.

Regan stopped nodding. 'You know I'll do anything you say, Mr Reilly.'

'That's all I wanted to hear,' Seamus told him, giving him a small, grateful smile, and pouring himself a cup of coffee.

Reilly carried his coffee to the table and sat down. 'Now,' he said, 'we don't know who actually planted the explosives but we do know who is behind it – '

'That bloody woman and McCluskey and Moran,' Regan said, if only to prove he was on the ball.

'Quite,' Reilly agreed, albeit a little testily. 'In your opinion which of them would break the easiest?'

'Oh McCluskey. No doubt about that, Mr Reilly. Everyone knows he's terrified of you.'

For an instant Reilly looked amused. 'Leaving me and my power to terrify out of it for the moment, Thomas – you still think McCluskey's the most likely to break?'

Regan took to nodding again. 'Yes. Moran's got family here. It wouldn't be easy for him to do a bunk if he gave anything away so they could get at him without trouble. McCluskey though could be gone before they laid a hand on him. Yea, McCluskey's your man, Mr Reilly.'

'Good,' Reilly said and tasted his coffee. 'Tell me this, Thomas. The place where McCluskey lives – what's it like?'

'Like? Well, he lives with his mother. Just the two of them. Not much of a place. Two up, two down. Dirty. The mother drinks a bit.'

'Any outhouses?'

'Oh I couldn't be sure about that, Mr Reilly. Probably there is though. Most of the houses on that street have a bit of a shed at the back. Used to be the piss house, the lavatories before they got inside ones. Most people use them as coal sheds now.'

'Find that out for me. As soon as possible, will you?'

'I can find out now if I can use your phone, Mr Reilly.'

'Good. Go ahead.'

Alone, Reilly finished his coffee and poured himself a second cup. Feeling guilty he opened the drawer at the end of the table and took out a tin of his small cigars and a box of matches. He argued with himself against lighting one but lost, and inhaled deeply, enjoying the nicotine.

'Yes, Mr Reilly. There is a shed. A lean-to thing.'

Reilly beamed. 'Fine. Can you get to it from the back?'

'Sure. There's a lane that runs right the way along. It's only a low bit of a wall. Easy to get at the shed if you want me to.'

'I do, Thomas. Tonight I want you to take Wilson's body and leave it in McCluskey's shed. Bring some sacks with you.

138

Cover the body up. Make it look as if someone was trying to hide it.'

Clearly Regan liked this idea. He grinned hugely. 'Sure I'll do that, Mr Reilly. No bother at all.'

'Good man. Just phone me when you have it done. Then we'll deal with Eddie McCluskey.'

'It's as good as done,' Regan said and finished his tea in one gulp. 'I'll be off, then, Mr Reilly, unless there's something else?'

'That's it for now, Thomas.'

'Right. And – well, good luck, Mr Reilly.'

Seamus Reilly was strangely touched: he looked almost embarrassed as he smiled at Regan. 'Thank you, Thomas. That's kind of you.'

'Yerra, you're worth any ten others, Mr Reilly.'

'Thank you, Thomas,' Reilly said again, making to open the front door, then changing his mind. He frowned. 'One other thing. You better phone me here this afternoon. About three. No, make it three on the dot. I might want you to pick up Fisher again. It depends how things go.'

'Will he be out, Mr Reilly? He's pretty scared now. He might just stay in the barracks.'

'He'll be out if I want him, Thomas. I'll see to that.'

'I might have guessed as much,' Regan said admiringly. 'Right then, I'll give you a buzz at three on the dot.'

So far so good. Reilly busied himself in the kitchen, putting the cups in the sink and the milk back in the fridge, running tap water on the butt of his cigar and tossing it into the bin. He had just finished when John Asher arrived. 'What a godawful mess,' he said by way of greeting.

Reilly grunted and led the way to the sitting-room. 'You could say that.'

'You should have been with me this morning and you'd know there's no supposing about it. The Chief Inspector's gone bloody berserk. You'd swear to God I'd put the bloody bomb there myself.'

Reilly could not prevent himself laughing.

'Huh, it's all very well for you to bloody well laugh, Seamus, but I'm telling you the laugh will be on the other side of your face if you're not damn crafty. You know what he said? He said he wanted every goddam Catholic in the province – the province, mind you – brought in for questioning before nightfall.'

'You'd better get a move on then, hadn't you, John?'

'What I'm trying to tell you is that we don't have a lot of time to sort this fiasco out.'

'I know, John. I know. I'm working on it already.'

'That's a relief.'

'By this time tomorrow I'll have someone for you to question.'

'Question!' Asher snorted. 'Seamus we have to nail someone for this, not bloody question them.'

'I'll give you someone to nail, as you put it.'

Asher squinted, immediately suspicious. 'You know who did this, don't you?'

Reilly shook his head. 'No. No I don't. I know who's behind it, just like you do. That's all. But – Look, John,' Reilly went on after a short pause. 'Later tonight I'll give you a call with a name, an address and something to look for. You can then arrest someone. From the questions you ask you should be able to find out what we both want to know. Mind you – you'll find out a lot quicker if I'm there,' he added with a twinkle.

'Why don't you just pick this nameless thing up yourself?'

'Not the same. We don't want to appear involved,' Reilly admitted. 'Far better for all of us that you be seen as the brains. I tell you what, though, if you just go along with me between us we'll soon have all the answers.'

'What charge am I supposed to use tonight?'

'Would murder do?'

'It would if I had proof.'

'I'll give you the proof.'

Asher shook his head. 'I've said it before and I'll say it again – you're a devious bastard.'

'I survive,' Reilly told him.

'You certainly do. So far.'

Suddenly Reilly went gloomy. 'Yes,' he agreed sadly. 'So far.'

' – Maddox to cope with,' Asher was saying.

'Sorry, John. I was – '

'I said I've also got Maddox to cope with. He was on to me at half eight this morning. He's convinced you deceived him and that you were behind the explosion. He wanted me to arrest *you* for Christ's sake.'

'Oh dear. What did you tell him?'

'I told him that I was seeing you this morning and if I thought you had anything to do with it I *would* bloody well arrest you.'

Reilly mockingly held out his wrists for handcuffing. 'I'll go quietly.'

'Very funny. He's damn jittery, Seamus, I can tell you.'

'Who? Maddox. Tell him not to worry. Tell him I have everything under control.'

'*That's* what he's afraid of.'

'You can say I'll phone him.'

'Better if you went and saw him.'

'I can't. I daren't leave home today. I've got to be within reach if any of my men want me.'

'I could bring him here,' Asher suggested hopefully.

'You can do that if you like.'

'I'll put it to him.'

'Just after lunch if possible,' Reilly said. Then he smiled. 'Actually, I might want him to do me a favour.'

'Just you do yourself a favour, Seamus, and stop buggering about. There's too many people in Belfast would like to see the back of you. They might just try and take their chance now.'

Reilly shrugged. 'Now or next year, what's the difference?'

'Twelve bloody months.'

Reilly stood up. 'Phone me if Maddox is coming.'

Asher, too, stood up now. 'I'll do that. And don't you forget: I need something by tonight.'

'You'll have it.'

'I'm banking on it.'

Declan Tuohy sat back from his desk, his feet balanced on the ledge of an open drawer, reading the first reports of the Brighton explosion. He found it all but impossible to concentrate. Something was wrong. It stank. Most of all the IRA claim stank. The bombing was sheer lunacy and, whatever else, the hard-core IRA were far from being lunatics. Especially Reilly. He would never in a million years have condoned such action, and he had the power to veto it. Besides, they had nothing whatever to gain except revulsion and appalling publicity which was certainly the last thing Reilly wanted, now that he was moving his section towards politics. Indeed, the whole trend of IRA publicity had been towards reasonableness, towards electoral success, towards, ultimately, peace.

Declan threw the reports onto his desk, and swung back and forth on his chair. Now, why the hell would the IRA claim responsibility if they didn't do it . . .? He looked at his watch. Then, from his inside pocket he took a small notebook, flicked through the pages, found what he wanted and reached for the telephone. When it was answered he stated: 'It's Declan Tuohy.'

'Ah.'

'Can you talk?'

'Of course.'

'Brighton. You've claimed – '

'I – Command claimed responsibility.'

'You knew about it beforehand though?'

Reilly hesitated. 'No.'

'Someone did.'

Reilly gave a small, tired laugh. 'Naturally.'

'What I meant was someone within your – '

'No.'

'Then you had nothing to do with it.'

'Nothing.'

'Well why claim – '

'There are reasons, Declan. Leave it at that for the moment.'

'Can we at least talk again later?'

'Perhaps.'

'Would it help if I came over?'

'Not really. Stay where you are. I'll be in touch. Who knows, you might even get that film you wanted,' Reilly said and hung up.

So that was it, Declan thought, and immediately burst out laughing as he realised he still had no idea whatever what *it* was.

'And I suppose you're going to tell me you believe him?' Colonel Maddox said.

Asher inclined his head. 'Yes. Yes, I believe him.'

Maddox threw up his hands in a gesture of exasperation. 'Well I don't,' he said.

'That's up to you, Colonel, but just think about it for a minute. Why should Reilly lie? Even if he was responsible, we could never prove it. He was in your office the other day. I've been in touch with him every day. How is that going to look if we charge him with something we can't even come near to proving?'

Maddox shook his head. 'I still think he had something to do with it. He's using us, John. He's twisting us round his little finger.'

Asher grinned. 'He would like to perhaps, but I don't think he is. Why not come and see him like I suggested. What harm can it do?'

The Colonel wagged a pencil at Asher. 'All right I'll come. But I'm telling you, John, if I'm not satisfied that he's completely innocent I'll have him arrested myself.'

So at 2.15 Maddox and Asher called on Reilly. Asher had already telephoned advising him of the visit, and had agreed to undertake the required security precautions, accepting Reilly's explanation that for him to do so would be 'tricky under the circumstances' meaning, presumably, that the streets were crawling with troops. When they were all seated, John Asher opened proceedings by saying: 'The Colonel is most displeased, Seamus. He thinks you're trying to hoodwink him.'

Reilly feigned surprise. 'Really Colonel?'

'Yes,' Maddox confirmed. 'There's too many coincidences. It reeks of your duplicity.'

'Oh dear,' Reilly sighed. 'I can assure you everything I told John this morning was the truth.'

The Colonel looked about the room as if hoping to find his next words painted on the wall. Seeing nothing, he stayed silent. It was all happening to him again. The damned intrigue was swallowing him. Already he was admitting to himself he could not cope. 'I simply want to know what is going on,' he said, perilously near to pleading.

Reilly was touched. One could not fail to like and be sorry for the unfortunate Colonel. Here was a man, he thought, who would have fulfilled his desires had he died heroically in battle. He was a brave man, and probably fearless when fighting anything he could understand. The trouble was his very decency and goodness left him naked and undefended in the face of the intrigue that was such a vital element in one's survival in Belfast. To him it was dishonourable, and life without honour was not something Colonel Maddox would wish for. Reilly appreciated that; he even admired the man for it; in truth he quietly envied him his goodness. 'Very well, Colonel, I will trust *you*. I will tell you what is going on. I will tell you on the condition that you allow me to pursue a solution without any interference, and with my promise that it will not involve any – eh – problems for the British forces here in Belfast. Do we agree?'

The Colonel surrendered. He nodded.

'What has happened is this. Some months ago we were forced to expel certain people from the IRA. They were thugs. Since then several things have occurred which made it clear they were going to take their revenge. They have, however, a following both here and in Dublin, and for them to survive as a viable entity it was vital that they prove their power by pulling off a coup, some grandiose action that would humiliate us and elevate them. We – John and I – are convinced they organized the Brighton explosion. They didn't *do* it themselves, but they were the brains, if that applies, behind it. In order to forestall the glory they hoped to reap among their supporters it was decided by my superiors that *we* should immediately issue a statement claiming responsibility. I had, and still have my doubts about the wisdom of this, but the decision was made and I must abide by it. For what it is worth I can tell you that we all are appalled and disgusted by the attack on the hotel. And that, Colonel, is the situation so far.' Reilly leaned back in his chair as if he had nothing further to say. But he had. He started speaking again almost immediately, keeping his eyes closed, and talking slowly, giving the impression he was reading the words from a screen somewhere in his mind; or it could have been that he was forging a plan as he went along. 'One problem that faces us,' he went on, 'is that we cannot be seen to be hunting anyone – that would simply put the lie to our claim. We have many members sitting on the fence, so to speak, members who could lean either way if it came to the crunch. If they got wind that we had *not* caused the explosion, that we were simply doing what we are, in fact, doing, they could very easily turn against us and make our future untenable. So, since I have been given the task of dealing with this matter, I have come to an understanding with John. I will supply him with the information he needs, but it will all appear to be an RUC operation. It starts tonight. Some time tonight, hopefully this evening, I will give John a man to arrest – one of those we suspect as organizing the bombing. John will bring him in for questioning. I will be there too.' At that point Reilly stopped, opened an eye and looked at Asher, who nodded. 'From this man we will, I hope, find out most of what we want to know. After that – ' Reilly sat up and spread his hands. 'After that who knows?'

'Who is this man you are going to question?' the Colonel wanted to know.

'Later. You'll be told later, Colonel. John, I'm sure will tell you. There are a few little arrangements to be made before he is arrested.'

'Does that satisfy you?' Maddox asked of Asher, clearly seeking an ally.

Asher nodded, 'I'm satisfied if everything works out as Seamus says.'

'Very well,' the Colonel said. 'I'll go along as long as John is happy.'

'Thank you, Colonel,' Reilly said politely, but in a tone that suggested he had known from the beginning he was going to have his way. 'There is one other thing.'

'Oh?' The Colonel didn't like the sound of that.

'Yes. Fisher. Your spy, Colonel. I may want to have another talk with him. He could be in danger now, and I gave him my word I would take care of him. If I contact you could you see to it that he leaves his barracks at a given time?'

'I could, but – '

'Thank you, Colonel,' Reilly interrupted.

Later as they drove home together Maddox turned to Asher, his shoulders heaving with mirth, but there was only a dry humour in his voice. 'You know what we've done, John? We've agreed to everything that damned Reilly wanted, and all he's given us is what is probably a cock-and-bull story about the righteousness of the damn IRA.'

Asher chuckled. 'I wondered if you had noticed that. Still, we'll know later tonight, won't we?'

As promised Thomas Regan telephoned Seamus Reilly at three on the dot. Their conversation was brief. 'No, Thomas, we won't need Fisher until tomorrow at the earliest. As soon as I know I'll get a message to you. Just you carry on and get Wilson's body into that shed. I'd like it done just after it gets dark if you can manage it.'

'I'll see to it, Mr Reilly.'

'Once you've done it get well away from that area and phone me. Don't phone me until you are well clear. Understand?'

'I understand, Mr Reilly.'

'Good man.'

It was well into the afternoon before Eddie McCluskey returned home. He was pretty drunk. He had spent several hours in a pub trying to drown the woman's screams that pierced his brain. And he was tired and scared, so the welcome he got was not what he wanted.

'And what time of the day do you think it is to be coming home?' his mother demanded, her hands on her bulging hips, her huge frame blocking the narrow hallway. Eddie ignored her question, pushing his way past her and climbing the linoleum-covered stairs.

In bed he shivered like an animal trying to warm itself. He was very frightened. He had thought of making off across the border but had soon realized the uselessness of such action. He curled himself up. No matter where he went if Reilly wanted him Reilly would find him, so bed, with its hope of oblivion, seemed as good a place as any to wait for the inevitable. And, indeed, he did manage to sleep, albeit fitfully. Once he opened his eyes and listened, trying to ascertain what had woken him. It was already dark, but there was no suspicious sound, only the laughter from the television downstairs as his mother watched some gameshow. Then, outside, a bin rattled, and he sat up, holding the blankets up to his neck, looking absurdly modest. There was silence again, and he slid back down in the bed, waiting to drift back into sleep.

Half an hour later Thomas Regan telephoned Seamus Reilly. 'All done, Mr Reilly.'

· FOURTEEN ·

FOUR RUC LANDROVERS and an unmarked car drove in convoy across the city. When they arrived at their destination they split up, one moving to each end of the street, blocking the entrance, the other two driving behind the car and stopping with as little noise as possible outside the dingy little house. Inspector Asher stepped from the car and directed the operation, not speaking, using only hand signals. But there was no mistaking his intent. In seconds the front door of the house had been smashed open and the security forces were piling in. Eddie McCluskey heard the rumpus from his bed. His reaction would have been comic were it not so pathetic: he pulled the blankets over his head and lay there, cuddled up, whimpering. Soon he was dragged from his bed and hustled down the stairs, his bare feet not once touching the ground. He saw his mother ineffectually trying to barge her way past two officers, heard her resort to verbal abuse. Then he was outside on the pavement. There was a strange eeriness about the place. Nobody spoke. The men's boots made no noise. The Landrovers, their engines cut, stood like grey, ghostly monsters waiting to be fed. He was kept standing on the pavement in his underclothes, and that was the worst part: waiting for something awful to happen. Then, far in the distance, an ambulance keened towards them. An engine was kicked to life and one of the Landrovers reversed, leaving the end of the street unobstructed. All the officers turned their heads and stared in the direction of the approaching ambulance, by now its blue winking light visible. Up the narrow street it came at full speed, looked, for a second, as if it was about to go screaming by, but in the nick of time skidded to a halt, swaying on its springs, the back doors already open. Asher pointed to the house with his hand, his arm at full stretch as though on traffic duty. Two men lifted a stretcher from the ambulance, and made for the front door, stopping for one stride to hear Asher's whispered instruction. McCluskey gaped. For a second he thought that perhaps, with luck, he was dreaming: when he saw Wilson's body on the stretcher he went to pieces, giving a long, high-pitched wail that belonged to a wounded animal.

Seamus Reilly waited at his home for Asher to pick him up as arranged. He sat at the kitchen table, a newspaper spread out in front of him. Across the top of the front page CONFERENCE HOTEL BLAST LEAVES 3 DEAD, 32 INJURED AND ONE MISSING was emblazoned, and under that, in even bolder print THATCHER DEFIES IRA BOMBER. There was a photograph of the damaged hotel, and scattered about the page were other headlines as though the editor had been unable to make up his mind which to use and hit upon the idea of using them all. TEBBIT AND CHIEF WHIP HURT AMID FALLING RUBBLE . . . FIFTEEN STAY IN HOSPITAL OVERNIGHT. . . JOSEPH SLEEPS THROUGH. . . CHIEF WHIP'S WIFE KILLED. . . INQUIRY ON SECURITY BLUNDER STARTS. . . FITZ-GERALD IS SHOCKED BY IRA . . . . And then, incredibly, with equal boldness the information that there was £22,000 TO BE WON in some oddity known as PORTFOLIO. Reilly smiled grimly, cynically wondering if it had anything to do with the price of death. It was something that had never ceased to amaze him: the view the British took of death. Of all the killings that had taken place in Britain the one that had most outraged them was the bombing in Hyde Park simply, it was clear, because of the injury to the horses. At that moment, John Asher arrived.

'No problems I hope?' Reilly asked as they sat together in the car, weaving their way through the evening traffic.

'None.'

'Where have you taken him?'

'Castlereagh.'

'Oh.'

Asher gave a little laugh. 'Don't worry. We'll let you out again.' Seriously he then asked: 'How do you think we should handle this?'

Reilly considered the question for a moment before speaking. 'I *think* the best thing would be for you to question him alone at first, John. I don't expect he'll tell you much. He wouldn't, you see, be all that afraid of the RUC. He might even have visions of martyrdom. Indeed, I can see that prison might seem very attractive to him – keep him out of my clutches, so to speak. And the longer you question him without result the more cocky he'll get. When he starts to smirk at you then I think you could bring me in,' he concluded with a satisfied, smug grin.

'And when you're finished?'

'When I've got the information I want you can do whatever you like with him. Charge him. Lock him up and forget all about him. Shoot him,' Reilly suggested, clearly joking. 'Any damn thing you want. He'll be no further use to me. Or to our plan of campaign,' he added thoughtfully.

As expected Seamus Reilly's prognostication was proved correct. McCluskey told Asher nothing. He sat on the wooden chair gazing glazedly at his interrogator. After half an hour his attitude started to change. He pretended to be bored, looking away and whistling through his teeth when posed a question. In an hour he was smirking. At his first smirk John Asher went to the door and whispered to the guard outside. Three minutes later the door opened and Seamus Reilly came in. Immediately he broke into a wide friendly smile. 'Ah, Eddie,' he said. 'You're just the man I want to see.'

Eddie McCluskey winced, but decided he might as well try and brazen it out. 'Hello, Mr Reilly.'

'Always the cool one, eh?' Reilly asked. 'And always the idiot. Well, I don't have time for any of your old crap, Eddie. You've had your little game with Inspector Asher here.' Reilly suddenly kicked the spare chair and sent it crashing into the wall. 'I've got questions, and I want the answers so you better come up with them.'

'Mr Reilly, I – '

Reilly's fist thumped down on the table, making McCluskey jump and cringe backwards. 'Shut up!' he shouted, then he turned away, licking the spots of saliva from the corners of his mouth, composing himself. When he faced McCluskey he was his calm, cold self again. 'First,' he said holding aloft one finger, 'in this – this – this coven of yours, how many are there besides you and Moran and that woman?'

'Nobody else, Mr Reilly. Honest to God. Just the three of us.'

Reilly nodded, accepting what he knew was the truth. 'Second, what do you know about the bomb in Brighton last night?'

Stupidly McCluskey tried to act innocent. 'What bomb, Mr – '

In a flash Reilly was round the table. He grabbed McCluskey by the short hairs on the nape of his neck and yanked him up (a painful but effective trick he remembered from his schooldays, a device perfected by the Christian Brothers), making him scream with pain. After a second Reilly released him, pushing him back into the chair. 'Second, what do you know about the bomb in Brighton last night?' he asked again.

'Nothing, Mr Reilly. I swear to God I know nothing.'

Reilly let that pass. 'Would Moran know?'

'Jesus no, Mr Reilly. Moran wouldn't know anything about a thing like that.'

'So we're left with your lady friend. She's the one, eh?'

McCluskey gritted his teeth, hesitated, but finally agreed, nodding.

'Now, wasn't that simple enough?' Reilly asked expansively. 'We're getting somewhere at last. She spoke to you about it then?'

'Only this morning. The first I knew of it was when she started cheering after a phone call.'

'Cheering, no less. Who was the phone call from?'

'I don't know.'

Reilly believed him, but there was something in his voice that suggested he might be able to make a pretty good guess. 'Make a guess, Eddie. Who do you think *might* have been on the phone?'

'Maybe someone in Scotland.'

'In Scotland?' Seamus Reilly feigned surprise. 'And why would you guess at someone in Scotland, Eddie?'

'She's been there a couple of times. By herself. I mean with kids. She takes kids over for a holiday. I was never with her. But she might have arranged something over there.'

'She might indeed. Names?'

McCluskey wilted again. 'I don't know any names. Jesus, if I did I'd tell you, Mr Reilly.'

'You might. You might. Where in Scotland?'

'Did she go? Glasgow. Always Glasgow.'

Now that he had capitulated Eddie McCluskey tried to ingratiate himself. He leaned forward on the table, looking intently at Reilly. 'You better watch that one, Mr Reilly. She really hates you. Especially now that you beat her to it and claimed responsibility for the bomb. She's mad you know. Crazy bloody woman. She'll kill you if she can.'

Reilly smiled. 'So would a lot of other people.' He glanced towards Asher who had remained leaning against the door through the entire inquisition. A silent affirmative message passed between them. 'Right,' Reilly announced. 'That's that. Now since you've been a good boy I'll give you a choice. Which would you rather do – live out your life peacefully if in somewhat restricted circumstances, in prison that is,' he explained as he saw McCluskey rummaging in his mind for an understanding, 'or be set free now and be dead within, say, ten minutes?'

Whether it was the lack of option or the precise, matter-of-fact manner in which Reilly offered them that made McCluskey break into a sweat it was impossible to tell. 'Jesus, Mr Reilly, I don't want to die. I haven't done anything. I – '

'So you would prefer to go to prison,' Reilly cut him off.

'I could be killed there too. Jeez – '

'Not by me or anyone connected with me you won't. If you fart-arse around and get your fellow prisoners against you that would be your problem.'

'You mean you wouldn't have me – '

'Killed in prison?' Reilly sounded hurt. 'Certainly not. I've given you the choice.'

McCluskey shrugged. As far as he was concerned there was no choice now. 'Yes. Prison, Mr Reilly.'

'Now that is very sensible, Eddie. I mean you at least stand a chance of getting out one day, don't you? Doesn't he Inspector?'

'Oh yes,' Asher said.

'Now, Eddie, the Inspector will take a statement from you. And what you will say in that statement is quite straight-forward. You will say that yourself and Patrick Moran hit Corporal Wilson over the head and knocked him out. This you did *after* he had left Carson's shop. You put him in the back of your van. You drove him back to your house and put him in the shed at the back of your house. Clear so far?' Reilly asked, speaking very slowly and deliberately as he might have to someone not quite alert or someone very old. Without waiting for an answer he continued. 'After you put him in the shed at the back of your house you shot him. Afraid that he was not quite dead Moran then shot him a second time with a different gun. Then you were sure he was dead. You were going to dump the body only Inspector Asher got to you first. Perfectly simple.'

Eddie McCluskey was so bewildered that he would have agreed to anything, particularly if it was proposed by Seamus Reilly.

'Yes, Mr Reilly I'll swear to that.'

'Now that's being sensible.'

153

As they walked back along the corridor Asher said: 'Was that what you wanted?'

'Oh yes. You can pick up Moran any time after McCluskey has made his statement. The woman is best left to me. And don't forget, John – pop another bullet into Wilson's body. There's supposed to be two. We'd look a right pair of fools if after all this they could only find one bullet.'

Reilly gave a small shudder as he went out of the gates, and bestowed a wary smile on Asher.

'Glad to be out then?' Asher asked.

'Damn place gives me the creeps.'

'It's your guilty conscience, Seamus.'

Reilly opened the car door and got in. Closing the door he lowered the window. 'I suppose,' he said, flicking his thumb towards the driver, 'he knows I'm an innocent?'

Asher laughed. 'He knows he can drop you off wherever you want, if that's what you mean. Good night, Seamus.'

'Hopefully.'

Alone in the back seat Reilly lit a cigar. He was, so far, well pleased. Not that he had gleaned much new information, but he had had it confirmed, if by guesswork, that the actual bomb planters had been brought down from Glasgow. That was one thing. Something else that satisfied him was that Major Fisher would not be thought of as having murdered his colleague. Not that Reilly had a soft spot for the Major. He hadn't; but he knew Fisher would be more – more manageable when he learned of Reilly's kindness; he would be far more likely to look kindly on what Reilly was going to suggest to him; he would fulfil his role in the scheme of things – of that Seamus Reilly was certain.

Reilly might, however, have been rather less certain of Fisher's malleability had he overheard the conversation that took place between Colonel Maddox and Fisher the next morning. Fisher was looking dismal as the day was cold. Colonel Maddox made a great show of making him relax. 'Do you know what my grandmother used to say, Fisher? Eh? She lived to be a hundred and one, and she always said there were only two things in life that kept a person sane: reading *The Wind in the Willows* and several strong drinks of whisky every day. Actually,' the Colonel confided. 'she said tea, but a small transposition is valid, don't you think? Now drink that,' he ordered, handing Fisher a tumbler half-filled with Teachers, 'and the world will seem a different place.'

Fisher took the tumbler and drank; and for a moment it looked as if it might work. Alas, only for a moment. 'Sir, I can't take it any more. Can you transfer me back to England?'

Maddox, his glass half-way to his lips, looked pained, and put the glass back on his desk without drinking. As ever when upset and seeking words he took to turning the signet ring on his little finger, rubbing it as if this would bring forth its magic powers; but there was no sign of magic when he spoke. 'I'm afraid that is not possible, Major. I only wish it was. I wish we could all get away from this place. But we are here for a reason and here we must stay. You know, this is the third time I've been here? It gets no easier, no less bitter.'

None of which was what Major Fisher wanted to hear. His hands were shaking and he had difficulty getting the glass to his mouth; when he did he gulped the whisky down, the tumbler rattling against his teeth.

'It has often struck me,' Maddox went on, somehow feeling that by just talking he could calm the Major, 'that there are only two kinds of people – the manipulated and the manipulators. From time to time both change sides and reverse roles. For the moment we, you and I, are the manipulated, but this is not always a bad thing. You will have to believe me when I tell you that you must stay, just as I must stay. Because of the – ' Maddox hesitated, ' – the situation, we have been forced to form links with strange allies, people who many would regard as our enemies, as terrorists. That is the real horror of war, you know – the hypocrisy, the intrigue and treachery, the survival of the guilty and the death of the innocent.'

If Maddox knew what he was talking about, Fisher certainly didn't. 'Sir, I – '

Maddox held up a hand. 'Please, Major, don't make me refuse you again. You are needed here, now more than ever. The two men who forced you to – forgive me – to kill Wilson have been arrested – oh, don't be alarmed,' he said quickly as he saw the look of consternation in Fisher's eyes. 'Indeed no. They have been persuaded – Seamus Reilly's word – to confess to the murder of Wilson. What you did in that barn is your secret. Even I have forgotten about it. Only you now know – you and your God if you have one.' Maddox paused. Then: 'But the third person, the woman, is still at large. Reilly believes it was she who organized that bomb in Brighton. He wants her. He is, really, doing our job for us – oh, not out of the goodness of his heart: for his own reasons, but he can do it far more efficiently than we could. He has told me he may require your help. I told him he could count on it.'

'I don't understand, sir.'

Maddox smiled gently. 'You will. Please trust my judgement. Just make your peace with yourself. Be patient. Help me in this matter.'

Bewildered and frightened Fisher was touched by the Colonel's plea for help. It had a kindness and loneliness about it with which he could easily identify. It was as though the Colonel, too, felt abandoned. 'Very well, sir. I'm sorry, sir. Sorry for making – '

Maddox held a finger to his lips. 'Shh,' he whispered. 'You'll come out of this all right, Major. I'm sure of it.'

Two hours later when Seamus Reilly phoned him and asked if he could arrange for the Major to be available at three o'clock, the Colonel agreed.

'Thank you, Colonel.' 'If possible outside St Enoch's.'

'Very well. Just one thing. I'm holding you responsible for anything that happens to him.'

'That is understood. I've already told him he will be safe in my protection.'

'For your sake I hope he is. I can promise you, Reilly, if anything happens to him I will have you crucified. I promise you that.'

Reilly sounded amused. 'Thank you, Colonel,' he said and rang off.

'That's fixed,' Reilly told Regan as he returned to his sitting room. 'Maddox has agreed. The Major will be at St Enoch's at three o'clock. Have O'Neill pick him up and bring him here, will you?'

'Certainly, Mr Reilly.'

'You have the woman covered?'

'Oh yes. I've had men watching her house all day. She's still in there. They've seen her look out of the window several times but she hasn't set foot outside the house.'

'I'm going to have to send Fisher to her. We'll have to take the chance that she believes what he tells her.'

'Will she?'

'Huh. I wish I knew. She might. She just might. He'll be the only contact she has. I hope to God Asher got that report of the arrests into the evening papers. It's vital she sees that.'

'Suppose she doesn't go out for a paper.'

Reilly tutted, irked that he had been misunderstood. 'No. I want Fisher to bring one with him when he goes. If he can produce that as evidence it will give credence to the story he'll tell her. God, I hope Asher got it in.'

The woman had calmed down, although it had taken her the best part of the day to do it. At first, alone when Eddie McCluskey had been unceremoniously ejected, her fury had sustained her, keeping the danger of her own position in the background of her mind. But in the evening, still alone, her solitude less bearable in the dark, the first creeping apprehensions started to surface. She had failed, and failure was like a sentence of living death: she would, she now realized, be an outcast. But she hadn't failed, dammit. She had succeeded, only Seamus Reilly had out-manoeuvred her, and the promises she had made with such bravado had been brought to nought, leaving her exposed and fair game to be ridiculed.

She made no attempt to sleep. All through the night she paced about. She thought about contacting McCluskey and Moran but rejected the idea, fearing although unwilling to admit it, that they, too, would have abandoned her.

By dawn she was scheming again, the full force of her loathing directed at attaining revenge on Seamus Reilly. No easy matter at the best of times; even less now. But somehow, somehow, somehow she would bring the bastard down. The more her rage subsided the more she was prepared to concede that it was her pride urging her on. So what? For far too long she had been 'tolerated'. That's all bloody Irish men did anyway: tolerate their women. Useful but brainless. She fixed herself a large gin and tonic. Purposefully she stood in front of the mirror as she drank, watching herself, eyeing her image, wondering what the nuns would have made of the dear little Catholic girl who had been so sweet, so pretty, so holy at Mass, so good at her catechism: the demure, shy, alert girl who had spoken so often of joining the convent. That was so long ago. Brutishly she stuck out her tongue at her reflection, aware that the silly action was only to counteract the tears she felt welling into her eyes. So bloody long ago . . .

– They've killed your Daddy, Mammy told her.

She had not understood.

– They've killed your poor Daddy and taken your brothers away.

Still it had meant nothing.

– They've left only you and me to fend for ourselves. Oh, Holy Mother of God how are we going to manage?

It wasn't until months later when her favourite brother died from hunger in prison that the awfulness began to sink in. Then her second brother, Peadar, never the bright one but harmless and kind, came home. He had changed terribly. Always afraid. Hiding himself away in dark places. And Mammy having to try and find him and bring him out to eat; sometimes not bothering and bringing his food to him, putting the plate on the floor in front of him like he was an animal. That was when she knew about the awfulness.

– Don't you worry, Mammy. They'll never do anything like that to us again.

– There's no one left for them to do it to, girl.

– They'll be sorry. I promise you, Mammy, they'll be sorry.

And Mammy had looked at her fondly and stroked her hair, her lovely long and shining hair . . . .

She shook herself away from the dreams and moved to the window, peering out. It was drizzling and grey and un-welcoming. A car drove past, its tyres hissing on the damp street. Two girls, giggling, hugging themselves together under an umbrella, trotted along the pavement apparently playing at two-legged racing. The woman shivered and left the window. *Do* something, she told herself. But what was there to do? Whatever there was it could not be done now, she decided. Later. Tonight. When it got dark. She would do something then, and she had until then to think about what to do. She added a drop more gin to her drink.

Major Fisher felt much the better for Colonel Maddox's pep-talk. He felt quite calm and at peace as the car drove him to Seamus Reilly's house, even to the point of asking good-humouredly: 'No blindfold this time?'

'Not this time,' Sean O'Neill told him. 'My orders didn't say anything about a blindfold.'

'And you always follow orders.'

'Yes. Yes I do.'

Seamus Reilly was waiting for them. He dismissed O'Neill to the kitchen with 'make yourself a cup of tea, Sean,' and, taking Fisher by the arm guided him into the sitting room. 'You'll never believe it,' he said chattily, 'but I got my first Christmas card this morning. From New Zealand. And you know something? I haven't a clue who it's from,' he admitted, finding this amusing and chortling away.

Encouraged by the friendliness, Fisher ventured: 'Perhaps it's one of last year's just arriving.'

Seamus Reilly enjoyed the joke. He threw back his head and

laughed. 'I never thought of that. You're probably right. I still don't know who sent it though.' Then, with a complete about-face of humour, his eyes darkening, he went on: 'Colonel Maddox has spoken to you?'

'Yes. This morning.'

'He explained that I need you to do something for me?'

'He said something about it.'

Again Reilly switched his humour, this time becoming paternal and concerned. 'You must be puzzled by the webs we weave,' he said. 'I certainly would be if I was you. The Colonel is – or he *was*, but I think he understands us better now. You see, we are not all monsters as some people would have you believe – the same people, mind you, who, for some unknown, perverse reason refuse to believe that we, too, only want peace. They think we *enjoy* killing.' Reilly stopped and shook his head as though still trying to fathom the reason for the folly. 'Nothing could be further from the truth,' he added, then paused again. Suddenly he became very businesslike. 'But you didn't come here to listen to me philosophizing, did you?'

Fisher managed a small smile.

'Of course you didn't. Right. You'll be wanting to know what it is I need you to do?'

Fisher nodded warily.

Reilly smiled. 'Still don't trust me? Never mind. Why should you? You don't know me. I never trust anyone I don't know. To tell the truth I'm not so sure I trust them when I *do* know them. But you can believe it when I say that I will take care of you. I won't ask you to do anything that might endanger your life.'

Fisher accepted this with another slow nod.

'Now, where was I? Ah. The Colonel will have told you about the two boyos? The ones who made you dispose of the unfortunate Corporal?'

'Yes. Thanks. He told me you made them confess to the shooting.'

'Well, in principle they did it, didn't they? Besides, it suited me that way. Which leaves us with one more to deal with.'

'The woman?'

'Exactly. That damned, accursed woman. A silly bitch really. Fancies herself as a sort of leader of the underdogs,' Reilly told Fisher scathingly. 'I'll tell you for nothing that she abominates me,' he went on, rubbing his hands together as though he relished being abominated. 'But I'm afraid she's bitten off a bit more than she can chew this time. With your help she is, so to speak, about to choke.'

Reilly rose to his feet and planted himself in front of the electric fire, warming his backside. After a few seconds he began to speak again in a slow, careful voice. 'What I want you to do is this. At eight o'clock tonight I will have you taken to her house. You will be given a newspaper in which there should be a report on the arrest of McCluskey and Moran – your two friends. If the report is not in the paper you won't have to bring one, but I am assured that it will be in there. She will be suspicious, of course, and the first thing she'll want to know is how you found out where she lives. You tell her – now listen to this carefully – you tell her that Sandy told you. She'll check on that but I'll have arranged that she hears what she wants to hear. The next thing you tell her is that you were hauled in before the Colonel – don't be specific – just the Colonel. If she insists on a name tell her Maddox. Now, the Colonel tells you he has reports that you have been seen associating – that's the word, isn't it? – with McCluskey and Moran. He further tells you that McCluskey and Moran have been arrested in connection with the bombing in Brighton. He also tells you that there is a woman involved and wants to know what *you* know about this woman. All right so far?'

Fisher nodded.

'Now, most importantly, the Colonel wants to know what you can tell him about certain people in Glasgow. He tells you their names but you can't for the life of you remember them since you don't know them in the first place. Clear?'

'Yes. I think so.'

'All through this you've got to look as though you're starting to panic. Try gibbering,' Reilly suggested with a little grin. 'I don't know how you gibber but try it. I am certain she will want to know the names the Colonel is supposed to have given you. I'm banking on that. I'm banking on her trying to jog your memory by suggesting a few names. She's no fool, though. She'll probably start off by giving you any old name. But I want you to memorize every name she suggests. Every single name. Got that?'

'Yes.'

'That's all I want. The names. When you've got those you can get out of there any way you can. You'll be picked up again on your way back to your barracks and brought here. But forget everything else. Just keep repeating the names over and over to yourself so that you can give them to me. As soon as you get here blurt them out. No hellos or how are yous or anything else. Just spit out the names. Can I count on you for that?'

'I'll do my best.'

Reilly shook his head. 'I'm afraid your best isn't good enough. I've got to have names,' he stressed almost vehemently.

'I'll get them.'

Reilly relaxed and smiled. 'That's just what I wanted to hear. Thank you, Major.'

From his tone of voice it was clear that Reilly considered the meeting over. Fisher stood up. 'Is that everything?'

Reilly nodded. 'Yes. That's everything. Enough I would think. You can, as we say, go in peace,' he said with a mischievous grin. 'Of course you would know that. You're Catholic, aren't you?'

'Yes.'

'Ah. More than ever difficult for you, then, this – what you've been through,' Reilly said, then his eyes twinkled and he added. 'Not that non-Catholics would have found it easy, but they're not quite as crucified to their religion as we are, are they? They seem to find it possible to escape now and then for a breather, for a breath of fresh heretical air. Whereas we – ' He shrugged. 'Go on. Off you go. You can make your peace with God in your own time.'

Fisher gave a hard, sharp laugh. 'You're the second person who said that to me. The Colonel said all I had to do was make my peace with God too.'

Reilly looked surprised. 'You surprise me. It's not something I would have thought the Colonel would say. Perhaps he *does* understand,' he added vaguely. 'Anyway,' he went on again, 'do what he says. It's always better to have the Lord on your side. And He's not as intolerant as He used to be,' Seamus pointed out, coming across the room and leaning close to the Major as if he was about to impart a deep secret. 'We've broadened His mind considerably,' he whispered in his ear.

Fisher looked as if he might be about to make some reply but was forestalled by the telephone ringing in the hall. Reilly excused himself politely and left the room; in no time he was back, beaming. 'The report I mentioned. It's in all the papers. That will help you no end.'

Fisher looked dubious still, but nodded none the less.

'Well, what can I say?' Reilly asked. 'Good luck and mind how you go. I'll see you later tonight when hopefully all this will be over and done with.'

'Yes. Hopefully.'

'O'Neill,' Seamus Reilly called, and when O'Neill came trotting from the kitchen he added: 'Take this gentleman back to where you met him.'

'Yes, Mr Reilly.'

Closing the front door behind them Seamus Reilly leaned his back against it and closed his eyes. That's all he had to live for, he thought. Hope.

It was with not much more than hope, too, that Major Fisher hammered on the door of the woman's house with his fist. He seemed to be left hammering for a long time, but he persevered, grinning once when he thought of Reilly's advice to gibber. There was a spyhole in the door and, though he could not be certain, he would have sworn he was being peered at. Finally the door opened. 'Christ!' the woman swore 'What the – come in for Christ's sake,' she whispered and dragged him into the hall by the sleeve.

Immediately Fisher began to blurt out his message. 'I didn't know what to do or where to go. When Sandy gave me your address I had to come round. What am I going to do? You've got to help me.'

The woman was taken aback by this onslaught, and for the moment the only thing she could think of to do was bring the wretch into her kitchen and give him a drink. 'What's the matter with you?' she asked absurdly as she started the kettle to boil.

'You don't know? You don't know those two blokes have been arrested?'

'What two blokes?' the woman asked still at a loss.

'*Your* two blokes. Look there's pictures of them in the paper,' Fisher told her and opened the paper for her to see.

Disbelieving and seeming to sense some invisible trap the woman came to the table and stared at the paper. 'Holy Jesus,' she whispered, her face growing pale.

'And that's not all,' Fisher went on, pushing his advantage. 'I've been hauled in to the Colonel.'

'What for?' the woman snapped.

'What for? For associating with those two,' Fisher said pointing to the photograph. 'You know what those two were up to, don't you? Only blowing up that hotel in Brighton. Not only them. There's a whole gang of them in Glasgow.'

The woman looked away. She walked to the far end of the table and sat down, ignoring the boiling water, allowing the kettle to switch itself off. 'Glasgow,' she whispered, possibly to herself.

'Yes Glasgow. He read me a whole list of names asking me which ones I'd heard of.'

The woman became immediately alert. 'Names? What names?'

Fisher put on a great act of exasperation. 'I don't know. I wasn't hardly listening. I don't know anyone in Glasgow,' he said. Then noticing what he felt might be her interest waning he added quickly. 'One I think I remember. Murphy, I think. Or Murray. Yea – Murray, that's it. Murray.'

'Any others?'

'I can't remember I tell you.'

'Jameson?' the woman suggested.

Fisher shook his head miserably. Jameson he memorized. 'Rourk?'

Again he shook his head. Rourk.

'Masterson?'

Better not be too dumb. 'What was that one?'

'Masterson.'

Fisher grimaced. 'That could have been one.' Masterson.

'Drumm?'

'No.' Drumm.

'Mulcahy?'

Fisher took to shaking his head again. Mulcahy.

The woman got to her feet and switched on the kettle again. 'What else?' she demanded.

'What else what?'

'Did they ask you.'

Fisher looked blank. 'Nothing. Jesus wasn't that enough? You've got to help me get out of this.'

Drumming her fingers on the worktop the woman said 'Yes, yes, yes,' but clearly without meaning it. 'What about me? Was I mentioned?' she demanded at last.

Fisher shook his head. 'I don't know. I don't even know your name, do I? There was nothing that sounded like a woman's name though.'

'I see,' the woman said, the fear in her eyes a little less.

'Yea, but what about *me*?' Fisher pushed on. 'What am I going to do?'

'You just sit still there a minute,' he was told. 'Make yourself some tea if you want it. I've a call to make.'

Alone Fisher ran through the names: Jameson, Rourk, Masterson, Drumm, Mulcahy. He repeated them over and over. He could hear the murmur of a voice coming from another room, and was on the point of going to the door to see if he could pick up any of the words when the voice stopped. Almost immediately the woman came back in. She looked, somehow, less tense, and when she spoke there was more confidence in her voice. Fisher was trying to make out the reason for this when she told him. 'That was Sandy,' she said. 'He says Eddie,' the woman pointed to the open newspaper, 'told him to send you here.'

Fisher looked at the paper. 'This one? Edward McCluskey?'

'Yes.'

Fisher shrugged. 'I don't know anything about that. All I know is that I went to Sandy's to try and find – eh – McCluskey after the Colonel had me in, and Sandy said I was to get round here as fast as I could.'

The woman smiled ominously. 'But what I can't understand is why the Colonel would let you wander off out of the barracks if he thought you were – '

Fisher decided to shout. 'He fucking well didn't. I *got* out. I'm not supposed to *be* out. I'm on the bloody run. That's why you've got to help me.'

For several seconds the woman stared into his pleading eyes without blinking. Then she blinked once. 'Well, you can't stay here, that's for sure. Can you make your way back to Sandy's without getting picked up?'

'I don't know. I expect so.'

'Well do that. I'll phone him again and tell him to expect you. He'll put you up for a day or two. Then I'll get you out.'

'You're sure?'

'Of course I'm sure.'

'You better. God knows what those two are saying,' Fisher pointed out, emphasizing his urgency by picking up the newspaper and shaking it.

'I said I'd get you out. Just you do what Sandy tells you to.'

'All right.'

'You better get moving. Out the back way. If you cut through the first street on your left it'll bring you back out onto the main road. You know your way from there.'

'Yes.'

Seamus Reilly had clearly been on tenterhooks. He opened the door before O'Neill had time to knock; and worried that Fisher might say something before giving him the names he took him by the arm and guided him immediately into the sitting room, all the while making a curious circular motion with his other hand as though he was winding an ancient, invisible phonograph. He sat Fisher in a chair and took a writing pad and ballpoint pen from the table by the fire. Holding the biro poised he said 'Now.'

Fisher closed his eyes and started the litany. 'Jameson. Rourk. Masterson. Drumm. Mulcahy.' He repeated the names again.

Reilly checked his list, his eyes shining. 'You did excellently,' he announced finally. 'No problems?'

Fisher shook his head. 'I'm supposed to be on my way to Sandy's now. He will get a call from the woman to tell him to hide me for a few days.'

'Good man,' Reilly told him. Then he turned to O'Neill. 'Get me Sandy on the phone.'

'I'm on the run from the army now,' Fisher contributed.

'Of course you are,' Seamus told him delightedly. 'Actually what you're going to do, Major, is stay in your barracks for the next few days. Colonel Maddox will see to it that you're relieved of all duties. He'll probably put you on the sick list.'

Fisher nodded.

'I've got Sandy, Mr Reilly,' O'Neill said, sticking his head round the door.

Reilly went immediately to the phone, coughing to clear his throat as he went. 'Sandy?'

'Yes, Mr Reilly.'

'Have you had a call from that woman yet?'

'I have. A couple of minutes ago. I'm supposed to stow someone for a few days. That Brit. He's on his way here now.'

'He isn't. He's here. Now listen. Give it ten minutes and call her back – you have her number?'

Sandy chuckled. 'Yea. She just gave it to me. I'm supposed to confirm that he's arrived.'

'Good. In ten minutes do just that. Tell her he's arrived safely and that you're sending him to the piggery later tonight.'

'Okay, Mr Reilly.'

'Now, at 10.15 exactly – exactly mind – I want you to call her again. I need her occupied for five minutes. What you say to her doesn't matter, just keep her on the phone for five minutes – got that?'

'Ring her at a quarter past ten exactly and keep her talking for five minutes. Yea, I've got that.'

'Fine. Now one more thing, Sandy. At 11.30 you're to call her again. This time you say that Fisher is causing trouble. Tell her he's refusing to stay at the piggery. Tell her he's going berserk and wants to get back to his barracks unless he can talk to her. You've got to make it sound desperate. I want that damn woman to go to the piggery.'

'I'll get her to go all right, Mr Reilly. You needn't worry about that.'

'She might just ask you to accompany her, Sandy. Don't. I want her to drive there alone. If she asks you to send someone else with her you'll have to wangle your way out of it. She's got to go alone. Clear?'

'Yes, Mr Reilly.'

'Good. I'll see to it that we don't forget this.'

'That's all right, Mr Reilly.'

'Thank you.'

When he came back to the sitting room, Seamus Reilly was his old businesslike self again; when he spoke his words were crisp and to the point. 'Right, O'Neill. Take the Major back. See him safely home. Then get in touch with Regan. Who's our mechanic?' he asked suddenly.

'Jimmy Doyle, Mr Reilly.'

'Tell Regan to pick up Doyle and bring him here. I want them here within the next hour. If you can't contact Regan, pick up Doyle yourself and bring him. You'll be able to find Doyle I suppose?'

'No problem. He's always in that garage of his in the evening.

Doing up some E-Type he got cheap. He'll be there without a doubt.'

'Good. Go on then. We don't have a lot of time.' Then Reilly turned to the Major. 'Thank you again,' he said, sounding sincere enough. 'I think you can safely say you'll be back in England before long. And don't forget what I told you – God is a lot more broadminded than they would have us believe.'

John Asher was peeved to be taken from his supper. His indigestion was bad enough without having his meals interrupted. But he soon forgot about his discomfort when he sensed the urgency in Seamus Reilly's voice. He listened intently, his eyes narrowing from time to time, then widening in surprise. He answered the few questions Reilly posed as briefly as he could, always in the affirmative. His longest statement came just before he hung up. 'I'll leave at once,' he said. And he did, throwing on his overcoat and leaving the house at the trot.

Colonel Maddox, also, was none too pleased to be called from the sparse comfort of his quarters. Indeed, when he came downstairs and confronted John Asher he was positively waspish. 'What is it *now*, John?' he asked.

'I'm sorry to disturb you, Colonel, but it is very urgent. I've just had Seamus Reilly on to me.'

'And what does *he* want?' Maddox demanded, sounding weary but keeping the sting in his voice.

Asher glanced about the hallway, obviously uneasy that he might be overheard. 'Could we – ?' he suggested, indicating a doorway.

'If we must.'

Maddox led the way across the hall and opened the door. Almost at once he backed out and shut it again. 'In use,' he informed Asher, now sounding thoroughly annoyed. 'We'll go in there.'

In there was the gents toilet, and Maddox strode towards it. 'Now what is so damned urgent?'

'The woman, Colonel. Reilly has arranged for us to pick her up. He's arranging for her to drive towards the border near Clones but he's had her car fixed so that it will break down before she gets there.'

'Well, pick her up, why don't you?'

'It had better be a military operation. To get sufficient men out I'd have to make too many explanations, and I don't have time to explain. '

'And on what excuse do I pick her up?'

'Not that you need one, Colonel, but Reilly has arranged that too. The boot of her car will be well stocked with explosives. If you could just have her taken in to Castlereagh we will do the rest.'

'And where is this car supposed to break down?'

Asher had been afraid of that. 'Reilly couldn't, of course, be absolutely sure. He thinks it should be about two miles this side of the border. You'd have to order her to be shadowed. A helicopter could do it nicely,' he concluded, slurring his concluding words upwards into a question.

'I'm sure it could,' the Colonel remarked sarcastically.

Feeling that time was being wasted and that he had not yet quite won the Colonel round, Asher went on. 'Major Fisher did everything he could to assist us in this matter, sir. He was most helpful. It would be cruel to have his efforts go to waste.'

'Very well,' the Colonel agreed at last. 'Wait in the hall, John, and I'll send someone down to you. Captain Young probably would be best. You can brief him.'

'Thank you, Colonel.'

'I just hope you two know what you're doing. The flak is already coming in from London. I'll have to give them something soon.'

'You can, Colonel.'

'You sound very sure.'

'I *am* sure.'

'Huh. I didn't think that was ever possible in this wretched place.'

The woman reversed her car out of the short, steep driveway. Sandy's phone call had been the final straw; although every instinct warned against going to the piggery, it was a risk, she told herself, she had to take: all she needed was that whingeing bloody Brit shooting off his mouth and then the shit really would hit the fan. She switched on the windscreen wipers as the rain suddenly bucketed down. Bugger Sandy for not coming. It was always the same: whenever you needed someone to help you in an emergency they always had excuses. Constantly she looked in her mirror as she drove through and out of the city. Nothing. All the good citizens were safely tucked up in their beds. Prods and Catholics alike needed their goddam beauty sleep. She slowed down at a crossroads and was about to curse as the engine coughed and almost stalled, but it picked up again grudgingly and on she went.

The nearer she got to the border the more relaxed she became, even dismissing the continued pinking of the engine as a minor hazard, putting it down to the damp: every year it gave the same trouble. When all this was behind her she would celebrate by trading it in for something more reliable. A helicopter flew overhead, quite low. More fucking Paras on their way to terrify the shit out of some poor unfortunate. She watched its winking lights veer away and disappear behind a hillock. Maybe it had turned back. Even the mighty fucking Paras hated the rain and the dark. Hopefully the bloody thing would crash.

She was about two and a half miles from the border when the car suddenly backfired loudly and came to a clunking standstill. Steam poured from the bonnet, and there were small metallic cracking noises. At first the full extent of her predicament did not seem to strike her: she sat in the car, staring out, strumming the steering wheel with her fingers. The rain had stopped as suddenly as it had begun. She got out of the car and stalked around it. The hissing steam had subsided, and it was probably this that suggested that the engine might hopefully, miraculously have recovered. She was on the point of getting back in behind the wheel and attempting to start it when the helicopter rose from behind the hillock, a glaring searchlight blazing from beneath its undercarriage, momentarily blinding her. Then a squawking megaphonic voice roared at her. '*Get out of the car. Put your hands on the roof. Spread your legs. Do not move.*' If further orders were given they were lost in the whirring whine of the descent, the great blades whipping up a storm, bending the bare branches of the trees that lined the narrow lane. She obeyed, still calm. They would search her, of course. They always started off by searching. And they'd take their time about it, their thick callous fingers groping about and lingering in all her nooks and crannies. They liked doing that, liked to cheapen people. Anything to humiliate. All the time making their lewd suggestions and sneering at one another, boasting of what they could do to her, already doing most of it in their minds. Oh, she'd been through all that. Several times. But she'd survive it yet again, using it to refuel her hatred. Fuck them all. They couldn't detain her. They couldn't do a damn thing. The car had simply broken down. Even here they could not make that an offence.

Three figures emerged from a gateway in the hedge, their faces smeared with black grease, their automatic-rifles thrust out before them. Two of the Paras walked round behind her, each of them grabbing one of her arms and twisting it behind her, yanking her away from the car. The third, seeming huge and sinister in the forged light of flashing torches, went directly to the back of the car and opened the boot. 'Corporal,' he yelled. 'Get that torch over here.'

There was a rustle behind the hedge. A radio crackled for a second and went dead. A fourth figure appeared and went to the back of the car. A flashlight was switched on. 'Take the bitch in.'

Immediately the woman went berserk. She tried to wrench herself free, screaming with the pain. She yelled obscenities and tried to spit at the two Paras holding her. 'You fucking Brit bastards. I've done fuck all.'

The Para left the boot, took two strides towards her, and hit her hard across the face. 'Shut your fucking mouth, you slut.

Done fuck all? What's all this then? Fucking Christmas presents?' He grabbed her by the hair and dragged her to the back of the car, shining the torch back into the boot.

The woman stared in total disbelief. At least half a dozen Armalite rifles. Hand guns. Grenades. Pounds of explosive. Suddenly it all became clear to her. A set-up. Seamus Reilly had set her up. It had to be him – nobody else could have manipulated everyone with such ease. Bloody Seamus Reilly. What a stupid goddam fool she'd been! Without warning she let her body go limp and started to laugh; a wild, crazed, hysterical laugh. And she was still laughing when they threw her into the helicopter and put their boots on her to keep her down.

'They've just sent her over here to Castlereagh,' John Asher told Reilly down the phone.

'Everything went according to plan?'

'Without a hitch.'

Reilly sighed. 'Good.'

'You want to come over now?'

'God no. I'm dead beat, John. Let her stew. She'll keep till the morning. Do her no end of good to wait.'

'Whatever you say. I'm done in myself. Goodnight.'

'Goodnight.'

· FIFTEEN ·

L ATE THE FOLLOWING afternoon the woman was taken in an unmarked car to the docks. Her hands were handcuffed behind her back, and she was made to lie on the floor. She had no shoes, and a woollen cap had been put on her head and pulled down, covering her eyes. John Asher sat on the seat above her, ignoring her for the most part. He was preoccupied, wondering what on earth Reilly had schemed up this time. He obviously knew what he was about: everything had worked like clockwork thus far.

As they approached the main gates a klaxon sounded, signalling the end of the day's work. Immediately, as if they had been on their marks for some minutes, men came streaming out, mostly on foot, but some on bicycles, and a few in cars. John Asher leaned forward towards the front seat. 'Make for number four,' he instructed, peering out over the driver's shoulder. As the crowd thinned the place took on the eeriness engendered by huge, abandoned machinery. Arc lights had been switched on, the massive cranes casting geometric shadows, their criss-cross metallic structure giving Asher the impression he was being driven through penetrable, ghostly chain-link fencing.

Soon the driver brought the car to a halt outside an enormous, low warehouse, the figure 4 painted on its sliding metal doors. Almost before the engine had been switched off Asher was out of the car and making for the entrance. He peered inside, squinting. There was only one small circle of light in the entire warehouse: a high wattage naked bulb suspended over what could have been a rostrum or high desk. Beside this, one arm resting on it, stood Seamus Reilly, flanked by Regan and O'Neill, with Jim Dowling standing a little further back. Asher looked back towards the car and signalled his driver to bring the woman in. He waited for them by the door. As they approached he gestured that the woman be taken towards the light. Then he followed, keeping several paces behind. Nobody spoke. Not even the woman made a sound when the cap was removed; her eyes sought and remained fixed on the small dapper figure under the light. Then Thomas Regan moved forward and took her by one arm, raising it behind her back. The driver unlocked the handcuffs and pocketed them. Reilly leaned a little sideways and nodded to Asher. John Asher spun on his heel and marched from the warehouse, followed by his driver. When Seamus Reilly finally spoke, his tone did nothing to disperse the macabre tension. 'You were told what would happen if you defied our instructions and undertook any action without our sanction, were you not?' he asked, politely enough.

The woman ignored him, transferring her gaze on the bulb over his head.

'We know it was you who masterminded the Brighton bomb,' Reilly went on undeterred. 'We know you got either Drumm or Mulcahy to plant the device. You kindly told us that. Of all the names you suggested to Major Fisher only those two correspond to men we have in the field, both, funnily enough, in Glasgow. We know you made several trips to the city.'

At the mention of Drumm's name, her eyes flickered towards Reilly.

'I might regret having to punish you had you not made Major Fisher shoot one of his colleagues. That was a heinous thing to do. Hence I have no regrets whatsoever about the punishment.'

The woman stared at Reilly with undisguised hatred.

'Have you anything to say?' he asked, being absurdly democratic.

There was a pause. Reilly had half turned away when the woman screamed: 'Yes, Reilly I have something to say. I say fuck you and your likes. You're all full of shit. You think you can talk the fucking Brits into giving us back what is ours. You can't. But you're all too shit scared to put up a fight. They've beaten you, Reilly. They've made you one of their bloody lapdogs. Well the fight will go on no matter what you do with me. There are still some decent fighting men left who won't rest until we've killed every last Brit who has a foot on our soil.'

'Finished?' Reilly asked.

'Fuck you Reilly,' the woman screamed as though she had practised this chant. Then she spat at him.

Seamus Reilly turned to O'Neill and jerked his head towards the woman. 'You and Dowling take care of this, please,' he requested. 'You come with me, Thomas,' he added, and walked quickly from the warehouse.

As arranged John Asher was waiting for him by the dock gates. When he spotted Reilly and Regan approaching he had a quick word with the security guard who promptly closed the door of his little hut and buried his head in a newspaper, holding it with some exaggeration high in front of his face, only emerging when he heard the two cars start up: he came out, locked the gates and, shivering with the cold, returned to his paper. It was a sombre Seamus Reilly who spoke first, not looking at Asher who sat beside him, but fixing his eyes on the reflection in the windscreen of the headlights of his own car that followed. 'You can have your men find her tomorrow, John. A couple of days' silence, I think. Then a brief report.'

Asher nodded. 'Very well.'

Reilly sighed, making a rasping, gargling noise in his throat. 'It never ends,' he said, almost as if he were just thinking aloud. 'Just when it seems – oh, to hell with it,' he concluded abruptly, taking out one of his cigars and lighting it.

They travelled almost half a mile before Asher spoke. 'It's almost over,' he said, trying to be a comfort but managing only to sound wishful.

Reilly shook his head. 'It's never almost over, John. There will always be someone who thinks they know better. Someone who longs for power. Someone who feels we are getting weak. The trouble is a whole generation has grown up in the shadow of violence. For them it is the most normal thing in the world to kill in order to achieve their ends. They don't *think* any more. They simply cannot see that our strength for the future is in politics. Words frighten them. They are tired of words having no immediate, concrete effect.'

'They'll learn,' Asher offered.

'I'm afraid they won't until it is too late. I sometimes wonder if we haven't reared a generation of monsters. And they have youth on their side, with all its rashness. He paused. 'I just don't know what should be done.'

Obviously neither did Asher. 'We'll just have to do what we've done for years – ride it out,' was all he could suggest.

'No. No. No.' Reilly said sadly, pausing between each word to shake his head a couple of times. 'Those days have gone.' Suddenly he gave a short, bitter laugh. 'The glory days we used to call them. Glory!'

The car braked suddenly, throwing the two men forward. Then it moved on slowly, passing two cars involved in a minor collision, both drivers gesticulating wildly at each other. It seemed Seamus Reilly had not noticed. 'Those were the days when even death was glorious,' he continued.

Perhaps in a genuine effort to comfort Reilly, or perhaps, more likely, to relinquish responsibility, Asher said: 'Well, there's not much we can do about it, Seamus. The best we can hope to do is keep things ticking along until some genius comes up with a solution. Just keep things ticking along,' he repeated.

Reilly was still shaking his head. 'It's not enough. It's not enough. Someone has got to take a stand. Someone has got to be *forced* to take a stand,' he said vehemently.

Asher grinned. 'Well, take one,' he said, and was surprised at the sad, tormented look he got from Reilly.

'I might *have* to,' Reilly said. 'That is what frightens me, John. I might just have to.'

The car drew into the side of the road outside Reilly's house. Gratefully John Asher sidestepped any involvement in his friend's remark, by asking: 'What happens next? About the bombers, I mean.'

Reilly chewed his lower lip. 'I'm not altogether sure. I have to clear that. My – my jurisdiction does not cover Scotland. A decision on that will have to come from higher up.'

'Oh. Yes.'

'There's no hurry anyway. They think they're safe. They won't be going anywhere – not without my knowing at any rate.'

'You're sure?'

'Oh I'm sure. Give me a day or two.'

Nobody paid much attention to the small report in the papers a few days later. Who cared if the unidentified body of a woman had been found floating in the docks, particularly when the police did not suspect foul play? Probably another suicide. Some old tart who couldn't make it any more.

It was early December before Seamus Reilly was summoned to the Republic to meet with the Commander in Chief of the Provisional IRA. As soon as he received the summons Seamus knew something was wrong. He was certain of one thing: that the plan he had put forward had been rejected, perhaps not in full, but sufficiently for him to have a fight on his hands. Indeed, the fact that the meeting was to be held in the Commander's own home suggested that he might be fighting for rather more than the acceptance of his strategy.

'Ah, Seamus. An uneventful trip, I trust?'

'Thank you.'

'Come in and get yourself warm at the fire. It's the only

problem with Wicklow. Too much water about. Always damp. Beautiful but damp. Still, one can't have everything.'

'No.'

The Commander settled himself in his armchair and lit his pipe, eyeing Reilly through the haze of smoke. Between puffs he said: 'We've considered your plan, Seamus. It's very ingenious. I thought very highly of it. It showed your undoubted flair for the – shall we say the subtleties of bargaining.'

For a second Seamus Reilly felt he had misjudged the reason for his visit. His spirits rose, only to plummet again as the Commander continued in the same pleasant voice. 'Unfortunately, I am only one voice in the Council. In a word I have been outvoted.'

'I understand. So what happens – '

The Commander studied the bowl of his pipe as he said: 'Nothing.'

'Nothing?'

'That's it, Seamus. Nothing. Drumm is not to be touched. Indeed, he is to be commended,' the Commander explained, a hint of irony in his voice.

'You can't be serious,' Reilly expostulated, perhaps foolishly.

'I am. For the good of everyone we have been – we felt it was necessary to make certain concessions, certain allowances. At all costs we must avoid a serious split in our ranks. God knows there is enough dissent already. Many consider the Brighton bombing as a considerable coup and made it abundantly clear that should any further action be taken against the perpetrators they would feel obliged to disassociate themselves from us. We cannot stand another rift, Seamus. Besides, it will soon be forgotten. Everything will quickly return to normal and we can pursue our political objectives as before.'

'And when they decide to have another – coup?' Reilly asked, loading the word with sarcasm.

'They won't. That has been agreed.'

Seamus Reilly could not contain his laughter although aware that he was infuriating his superior. 'They *will*,' he said flatly.

'Don't you see? They have simply been testing your strength. If you give in to them on this they will see it as weakness, and before you know it they'll be blasting all hell out of what they consider to be legitimate targets all on the mainland.'

The Commander shook his head, trying to remain reasonable. 'They have agreed not to. They have been warned what will happen to them if they do.'

Seamus Reilly was dumbfounded at what he regarded as incredible naiveté. 'We gave them that warning before the Brighton bomb. They paid not a whit of notice. Why should they do so now? I'm sorry, but you're wrong, Commander. You've *got* to let me deal with Drumm and Mulcahy the way I suggested. I know the way they think. God Almighty I've been keeping people like that under control for the last fifteen years. You can believe me when I tell you they've – '

The Commander silenced him with a wave of his hand. He stroked his beard thoughtfully. When he spoke it was quietly, as though he was making an effort to be friendly and understanding, but his voice had a cold quality to it that Reilly recognized. 'Seamus, we've known each other a long time. We've been friends for a long time – far too long for us to allow something like this to destroy our friendship. As I have told you on many occasions, I admire you greatly. You are loyal. You are trustworthy. You are dedicated.' The Commander paused to let the compliments sink in. 'However,' he then went on, 'despite my admiration and fondness I must tell you that I will not tolerate your questioning the agreement that has been reached. I hope that you will accept the fact that we have decided it is for the best. Learn to live with it. I would grieve were it necessary for me to be forced to ensure your agreement. You understand what I'm saying?'

Reilly understood. For what seemed a very long time he just stared at the Commander, saying nothing, allowing his head to nod backwards and forwards. 'I understand,' he said finally.

Immediately the Commander cheered up, tapping his pipe vigorously in the ashtray. 'I knew you'd finally see things our way. We are only cogs in the great machine,' the Commander informed him in a mildly mocking way. 'Our destiny is determined by mere whims. We must adapt. Always be prepared to adapt, Seamus. Take my word for it. Adapt and you'll survive. Now, a drink?'

Reilly stood up. 'Thank you. No. I better be heading back.'

'Oh. You're sure?'

'Quite sure. Thank you.'

The Commander saw him out, even opening the car door for him. Just as Reilly was about to get in he felt a hand on his arm. 'We *have* reached an understanding, Seamus?' the Commander asked.

Reilly, bent to get into his seat, looked up. 'An understanding has been reached, Commander,' he said.

Seamus Reilly could never quite pinpoint the moment he decided he had to defy the Commander. Sometimes he believed it was the instant he had felt deliberately threatened; then again it could have been when the Commander had displayed a shocking misconception of the men he was so willing to barter with; or it might have been when it was declared that his destiny was determined by whims. Most likely, he ultimately thought, he had known from the moment he had received the message to visit the Commander, some small part of his mind tucking the defiance away for the moment it was confirmed that his plan had been rejected and a deal had been struck. Not that the actual timing made any difference: it didn't. What mattered to Seamus Reilly was why he had decided to choose his solitary, dangerous path. It was not vanity. Nor was it simply anger. When it came down to it Reilly knew his already exhausted spirit had rebelled at the prospect of continued violence, at the images of more and more maimed and crippled and dead people that haunted his mind. Innocent people. People who had simply tried to live out their lives, causing no harm to anyone. Perhaps a trifle too arrogantly, Reilly prided himself in the fact that he had never been responsible for the death of anyone who was truly innocent or uninvolved. Everyone had to accept the risks.

The evening of his return from Wicklow, Reilly went to bed early. He did not sleep. He did not want to sleep. He wanted to think. And in the quiet darkness of his room he allowed both the prosecution, so to speak, and the defence to argue their case, stating the pros and cons aloud. He was breaking the rule he had so vigorously enforced, and by so doing his death was a practical certainty. Oddly, this did not worry him for the moment. But the rule no longer applied, he decided. Not to him. And from long forgotten recesses in his mind he found a strange explanation for this. Something he had read, or had been told, but where he had read it or who had told him he could not, for the life of him recall – probably Arthur Apple. It sounded like Apple. Yet it was very clear '. . . *There seems to be no one to guide them towards human dignity, no one for them to admire, no one worthy of emulation.*' That was one thing. And having recited this, Seamus Reilly realized there was more to it, from somewhere else, some other voice was crying out, yet it was, strangely, the same voice. *Man dies in peace – reward enough; or with an awful darkness in the eye he dies screaming for the power of Shekinah to protect him. Alas, by then, it is too late for mercy, too late, even, for pity . . . .*

Seamus Reilly sat up and switched on the light, the evocative, frightening words echoing in his head. Too late for mercy. Perhaps that was so. He opened the drawer in the bedside table and pulled out his telephone book. He thumbed through it, then lifted the phone and dialled.

'Declan?'

'Yes. Who's that?'

'Seamus. Seamus Reilly.'

'Oh. What a surprise. How are you?'

Reilly ignored the question. 'Declan you remember what you wanted me to do? That film thing?'

'Of course.'

'I've decided to do it.'

'You – well, great. I wasn't – '

'There are conditions you might not agree to.'

'I've been told to agree to any conditions.'

'Perhaps not mine. Is there any chance you might come over for a day?'

'No bother. As soon as I tell – '

'You must tell no one, Declan. Not a living soul. Not until I've spoken to you at any rate.'

'I see. Okay. Fine. What's today? Say Friday next, would that do?'

'Yes.'

'I'll go straight to Rose's. I'll phone you from there.'

'Thank you, Declan.'

'Is something wrong, Seamus? You sound – '

'No. Nothing's wrong. I'll explain everything when I see you on Friday. Thank you again for coming.'

'Think nothing of it.'

So that was it. The first step completed, or almost. He could still change his mind, of course. He had a couple of days in which to do it. As though to eliminate such a possibility, Seamus Reilly now phoned John Asher.

'John. I'm sorry to disturb you. It's Seamus.'

'Yes, Seamus?'

'I need to meet with you. With you and Maddox. Tomorrow. Can you arrange it?'

'I'm sure I can. I'm free anyway, whatever about the Colonel.'

'I would prefer to see you both together. In the evening if that's at all possible.'

'I'll have to call you back on that.'

'Thank you. I would be grateful if you can organize it. It's important.'

'I'll phone Maddox now if you like and come straight back to you.'

'No. The morning will do.'

'Whatever you say. You sound – funny. What's happening?'

Reilly gave a little laugh. 'I'm not feeling very funny, John. Far from it. But nothing has happened. Well, not yet. I'll speak to you in the morning.'

The second step. Now he had dragged his self-imposed

ultimatum yet closer: only twenty-four hours, give or take an hour, to change his mind. He switched off the light and lay down again, pulling the blankets up under his chin. And he managed to doze.

If anyone had seen Seamus Reilly during the next five hours they would have thought, quite reasonably, that he was planning to move house. Methodically he went from room to room, clearing out drawers and cupboards, reading everything and stuffing all unwanted papers into a large black plastic bag, turning out pockets before consigning his old clothes to the sack also. Everything he wanted to keep he carried to the sitting room and stacked in a neat pile on the floor under the window. Fortunately he had never been a hoarder: there were few photographs in the house: nothing that connected him with his childhood, little to suggest he ever had a private life. There were some books (among them Declan Tuohy's single slim volume of poetry), an old tin box filled with foreign stamps, some magazines (dealing, mostly, with the tragic deaths of tragic men: Kennedy, King, Ghandi), and a collection of oddments he had picked up here and there: a meerschaum pipe, its bowl carved in the image of Lincoln, memorial cards held together by an elastic band, a tiny figure of a clown-like doll.

At six-thirty he was shaved and dressed ready for Asher and Maddox. He was wearing his black suit, the one he kept for funerals. He enjoyed the contrast of his scarlet tie and socks, an unusual urge to be devil-may-care triumphing. He was just checking that his hair was neatly combed when John Asher arrived.

'Ready?' he asked as Reilly opened the door. 'Maddox will be waiting for us at the barracks.'

Reilly gave him a twirl, coming to a standstill with a quick little tap dance. 'As ready as I'll ever be, John.'

Asher shook his head in quiet amazement at the antics, and grinned. 'I'm glad you're in such high spirits. Maybe you can cheer Maddox up. What I didn't tell you was that they're hounding him from London.'

As they settled themselves in Asher's car, Reilly asked: 'Why should they?'

'Because they want results. That's why. The only way Maddox could get Fisher back to England without too many questions was to tell them he had developed his own contacts – us, in case you don't know – and that he would have the names of the bombers within days. That was weeks ago. That's why they're hounding him.'

'Oh,' said Reilly, hunching his shoulders, and sinking lower in the seat. 'Well, that's part of what I want to talk to you both about.'

'He'll be pleased to hear that. So will I.'

Seamus Reilly looked at the clock on the dashboard. Time was almost up.

· SIXTEEN ·

WAITING FOR THEM to arrive, Colonel Maddox stared out of the window into the cold frosty night. He had chosen to wear his uniform, perhaps to stamp his authority on the meeting. Below him army vehicles reversed out and drove round the corner of the building and out of his sight, filled with young men who could possibly not return alive. Still, the city had been remarkably free of violence since the bombing in Brighton. It always was after a major offensive, but one could take nothing for granted: someone, perhaps from nothing more than boredom, could hurl a petrol bomb and the whole bloody mess would erupt again. God, how he wanted to be away from it all! He turned from the window and sat on the corner of his desk, swinging one leg. Life, he thought, had simply passed him by. It had used him. Like Seamus Reilly had used him. It was unfortunate that this thought was uppermost in his mind when Reilly and Asher knocked on his door and came in.

'You've arrived, then,' Maddox said gruffly, heaving himself from the desk and sitting down in his chair.

'As you say, Colonel,' Asher said. 'We've arrived.'

The Colonel put the palms of his hands flat on the desk in

front of him, looking directly at Reilly. 'You'd better explain what this is all about, Reilly. And I hope for your sake that it's not to suggest another damnable scheme. I'm in no humour for any more of that. From now on I want answers from you. And don't think I won't have you arrested if you try and play the fool.'

As soon as he had said it the Colonel realized he had made an ass of himself, had chosen quite the wrong approach, and certainly the wrong words. He felt himself start to blush as he noted Asher and Reilly glance at each other and laugh.

'I'm sorry, Colonel,' Reilly apologized as soon as he could control himself, waving his hand in front of his face as though to whisk away the last traces of merriment. 'It was just so unexpected – what you said.'

Maddox spotted his way out. 'Be that as it may, what is the reason for this meeting?'

'May we?' Reilly asked, indicating the two vacant chairs.

'Yes. Yes. Sit down.'

Reilly produced one of his small cigars, taking his time about lighting up, blowing out a stream of smoke before he spoke. When he did his voice was very quiet and tight. 'You will probably immediately object, Colonel, but before I tell you what I have to say I must first have your assurance – and yours John – that it remains within these four walls until I have completed all my preparations. You will not be able to use the information for at least another month.'

The Colonel jumped to his feet. 'No. No more deals, Reilly. I'm sick and tired of you and your deals.'

Reilly grimaced, shrugged and stood up also. 'I was afraid of that. I'm sorry that I wasted your time,' he said apologetically, already making for the door.

'Hang on a minute,' Asher said quickly. Then, turning to the Colonel, he went on. 'Colonel I don't believe this is another deal.' He swung back to Seamus. 'Is it?'

'No.'

Now Asher faced the Colonel again. 'No deal, Colonel. I think you should hear Seamus – Reilly – out. He has tried to co-operate with us. You know that. He needn't have taken care of Fisher the way he did.'

'No deal?' the Colonel demanded looking hard at Reilly.

'No deal. A request, Colonel. A request that you respect my confidence for one month.'

Nodding, the Colonel agreed. Annoyed with himself for being browbeaten yet again, he sat down and folded his hands under his chin.

'Yesterday morning I had a meeting with my Commander in Chief,' Reilly began, stopping there for a second to clear his throat. 'I was told that those who planted the bomb in the Brighton hotel were not to be punished, – that they were, in fact, to be commended. I think that was the word used. I was told that any plan I might have for effecting their punishment was to be scrapped. I was also told that should I attempt to disobey this order I would find myself as the one being punished.'

Reilly paused to take in another lungful of cigar smoke, to take, also, a look at the faces of his audience. It seemed that Maddox might interject so he continued immediately. 'I argued with the Commander. I explained why I thought the decision to let the bombing go unpunished was against everything I have fought for. I explained the devastating effect it would have on our chances in the elections. The Commander listened, but in the end he insisted that I accept the decision of the Council.' Reilly stopped again, this time to squash the remains of his cigar into the ashtray on the desk. Then he sat back. 'I have decided *not* to accept that decision.'

It took several seconds for the full import of what Seamus had said to sink in. Asher and Maddox looked at each other, one frowning, one with his eyebrows raised. Oddly enough, the realization of what had been said struck them both at the same time, and slowly they both turned their heads and gazed at Reilly. Reilly gazed silently back, faintly amused.

Asher was the first to recover. 'You mean you're breaking with the IRA?' It was as though he could hardly believe he was asking such a thing of Seamus Reilly.

Reilly shook his head. 'No, I don't mean that. I mean that I am going to make a stand against certain policies that have been adopted by the IRA. It is possible they will break with me, however,' he added wearily.

'You know what you propose to do will – ' Maddox began but stopped as Reilly held up his hand.

'I know,' Reilly told him.

'It is a far, far better thing,' Maddox decided to quote, and might even have finished the quotation had not Reilly winced.

'Nothing so dramatic, Colonel, I fear. Nor for such noble reasons.'

'Sacrifice is always noble,' Maddox countered, his tone distant, almost as if he was longing that the opportunity for sacrifice would step his way.

Reilly was cynical. He chuckled. 'You're still missing the point, Colonel. It has nothing to do with sacrifice. Years and years and years ago I swore I would do everything in my power to see to it that Ireland was united. And, from time to time, violence has been the only option.'

'I don't – '

Again Reilly held up his hand. 'You know that's true, Colonel. You won't – can't – admit it, but you know it's a fact. You saw for yourself how things worked when you were stationed here last time.'

The Colonel nodded. 'Yes. Yes, indeed I did.'

'Well,' Reilly went on, 'things have slowly changed. There is just a glimmer of hope that we can achieve our dreams by political means, so the violence has got to stop. Unfortunately there will always be those within our ranks who disagree. They see negotiation as weakness, terror as strength. Someone, finally, has to take a stand against the wasteful violence. Someone from within the IRA. So . . . .' Reilly smiled thinly and raised his eyebrows.

'Seamus you can't just barge blindly into a decision like that.' It was Asher who spoke, leaning forward and touching Reilly on the knee.

'Oh there's nothing blind about what I'm doing, John. I

189

shall be taking precautions. I'm a cautious bugger – as you've so often told me.'

Asher drew back, shaking his head.

'As to the bombers themselves,' Reilly went on, 'I'll give you the names I have soon, John. You know where they are; you can make your own cross-channel arrangements for their apprehension. But not until I say you can. It won't be long. Probably not as long as a month – that rather depends on a meeting I have tomorrow night.'

'To hell with that for the moment. What about you? For Christ's sake, Seamus, you can't just suddenly take on the role of martyr on us. We've worked together for too long for me to let you waltz into – '

Reilly stopped him. 'It's not a question of waltzing into anything, John. The probable truth is that I am just tired, tired of trying to maintain this interminable, uneasy peace when everyone around me seems bent on their own destruction. Besides, it is something I *want* to do; something I *need* to do.'

Asher protested: 'But – '

'And speaking of Christ – I remember reading once – it *is* strange the things you remember when you take the time to think – I remember reading somewhere that there is a legend among some tribe in Borneo – I believe it was Borneo, but maybe not – a legend, anyway, that God didn't really want to be bothered with us at all. It was up to *us*, you see, to attract *his* attention by whistling and dancing and singing. This, in an odd way, might be my little jig, my little hymn. But what I'll do if I ever do get His benevolent eye fixed on me I have no idea.'

Maddox and Asher seemed totally flummoxed, embarrassed even. Unabashed, Seamus was off again. 'It's the Irish Catholic circle, you see. At baptism you scream your head off and fight like mad to get away from the sacrament, but when death approaches you fight again but this time to partake of the sacrament that will give you at least a reasonable chance of a peaceful departure.'

Asher was shaking his head, completely baffled, but

determined to argue on. 'Look, so you don't agree with the decision. I understand that. But you don't have to – '

Again Reilly stopped him. 'But I *do*. I do. Won't you let me do one decent thing in my life?'

Declan Tuohy stopped the senior editor in the corridor. 'I won't be in tomorrow, Myles,' he said. 'I've got to go away for the day. Belfast.'

'Oh? Anything I should know about?' Cravan asked, smiling.

'No. Not really. Not yet at any rate. If anything comes of it we'll have to have a talk.'

'That means it could spell trouble.'

'It could. Well, not trouble. Controversy would be a better word.'

'That I can cope with.'

'I'll remember you said that.'

Now, still wearing his safety belt, a cup of lukewarm, weak coffee in a plastic cup in his hand, Declan stared out of the window at the sea below, thinking of the city they were fast approaching. The city of his birth. The city he feared. The city, as he had called it, of Moloch. The city he loved, too . . . .

It looms a far-off skeleton
And not a comrade nigh,
A fitful far-off skeleton
Dimming as days draw by.

. . . Well, perhaps Hardy was right even if Belfast had been the furthest thing from his mind. And it didn't dim either, for that matter. Far from it. That was the astonishing, the most admirable thing. Bombed and battered it might be, but there it still stood, sheltering its people. And what people! The most cheerful, friendliest people in the world, defying the world to beat you down with a laugh and a grin and a rose in your teeth and a clackety-clack-clack of your fingers.

Already the lights of the city were whooshing up towards

them. It could be anywhere, so peaceful and serene did it look. But it wasn't. It was Belfast, each tiny light like a candle lit to a personal tragedy, to a private agony. And, thinking of agonies, what agony, or, rather more likely, what devilish enterprise had made Seamus Reilly even consider putting himself at risk? Declan smiled to himself. God alone knew what he was up to! Well, he would be told too, soon enough. An hour at most.

Reilly could not settle. Even his beloved Mahler could not calm him down; *Das Lied von der Erde* sounded more than ever as if it was coming from the grave. Now that he had started the ball rolling he wanted desperately to get the whole thing over and done with. He walked from room to room, always returning to the hall and glaring at the phone, waiting for Declan to call. His tiredness made him irritable. All night long he had lain in bed, gazing at the myriad of tiny lights that seemed to flicker in the darkness, sometimes squeezing his eyes closed and opening them suddenly to intensify those lights. He had rehearsed, carefully, what he would say during the proposed interview. He was going to be open and frank. He would not hedge. He would answer every question as honestly and truthfully as he could: if retribution was to follow he would prefer to be hanged for telling the truth than for lying.

At last the phone rang.

'I've arrived, Seamus. Just this minute. I'm with Rose.'

'Ah, Declan. Thank you for coming.'

'You asked me to, didn't you?'

'How soon can we meet?'

'As soon as you like. Now if you want.'

Seamus jumped at the suggestion. 'Yes. Now. I'll come right over.'

'Fine.'

Declan was shocked when he opened the door to Reilly's knock. It was hard to believe that anyone could have aged so much in just a few months. He was no greyer, no more stooped, no less vigorous in his actions. His voice had the same crisp sharpness and he looked fit enough. It was only when Declan concentrated on his eyes that the trough of decline was indicated. There was no fire in them now, a veil of grey filtering the sparkle, leaving a residue of sadness. 'Come on in Seamus,' he invited.

'Thank you.'

'In here,' Declan said, leading the way to the small dining room. 'I've set a real fire in here. I thought it might be friendlier.'

Seamus followed him into the room, removing his overcoat as he went, hanging it on the back of a chair when he got there. 'Yes,' he answered.

'Can I get you anything? Tea? Coffee? Something stronger?'

Reilly smiled gratefully. 'Thank you, no. I've been drinking coffee most of the night.'

'Well, take a seat then. Rose is upstairs,' he added. ' "Doing" my room, as she puts it.'

'Ah.'

For several minutes they sat in silence, looking rather odd and uncomfortable side by side in front of the fire, perched on the straight, high-backed dining room chairs.

'Declan, I've decided to give you your interview,' Reilly said quietly at last.

'What made you change your mind?' Declan asked.

Reilly gave a tiny shrug, but did not answer.

Declan did not press the point. He leaned forward and poked at the fire. 'You mentioned conditions.'

'Yes,' Seamus agreed, and then laughed. 'I always make conditions, don't I? Habit, I suppose. I've done it all my life. Even with God. My prayers were always loaded with conditions. If *He* did this, I would do that. Even at school I tried to barter with Him. If He helped me pass such and such an exam I would – I think I promised a decade of the rosary every day. Anyway, yes, there are conditions,' Reilly confirmed and stopped talking again.

'Well, let's have them,' Declan said, trying to introduce a note of lightheartedness, putting a little laugh into his words.

Seamus Reilly held one of his hands out in front of him, palm upwards, and when he spoke he ticked off his conditions on his fingers. 'It will have to be done in absolute secrecy. You will have to vouch for everyone involved. It will have to be screened without editing. And, finally, it cannot be screened until I give you permission.' Reilly looked at Declan for his reaction.

Declan stared pensively at the flames. Finally he asked: 'Just one question – why the secrecy? That could be difficult.'

'Because, Declan, I have decided to do this without the knowledge or the permission of Command. So I need a certain amount of time. I have things to do. I have, as the poet said, promises to keep and miles to go before I sleep. Not too many miles, mind you.'

Declan stood up and walked across the room, turned, and stared down at the back of Reilly's bowed head. 'Why?' he asked, his voice suddenly strained. As he stood up he had thought about protesting, about saying he couldn't let Seamus do it, about insisting that he wanted no part of it. He had rejected these thoughts. He knew Seamus only too well. Reilly would not have undertaken such an action without very good reason.

'Why?' Seamus asked, turning and looking over his shoulder. 'You know, I wish I knew the *real* reason. Suffice it to say I believe it is the right thing to do. There is always a moment in one's life – everybody's life – when a single decision has to be made, and although we may not know it at the time, that decision is the one, vital, monumental task set to us. The result might be glorious or infamous. It doesn't matter. Destiny or fate or what you will has decreed that *you* must decide, and in deciding imprint your existence on the world. It makes not a whit of difference how insignificant it may strike you at the time, but if you fail to decide you are doomed.'

Declan walked slowly back to his chair and sat down again. He put his hand on Reilly's arm, but did not look at him. 'Seamus, Seamus, Seamus.' He was lost for words of comfort.

Reilly brightened. 'Sorry about that. I didn't mean to be so gloomy. Let's just say I *want* to do it. Now, can you meet my conditions?'

'I think so. I can get a crew who are used to keeping their mouths shut. It's back in London that worries me. I would have to tell my editor in chief.'

'And?'

'And – well, you know how the BBC feel about IRA interviews. They have to be cleared usually. And having you on film will be quite a coup. He might feel he *has* to go higher up . . . . I'll tell you what I *can* do. We could do the interview. When I have it in the can I'll tell him. If he doesn't agree to what we've agreed I'll destroy the film.'

'Can you do that?'

'I can do it. There'll be a lot of screaming, but I can do it.'

'And what happens to you?'

'Sent to the bloody Tower probably. Don't you worry about me. I'll ride it out. Maybe that is *my* monumental decision.'

Seamus Reilly patted the hand on his arm. He was just thinking what a strange thing friendship was when he heard Declan saying: 'You've split with them, haven't you?'

'No. Disagreed. Not split.'

'Same thing.'

'I suppose it is. The wrong people are getting too powerful again, Declan. Someone has to try and put a stop to that. I've elected myself.'

Declan shook his head. 'They won't like it, to put it mildly.'

Seamus managed a little laugh. 'I don't expect they will. But, you know, my friend, I've just realized that my usefulness is over. I may as well go out on a mildly human note.'

'When do you want us to do it, Seamus?'

'As soon as possible.'

'I'll make a few calls. With a bit of luck I might even be able to assemble the crew I want and get them over by tonight.'

'How efficient you are. That would be excellent.'

'I'll know by lunchtime.'

'Excellent,' Seamus said again. 'I'll be at home.'

'If you change your mind I'll understand, Seamus.'

Reilly stood up and put on his coat. 'No changing of my mind, Declan. The dye, as they say, is cast.'

At that moment, the Commander in Chief of the Provisional IRA was offering Thomas Regan a seat. He had driven to Clones the night before, and had slept badly in the unfamiliar bed. His humour was tetchy. 'Sit, Regan,' he said.

Regan sat, dropping quickly into the seat as though pole-axed.

The Commander was in no mood to beat about the bush. 'How long have you been working with Seamus Reilly?' he asked.

Regan cleared his throat. 'About ten years now.'

'Good. I have something I want you to do. I want you to keep an eye on him. We have cause for concern. If he does anything out of the ordinary, anything that causes *you* the least concern I want to know about it immediately.'

'Yes.'

'As from tomorrow you will stick to him like a limpet. And I want a written record kept of his movements. Who he sees, what time, where, and for how long. Is that clear.'

'Yes.'

'In particular I want to be informed as to any action he might be contemplating against Dermot Drumm or Joe Mulcahy in Glasgow. I can tell you that he has been ordered to take no action whatsoever. I want to be sure that order is obeyed. He might even instruct you to go over there. If he does, say that you'll go and let me know.'

'Very good.'

'And don't forget: I want to know *everything*. Every single detail of his movements.'

'I won't forget.'

'But be careful. If he suspects you *are* watching him, you could find yourself receiving the full extent of his wrath – and I need hardly tell you what that entails.'

John Asher was surprised when Reilly asked him to call round. He had not expected to hear from him just yet. He was even more surprised when Reilly told him the reason for the request, although he took his time about it, delaying it with a series of questions. 'How long do you think, John, it would take you to get the mainland police to react to information?'

Asher made a rather moronic face, indicating, more or less, that such a thing was debatable. 'That depends on the information, really. Depends on which branch would be dealing with it.'

'Anti-terrorist.'

'Oh they'd move on that.'

'Within hours?'

'Within bloody minutes.'

'Good. The name of the person who set off the Brighton bomb is Drumm. Dermot Drumm. You'll find him in a flat in James Gray Street, Glasgow. His accomplice is Joe Mulcahy. He lives in Shawlands also. With a woman. A Peggy Dunne. They actually planted the bomb. In three days I want you to get in touch with your colleagues in the special branch and pass on that information. But not for three days. I need that time.'

'Three days. And it's Dermot Drumm, Joe Mulcahy and Peggy Dunne.'

'Yes.'

John Asher wrinkled his brow, scribbling the names on his mind. Then he looked at Reilly, an uncharacteristic fondness in his eyes. 'This is it, Seamus, isn't it?'

Reilly gave a wan smile. 'Yes. I suppose it is.'

'I'll keep this to myself if you want.'

'Thanks, John. But no. Go ahead in three days. God alone knows how many lives you might save.'

'*You* might save.'

'Well, we might save.'

At the hall door but before it was opened they shook hands. It was a poignant gesture, a moment of shared sadness.

'If you need me – ' Asher began.

Reilly silenced him with an understanding nod. 'Thank you, John.'

No sooner had Asher left than Declan phoned to say he had

mustered his crew and that they would be arriving in Belfast at 4.15: where did Seamus want the interview done? His house would be fine. Yes, he understood why he would want to do it there. Yes, he would see to it that they did not all arrive at once. Yes, he, Declan, would be acting as interviewer. No, it made no difference: he would ask the right questions, be impartial.

Reilly spent the afternoon tidying up. He moved his stack of belongings away from under the window in the sitting room and put them behind the kitchen door. He hoovered and dusted. He arranged the furniture, pushing his favourite armchair back against the wall and under a copy of a print by Alken. Beside it he set his small table with an ashtray, a full tin of small cigars and a lighter. As an afterthought he put a couple of books on it also, giving it tone, as he gleefully saw it. Then he went upstairs and took a shower, humming to himself all the while, admitting that he was so doing to forestall the doubts that niggled at his mind. He took particular care in dressing, choosing a plain grey suit, blue shirt, striped tie. Nothing flashy, nothing too glum.

They started arriving at half-past five: Declan first, with the cameraman carrying his camera already loaded. Twenty minutes later, by taxi, came the lighting and sound men, each with what looked like an ordinary suitcase; and a quarter of an hour after that, in another taxi, an efficient young woman with a briefcase.

Seamus watched as they set themselves up, pleased when he saw the nod of approval at his arrangements. The curtains were tightly drawn and a single spotlight, produced from the suitcase, focused on the chair. He was asked to sit down. A small microphone was clipped to his tie. He was asked to say a few words, any words, for a voice level, it was explained. Seamus said: 'Where there is great power or great government, or great love and compassion, there is error for we progress by fault', and they all looked at each other, seeming to wonder if he had said something significant, but finally accepting it as just words and smiling with relief.

'Fine,' the soundman said and held up one thumb.

'Ready?' Declan asked the cameraman.

'Ready,' he answered putting his eye to the camera.

'Ready Seamus?' Declan asked.

Seamus nodded. 'As ready as I'll ever be.'

Declan smiled encouragement.

The clapperboard was clapped.

'Interview Seamus Reilly. Take one,' the young woman said brittlely, and went and sat beside the soundman, a clipboard on her knee, her pen poised, her ankles crossed.

The camera whirred.

Another thumb went up.

Declan Tuohy began to interview Seamus Reilly.

Driving home from Clones, Thomas Regan felt elated. That he had been summoned alone to the Commander was honour enough; to be his eyes and ears was more than Regan could have hoped for. Already the downfall of Seamus Reilly danced in his imagination and he saw himself taking Reilly's place in the hierarchy. Unconsciously he licked his lips as though already tasting the power. In a way, he admitted, he was sorry it was old Reilly. He quite liked him. Feared him, certainly, but liked him as much as that fear would allow. Still, one had to think of oneself first. Reilly had had his day. His was yet to come. As from tomorrow . . . that was what the Commander said. Regan toyed with the idea of calling on Reilly: he could easily find some pretext. It would, perhaps, show his enthusiasm if he could date his first report a day earlier than asked. On the other hand it might be seen as disobedience, and the last thing Thomas Regan wanted was to start off his mission on the wrong foot. No. He would go home. Have a nice meal. Play with the kid. Do what he was told. Tomorrow would obviously be time enough if that was the way the Commander saw it. Nevertheless he decided to drive past Seamus Reilly's house. Case the joint, he told himself, laughing at his little game.

He turned left and drove slowly down the street; even slower as he came close to the house. Not a light. The curtains tightly drawn. He must be out. Or gone to bed early. Probably out. Well, let him enjoy himself. Poor old bugger.

By ten o'clock they had finished, the equipment dismantled and stowed back in the cases.

'Is it safe to call taxis?' Declan asked.

Seamus shrugged. 'Does it matter now. Still, perhaps if you could – '

'Sure. I'll ferry them.'

They started filing from the house, each shaking Reilly's hand in turn. Declan was the last to leave. 'How do you feel now, Seamus?' he asked.

'Naked. How about you?'

'Frightened for you. The interview was terrific.'

'Don't you worry your head about me. Just see to it that you keep to our agreement.'

'I will. You have my word.'

'Good.'

'I'll have a transcript with you as soon as possible.'

'Thank you.'

'Well. That seems to be that.'

'Yes.'

Suddenly they embraced, patting each other gently on the back. Then Declan was gone.

· SEVENTEEN ·

FOUR DAYS LATER Seamus Reilly received a note from Declan Tuohy (a postcard of the Tower of London in an envelope, the significance of which was not lost on him), saying that the transcript had been sent to Rose, and would he collect it there, although for 'transcript' he had written recipe. Seamus smiled to himself at the silly subterfuge. It was proving to be a momentous day. Already the early morning newscasters had broken the story that two men and a woman had been arrested by the anti-terrorist squad, and, amid 'unprecedented security' had been taken to London from Glasgow to be charged with a number of IRA bomb incidents going back seven years and including the explosion at the Grand Hotel. They were to join two other men already being held in the special terrorist-proof unit inside Paddington Green police station. At the time of the arrest in Glasgow an unconfirmed report said police had found under the floorboards in a flat in the Shawlands district of the city a cache of weapons and enough explosive (estimates put as high as 150 lbs) to make between thirty and fifty bombs.

The next afternoon Seamus collected the transcript, at the same time giving Rose the money from her dead husband's supposed pension. As he was leaving he said quietly: 'Rose, I might have to go away for a while. I – '

'Oh good, Mr Reilly,' Rose interrupted, her eyes brightening. 'You need a little holiday. You haven't been looking yourself for quite a while now. A break will do you the world of good.'

For a moment Reilly thought of protesting. 'Yes,' he said finally. 'I'm sure it will.'

'You'll see,' Rose went on cheerfully. 'You'll be a new man when you come back.'

'I'm sure I shall. I just wanted to say that your pension will come in just the same while I'm away.'

'Thank you, Mr Reilly. Tell me, is it somewhere nice – where you're going?'

Seamus frowned. 'I don't know, Rose. I just don't know.'

Back home Reilly made himself a cup of coffee and carried it and the transcript upstairs. He went into the small back bedroom and shut the door. The mattress had been folded over on itself, so he unfolded it and sat down. There was no other furniture in the room: it looked for all the world as barren and impersonal as a cell. Appropriate, he mused grimly. Then he lit himself a cigar, and started to read. It was headed simply 'INTERVIEW' and the date of April 29th had been typed alongside. Seamus scowled and wondered what significance there could possibly be in the false date. Underneath that, in capital letters, was SEAMUS REILLY/DECLAN TUOHY. And then the actual interview began using his own and Declan's initials to identify the interrogator and his victim.

DT:Can we start by my asking you why you have decided to grant this interview.

Seamus chuckled. Grant, indeed! He recalled the sardonic glance he had given Declan and the almost apologetic look he had received in return. Well, why *had* he granted the interview. His official reply had been straight enough. He believed it was time someone explained certain facts about the IRA although, now, in the clinical loneliness that surrounded him, he found himself wondering if it hadn't been something of a last ditch stand by someone who was forced to admit that his life was a failure. He had pointed out that anything he said was a purely personal opinion although he believed those he labelled the 'majority of our right-thinking' members shared his views. Not that they would dare admit it. Certainly not now. Indeed, Reilly was only too well aware that by speaking openly about IRA affairs without the sanction of the Council he had alienated all those who might have reasonably been seen to be his supporters. And he could hardly blame them. He knew the rules better than anyone. He gave a small laugh. He had drafted many of the rules himself with youthful, uncaring eagerness. Once he chose to disobey them he automatically isolated himself.

Reilly stood up and walked across the room to the small window. He stared out at the neglected garden, watching an old tabby cat with a stiff back leg lopsidedly stalk a plump missel thrush. It was as though the bird was alert to the cat's incapacity as it managed to stay just out of reach, unflustered. Seamus smiled. That was what his own life had been like: just keeping one step ahead. That was all one could reasonably be expected to do, and he had done it adroitly.

Another of Declan's questions filtered into Reilly's mind. Most people would consider you a dangerous terrorist, he had stated. How do you react to that? He returned to the bed. This time he lay back. Terrorist. He winced. It was one of the more implacable aspects of his character that Seamus Reilly had never considered himself to be a terrorist. He believed himself to be a freedom fighter: the fact that the 'fight' had deteriorated in most people's eyes into an incomprehensible circle of murders and reprisals could not detract from the original well-meaning intent. Seamus ran his fingers across his brow. The truth was, he reflected, that governments only paid attention when violence disrupted the calm. Politicians could convince themselves that everything in the garden was rosy if people silently and submissively accepted oppression and hardship. He closed his eyes, sighing, feeling suddenly cold. Faces from

203

the past loomed into his consciousness and then disappeared again, recoiling. His brother, pleading for his life, his eyes remorselessly accusing; Martin Deeley, a young killer nurtured on the hatred and violence that had surrounded his youth, still arrogant and cocky, winking at him, keeling over, toppling from life; Fergal Duffy, Declan's nephew, sprawled on the pavement, reaching out towards something only he could see, bearing an expression of total puzzlement. Seamus opened his eyes abruptly, dismissing for the moment his tormentors. Perhaps that was all death was in the end: a puzzle.

Thomas Regan was answering the Commander's questions as best he could: 'I've had someone watching him morning and night. He's not been out of the house once. Oh. Sorry. Once. He went to Rose Duffy's house, but that was nothing. He goes there once a week anyway to see her.'

'I'll decide if it's nothing or not,' the Commander snapped. 'And that's the only place he's been?'

'Yes.'

'Visitors?'

'None. It's like he's become a recluse.'

The Commander was furious. Damn Reilly and his meddling, righteous ways. It simply had to be him. It was too much of a coincidence. The Glasgow arrests had been too swift, too clean. Over and done with before even a hint of their possibility emerged. Worse still: his own tacit agreement with those who had demanded that Drumm and Mulcahy be kept active was being called into question; there were hints dropped that he was losing his grip on things. 'Go back to Belfast and bring Seamus Reilly here,' he said icily. 'I want him here this evening.'

Reilly sat up and glanced at the open transcript. He was amazed at how honest he had been in his answers to some of Declan's questions. He was, also, suddenly afraid. The more he read the more he realized the inevitable outcome of his replies. He let the pages flip through his fingers until, nearing the end, another question caught his eye. 'Could you yourself be killed for giving this interview without permission?' Declan had wanted to know.

Reilly gave a wan smile, recalling kindly Declan's gentle tone. His reply had been simple. He had nodded and said yes. You seem very fatalistic about it, Declan countered. Again Seamus had nodded. I am.

He threw the transcript onto the bed. If only they had known that the prospect of death terrified him. It had haunted him for years in a million guises. Dreams peopled by spectres who linked arms and prevented him from reaching God; pushing him away and downwards into an abyss. There had always been a glimmer of escape in the shape of a horny hand that reached down to save him from almost certain damnation; a hand, and above it that face, gaunt and haggard yet continually smiling, mouthing the words that Seamus Reilly had lived with for several years: *'You are already dead'*. It always struck him as particularly baleful that God seemed to play such a minor role. Perhaps, indeed, God had no say in the matter.

Myles Cravan looked particularly pleased with himself, grinning like the Cheshire cat. 'I've had it cleared,' he told Declan. 'The dear old DG likes the idea. *And* we get full treatment – coverage on the front page of the *Radio Times*.'

Declan was far less enthusiastic. 'You warned the DG we had to wait until we get Reilly's okay?'

Cravan hesitated. 'Sure,' he said.

'Myles,' Declan said, a warning of oncoming anger in his voice. 'Did you or didn't you?'

'Yes. Yes I did.'

'And you told him we couldn't even let a hint drop about the material we have in the can?'

Cravan looked away, his grin freezing to an embarrassed leer. 'Yes.'

'You're lying to me – '

'I told him we had to be careful.'

'Shit, Myles, that's not enough. We promised Reilly – '

'It's all right. It's all right,' Myles Cravan insisted. 'The DG just has to cover himself.'

'What's that supposed to mean?'

'He has to put the Governors in the picture. The IRA and the whole Ulster bit is too damned sensitive a subject at the moment.'

'Oh Jesus. You're a bastard, Myles. I promised Reilly – I gave him my word, dammit, that no hint of this would get out until he said it was okay.'

'Word won't get out, Declan. I'm sure of that. The Governors aren't going to blab to all and sundry about what we've got.'

'Oh, aren't they?' Declan asked sarcastically.

Reilly had nearly finished reading the transcript. It appalled him that at times he had appeared so ridiculously pompous, at times pathetically naïve. Still, what was done was done. He got up and carried the last few pages to the window, bending them towards the light.

DT: What in your opinion is the solution to the troubles in Northern Ireland?

Seamus threw back his head and laughed out loud. Solution! For whom? Britain? The Unionists? Sinn Fein? He remembered he had felt like shouting: 'There is no damn solution!' The possibility of agreement remained forever remote, but not unattainable. From time to time, it seemed almost within reach, there for the taking. Alas, something always went wrong. Bigotry, as the saying went, raised its ugly head.

Someone knocked on the front door, making him jump. Without hurrying he went downstairs. He was at first surprised when he saw Thomas Regan, but his surprise faded when he heard the Commander wanted to see him: now, 'I'm to drive you there myself, Mr Reilly.'

They drove rapidly towards Clones at a speed Regan would never have dared only two or three days before. Reilly observed him silently from the back seat, quietly, sadly amused. Poor Thomas. Illusions of power and grandeur were already getting the better of him it seemed. He would soon learn that there was a terrible price to pay for having power, but probably not until it was too late.

The Commander welcomed Reilly with a curt nod, and ordered Regan to stay by the car. So much for power, Reilly thought, and followed the Commander into the room.

'Just one straight answer, Seamus,' the Commander said immediately, not even bothering to be seated. 'The Glasgow arrests. Had you anything to do with that?'

For an instant Seamus Reilly felt like shouting out his involvement at the top of his voice. However, wily as ever, he decided to play a dangerous game of cat and mouse. 'I've only been out of my house once since we last spoke, and that was to visit a friend.' Irritation got the better of the Commander, who blurted: 'I know that.'

Reilly narrowed his eyes. 'Ah.'

Recovering, and seeming only slightly flustered, the Commander continued: 'That's not what I asked you.'

'My influence does not extend across the channel, Commander. The police, as we well know, are not stupid. Two and two makes four even in their book. You cannot expect to try and exterminate the entire British Cabinet and not have the police find you. Drumm, as I warned you several times, is a clumsy fool. Mulcahy isn't much better. They obviously gave themselves away.'

'And you had nothing to do with it? You didn't strike one of your deals with that RUC conspirator of yours?'

'You told me to do nothing. You said they were to be commended, I recall. Have you ever known me to disobey your orders?'

The Commander was forced to admit: 'No.'

Seamus felt the muscles in his stomach relax. 'That should answer your question.'

The Commander moved across the room and put an arm about Seamus's shoulder. 'I'm sorry, Seamus. I had to ask you.

We are under the severest pressure from our intelligence to find out what happened. The arrests were too – too clean.'

'I did warn you to have no truck with the hard-liners, Commander,' Seamus pointed out somewhat complacently.

'Damn it, Seamus, we had no choice.'

'There is always a choice,' Reilly told him, moving away. 'Always,' he repeated, almost to himself.

'Not always,' the Commander said, sounding sad.

'Always,' Seamus reiterated.

Three hours later he was back home. He decided to leave the final couple of pages of the transcript for the morning, and headed for bed. Once undressed, he put out the light and moved to the window, peering through a narrow gap in the lace curtains. The street was deserted. He was about to turn when he spotted a tiny movement of the curtains in the upstairs window of the house opposite.

'Jesus, I said I was sorry, Declan,' Myles Cravan protested.

'You're sorry? Well, that's just bloody great. *You're* sorry. What about Reilly? What do you think is going to happen to him when this breaks? He's going to be a hell of a lot sorrier than you I can tell you.'

'It couldn't be helped, Declan,' Cravan said lamely.

'Shit, of course it could have been helped. What a stupid fucking thing to say. It couldn't be helped! You know what we've done, don't you? We've killed Reilly, that's what we've done.'

Seamus Reilly was awoken by the phone jangling at his bedside. It was 2.30 a.m. 'Hello?'

'Seamus. It's Declan. Christ, I'm sorry, Seamus. They've cocked up everything over here.'

Seamus heaved himself up onto one elbow.

'It'll be in all the papers tomorrow. The fact that you gave us an interview. The government got wind of it. Someone must have told some gobshite looking to make points. Anyway, the

Governors have been got at. They've reversed the DG's decision to show the film. Seamus – you've got to get out.'

Reilly went cold, his muscles stiffened. 'Get out? And where do you suggest I "get out" to?'

'Anywhere. Over here for a start.'

Suddenly Seamus burst out laughing. 'Over there,' he said flatly. Then with equal suddenness he was serious again. 'And what would be the point of that?'

'Seamus you must – '

'I knew what I was doing. I knew the risks. To get out, as you put it, would be defeating the whole – '

'For Christ's sake, Seamus, will you wake up? Your name will be splattered across every front page in the morning – *this* goddam morning. You told me yourself what would most likely happen.'

'I said it *could* happen, Declan.'

'Could or would. Bugger the difference. We both know damn well what *will* happen. Jesus, Seamus, if you just stay there you're as good as dead already.'

'I am already dead,' Seamus replied, his voice curiously echoing. 'I am already dead,' he repeated as though recalling the words from long ago. Then abruptly and firmly he said simply: 'Goodbye, my friend,' and replaced the receiver in its cradle.

Alone, Reilly pondered what Declan had said. It was difficult not to distance himself from the truth; far easier to regard himself as someone else and commiserate with the plight of that unfortunate person, comforting him, telling him not to worry, that things could be worse. Not that they could be much worse, he admitted grimly as he came to himself, getting out of bed and slipping on his dressing-gown. What *was* strange was that all sense of fear suddenly vanished. It was as though he *was* already dead as predicted, patiently waiting for it simply to be confirmed.

· EIGHTEEN ·

OVER THE NEXT few days, the newspapers had a field day, delighting in the procession of incredible blunders that were made. HOME SECRETARY ASKS BBC TO BAN REILLY FILM. That was the start of it. BBC AGREES TO DROP IRA INTERVIEW – GOVERNORS BOW TO CABINET PRESSURE, soon followed. Then: STRIKE OVER BANNED PROGRAMME – BBC ULSTER CHIEF TO GO. Inevitably, next: BBC ULSTER CHIEF NOT TO RESIGN OVER BANNED PROGRAMME.

Seamus Reilly read the headlines in utter astonishment. He would never have believed such a furore could have resulted. If this was the Prime Minister's way of 'starving the terrorists of the oxygen of publicity' long may she reign. Most ridiculously of all came the news that the BBC TO SHOW IRA FILM – MY BOARD WAS READY TO RESIGN SAYS DG. Reilly knew now that he would be 'dealt' with, and for a moment he felt sorrow for those he had himself been obliged to punish. He recalled that his favourite tactic was to make them wait. It was, he now discovered, the waiting that was worst: the time to reflect on one's possible foolhardiness, to reflect, too, on the uselessness of one's life.

One week after the story broke an emergency meeting of the IRA Council was called. It was fully attended. The Commander sat at the head of the table looking tired and sad. 'There is no need to reiterate the reason we are here. I am sure I speak for all of us when I say how deeply I regret the decision we have to make.'

Everyone nodded.

The evening was filled with anticipation. The streets were deserted. Everyone was glued to their television sets watching young Barry McGuigan fight the fight of his life.

Seamus Reilly, too, decided to watch, but before settling himself comfortably in his chair he went into every room that had a mirror and turned each face to the wall. The sixth round had just ended and the boxers returned to their corners when the doorbell rang. He stood up slowly and deliberately: smoothed down his jacket and straightened his tie. He brushed a thread from his trousers, and flattened the hair on his temples with the palms of his hands. Then he walked deliberately to the door and opened it. Thomas Regan and Sean O'Neill stood there, looking solemn. 'Ah, Thomas – and Sean,' Seamus said without surprise. 'Not watching the fight? Come in. Come in. You can watch the finish from here if you've the time.'

He led the way into the sitting room, and sat down again in his chair. 'Sit down, sit down,' he invited, aware that he was repeating himself, aware, too, that neither man accepted his invitation but remained standing just inside the door. 'You see that man?' he asked quietly without looking round, pointing a finger towards the television screen. 'He's done what none of us could do. And without a word. It really is amazing when you come to think of it. Listen to them cheer! Every make and shape of religion, all together, cheering. Wonderful!,' he exclaimed.

That was when the first bullet hit him. He didn't move immediately. His eyes remained fixed on the screen. He felt no pain. He was just beginning to wonder if he had imagined the shot, was just rising from his chair when the second bullet ripped into him. Again there was no pain, but his knees buckled and he slid to the floor. He felt, suddenly, very tired. He could hear noises above him, noises he could no longer quite interpret. Someone touched him, feeling his neck, perhaps straightening his tie, making him presentable for whatever was in the offing which was kind of them. Then a mighty, uproaring cheer went up as Barry McGuigan pummelled his opponent sending him to his knees. For Seamus Reilly, now unaware of the impending victory, it was a frightening, hurtful sound, leaving him to slip into death bewildered that everyone should be so elated to see him die.

ROBERT RANKIN
The Brentford Trilogy

Can that be Jim Pooley himself? Layabout, bookies' best customer and dedicated pint-of-Large-fancier? Yes, unquestionably, it is he.

And by his side, isn't that the professionally unemployed ladies man. Flying Swan worshipper and bike rider, John Omally? Indeed. It is that lad.

Once more the dauntless double-act must outwit the fiendish Unknown Powers of Darkness, and defeat alien superpowers, crushing the legendary ancient Evil which, from time to time, crawls out with a new game plan, intent on nobbling life On Earth As We Know It! But the plucky Brentonians are never alone – even when facing the Big One. There's back-up from Professor Slocombe, Norman, Neville and Soap Distant – throw in a camel, some magic beans, Penge, the Great Pyramid, Norman's Morris Minor, a fleet of robots and a uncanny feeling for atmosphere – with expert consultation and guest appearances from Edgar Allan Poe and Sherlock Holmes . . . it all makes you wonder why Evil ever bothered to have a go!

'A born writer with a taste for the occult . . . Robert Rankin is to Brentford what William Faulkner was to Yoknapatwpha county'
TIME OUT

0 349 10028 4   FICTION   £3.99

Donn Pearce
COOL HAND LUKE

Lloyd Jackson was caught red-handed, abusing the system. So he was brought before the wrath of the Law. And he left an anguished chorus of forlorn voices praying behind him, and danced his way heel and toe right into his cell and on to the chain gang.

Donn Pearce's own experience on a chain gang in central Florida created COOL HAND LUKE and later the screen play to the classic film, starring Paul Newman. This story of one man's refusal to let the prison system grind him down has a poignancy and vitality which immediately caught the imagination of everyone who read the novel when it was first published in 1965. It remains just as powerful today.

'Rhythmic prose, tragic drama, and realism made larger than life'
PUBLISHERS WEEKLY

0 349 10004 7   FICTION   £3.99

S·U·M·M·I·T

D. M. Thomas

Age and soggy brain cells are not a safe combination for a US president, and 'Tiger' O'Reilly's got a big helping of both. Let's just say he makes a big blunder and impeachment looms. In the circumstances, a summit meeting with the new Soviet leader, Grobichov, seems a good thing to go for.

Quickly, the two world leaders take protocol into their own hands, dismissing the ranks of fawning advisors and second-rate interpreters, deciding to hold discussions on a private man-to-man basis, to cut the cackle and really get to know one another. And it has to be admitted – Alexei and Larissa, 'Tiger' and Wanda make a great double-date. A couple of Class A misunderstandings *do* slip through the fine mesh of presidential intelligence . . . something to do with twenty million contraceptive coils and California being presented to the Soviets . . . but world leaders are only flesh and blood, after all . . . anyone can make mistakes!

'With its canny political satire, its hilarious insights into the sex of politics and the politics of sex will delight and amuse even Thomas' most devoted readers.'
Erica Jong

0 349 10024 1   FICTION   £3.99

Also available in ABACUS paperback:

FICTION

AHAB'S DAUGHTER	James Thackara	£3.99 ☐
CHATTERTON	Peter Ackroyd	£3.99 ☐
SUMMIT	D. M. Thomas	£3.99 ☐
THE BRENTFORD TRILOGY	Robert Rankin	£3.99 ☐
COOL HAND LUKE	Donn Pearce	£3.99 ☐
STRAIGHT CUT	Madison Smartt Bell	£3.99 ☐

NON-FICTION

ZOO STATION	Ian Walker	£3.99 ☐
THE PANAMA HAT TRAIL	Tom Miller	£3.99 ☐
UNDER A SICKLE MOON	Peregrine Hodson	£3.99 ☐
AN UNFINISHED JOURNEY	Shiva Naipaul	£3.50 ☐
METROPOLIS	Jerome Charyn	£3.99 ☐
IN THE LABYRINTH	John David Morley	£3.99 ☐

All Abacus books are available at your local bookshop or news
agent, or can be ordered direct from the publisher. Just tick the title
you want and fill in the form below.

Name _____

Address _____

_____

Write to Abacus Books, Cash Sales Department, P.O. Box 11
Falmouth, Cornwall TR10 9EN

Please enclose a cheque or postal order to the value of the cover
price plus:

UK: 60p for the first book, 25p for the second book and 15p for each
additional book ordered to a maximum charge of £1.90.

OVERSEAS & EIRE: £1.25 for the first book, 75p for the second book
and 28p for each subsequent title ordered.

BFPO: 60p for the first book, 25p for the second book plus 15p per
copy for the next 7 books, thereafter 9p per book.

*Abacus Books reserve the right to show new retail prices on covers
which may differ from those previously advertised in the text or
elsewhere, and to increase postal rates in accordance with the P.O.*